University Reader

英汉对照·中国文学宝库·现代文学系列
English-Chinese·Gems of Chinese Literature·*Modern*

鲁迅小说选
Selected Stories by Lu Xun

鲁 迅 著
Lu Xun

中国文学出版社
Chinese Literature Press
外语教学与研究出版社
Foreign Language Teaching and Research Press

图书在版编目(CIP)数据

鲁迅小说选:英、汉对照/鲁迅著. —北京:中国文学出版社;外语教学与研究出版社,1999.8
(中国文学宝库·现代文学系列)
ISBN 7-5071-0561-X

Ⅰ.鲁… Ⅱ.鲁… Ⅲ.鲁迅小说-中国-现代-对照读物-英、汉 Ⅳ.H319.4:I

中国版本图书馆 CIP 数据核字(1999)第 29852 号

中文责编:文 钊
英文责编:殷 雯

英汉对照 中国文学宝库·现代文学系列

鲁迅小说选

鲁 迅著

中国文学出版社
(北京百万庄路24号)
外语教学与研究出版社   出版发行
(北京西三环北路19号)

北京市鑫鑫印刷厂印刷
新华书店总店北京发行所经销

开本 850×1168 1/32 10.5印张
1999年8月第1版 1999年8月第1次印刷
字数:160千 印数:1—5000册

ISBN 7-5071-0561-X/I · 499
定价:12.90元

总编辑 杨宪益 戴乃迭

总策划 野 莽 蔡剑峰

编委会（以姓氏笔划为序）

　　　　吕　华

　　　　李朋义

　　　　赵文炎

　　　　凌　原

　　　　野　莽

　　　　蔡剑峰

目 录
CONTENTS

大学生读书计划 ·················· 编 者（Ⅰ）
　　——中国文学宝库出版呼吁
A Madman's Diary ····················（ 2 ）
狂人日记 ·····························（ 3 ）
Kong Yiji ·····························（ 36 ）
孔乙己 ·······························（ 37 ）
Medicine ····························（ 50 ）
药 ··································（ 51 ）
The True Story of Ah Q ···············（ 74 ）
阿 Q 正传 ····························（ 75 ）
The New Year Sacrifice ···············（198）
祝 福 ·······························（199）
In the Tavern ························（246）
在酒楼上 ····························（247）
Regret for the Past ···················（276）
伤 逝 ·······························（277）

大学生读书计划
——中国文学宝库出版呼吁

在即将开机印刷这第一批 50 本名为中国文学宝库的英汉对照读本时,我们的心情竟然忧多于喜。因为我们只能以保守的 5000 册印数,去面对全国 400 万在校大学生。

虽然我们并非市场经济的局外者,若仅为印数(销售量)计,大可奋起而去生产诸如 TOFEL 应试指南,或者英语四六级模拟试题集一类的教辅图书,但我们还是决定宁可冒着债台高筑的风险,也有责任对大学生同胞发出一声亲切的呼唤:请亲近我们的中国文学。

身为向世界译介中国文学和向国内出版外语读物的,具有双重责任的出版社,我们得知目前大学生往往仅注重外语的学习而偏废了母语的提高,以及忽视了中国文学的阅读,放弃了人文知识的训练。有统计表明,某理工院校 57% 的同学不曾读过《红楼梦》等四大名著,以致校园内外流行着"样子像研究生,说话像大学生,作文像中学生,写字像小学生"的幽默。还有一副这样的对联,说大学生的文章是"无错不成文,病句错句破残句,句句不堪入目;有误方为篇,别字错字自造字,字字触目惊心",横批"斯文扫地"。作为未来社会中坚和整个社会发展关键力量的大学生,这种"文弃"现象的流行,势必导致一场人文精神危机的爆发。对照以科学与人文精神追求为主题的五四新文化运动,八十年的历程告诉我们,以上提醒绝非危言耸听。

我们已经迈入知识经济时代,在追求科学知识的同时,创新精神已成为关键;而创新的源泉其实有赖于多学科多领域知识的交融,依靠的是新型的复合型人才,所以,文学对于新一代的大学生来说绝非装点,而是沟通自然科学与人文科学的桥梁,使我们在汲取知识的同时更能获得智慧,于创造物质的同时还进一步丰富和完善着精神;无怪乎爱因斯坦认为自己受影响最大的竟是陀思妥耶夫斯基。由此证明,一个真正的科学家应该拥有丰富的文学和文化知识以及完整的人格。十年前,七十五位诺贝尔奖得主聚会巴黎,当时他们所发表的宣言开篇就是,"如果人类要在21世纪生存下去,必须回首2500年去吸收孔子的智慧。"确实,十年的时间让我们有目共睹,现代经济科技的飞速发展何尝不是一柄双刃的剑?只有文化的力量才能抵消随之而来的负面后果。可见,知识的获取与技能的训练对于大学生来说固然重要,但文化与修养却尤需关切。正因为大学生代表着社会先知先觉的知识力量,置身当前的文化现实,就应有一分责任感与使命感,力求对知识技能以外许多带有根本性质的精神追求形成明确的意识,从而具备一种对生命意义进行探索与追问的精神,一种以人文精神为背景的生存勇气和人格力量。那么,能够引导我们探索前行的一盏明灯,不就是闪烁着理想光芒的不朽的文学名著吗?

一个人乃至一个民族,从其对文学的亲疏态度,可以衡量出其文化素质的程度。文学应是从人类文化中升华出的理想的结晶,她"使人的心灵变得高尚,使人的勇气、荣誉感、希望、尊严、同情心、怜悯心和牺牲精神复活起来"(威廉·福克纳);无疑,只有文学才能从更高的层次上提升人的文化素质和整体素质,充实人的内心世界,焕发人的精神风貌,带给人们真善美。而亲近文学,特别是热爱祖国灿烂的文学以及文化,正是当代中国大学生加强文化修养,弘扬人文精神的有力脚步。

"越是民族的,就越是世界的",中国文学属于中国,也属于世界。和平是人类的共同愿望,交流与共享则是新世纪的潮流。

中国当代大学生的血液里流动着数千年的文化积淀,没有理由在让世界了解中国大学生聪明才智的同时,却无缘分享我们的骄傲——中国大学生不但能够读懂英语的莎士比亚,而且能让世界感动于中国文学的伟大。

  这是我们作为出版者的理想。我们原有一个世纪礼物的构想,是同大学生一起做一个"读书计划"。这一次将中国文学的最新荟萃配设高水平的英语译文,是其中推荐给新世纪大学生的第一批读物。盼望着您——我们无数知音中的5000名先来者,给我们鼓励,也给我们意见和批评。

编者
一九九九年五月三十日

只有文学才能从更高的层次上提升人的文化素质和整体素质,充实人的内心世界,焕发人的精神风貌,带给人们真善美。而亲近文学,特别是热爱祖国灿烂的文学以及文化,正是当代中国大学生加强文化修养,弘扬人文精神的有力脚步。

A Madman's Diary

Two brothers, whose names I need not mention here, were both good friends of mine in high school; but after a separation of many years we gradually lost touch. Some time ago I happened to hear that one of them was seriously ill, and since I was going back to my native place I broke my journey to call on them. I saw only one of them, however, who told me that the invalid was his younger brother.

"I appreciate your coming such a long way to see us," he said, "but he recovered some time ago and has gone elsewhere to take up an official post." Then, laughing, he produced two volumes of his brother's diary, saying that from these the nature of his past illness could be seen, and that there was no harm in showing them to an old friend. I took the diary away and read it through, and found that he had suffered from a form of persecution complex. The writing was most confused and incoherent, and he had made many wild statements; moreover he had omitted to give any dates, so that only by the colour of the ink and the differences in the writing could one tell that it was not written at one time. Certain sections, however, were not altogether disconnected, and I have copied out a part to serve as a subject for medical research. I have not altered a single illogicality in the diary and have changed only the names, even though the people referred to are all country folk, unknown

狂人日记①

某君昆仲,今隐其名,皆余昔日在中学校时良友;分隔多年,消息渐阙。日前偶闻其一大病;适归故乡,迂道往访,则仅晤一人,言病者其弟也。劳君远道来视,然已早愈,赴某地候补②矣。因大笑,出示日记二册,谓可见当日病状,不妨献诸旧友。持归阅一过,知所患盖"迫害狂"之类。语颇错杂无伦次,又多荒唐之言;亦不著月日,惟墨色字体不一,知非一时所书。间亦有略具联络者,今撮录一篇,以供医家研究。记中语误,一字不易;惟人名虽皆村人,不为世

---

① 本篇最初发表于一九一八年五月《新青年》第四卷第五号。作者首次采用了"鲁迅"这一笔名。它是我国现代文学史上第一篇猛烈抨击"吃人"的封建礼教的小说。

② 候补:清代官制,只有官衔而没有实际职务的中下级官员,由吏部抽签分发到某部或某省,听候委用,称为候补。

to the world and of no consequence. As for the title, it was chosen by the diarist himself after his recovery, and I did not change it.

April 2, 1918

间所知,无关大体,然亦悉易去。至于书名,则本人愈后所题,不复改也。七年四月二日识。

英汉对照
English-Chinese
中国文学宝库
Gems of Chinese Literature
现代文学系列
Modern Literature

A Madman's Diary

1

Tonight the moon is very bright.

I have not seen it for over thirty years, so today when I saw it I felt in unusually high spirits. I begin to realize that during the past thirty odd years I have been in the dark; but now I must be extremely careful. Otherwise why should that dog at the Zhao house have looked at me twice?

I have reason for my fear.

2

Tonight there is no moon at all, I know that this bodes ill. This morning when I went out cautiously, Mr Zhao had a strange look in his eyes, as if he were afraid of me, as if he wanted to murder me. There were also seven or eight others, who discussed me in a whisper. And they were afraid of my seeing them. All the people I passed were like that. The fiercest among them grinned at me; whereupon I shivered from head to foot, knowing that their preparations were complete.

I was not afraid, however, but continued on my way. A group of children in front were also discussing me, and the look in their eyes was just like that in Mr Zhao's, while their faces too were ghastly pale. I wondered what grudge these children could have against me to make them behave like this. I could not help calling out: "Tell me!" But then they ran away.

I wonder what grudge Mr Zhao can have against me, what

一

今天晚上,很好的月光。

我不见他,已是三十多年;今天见了,精神分外爽快。才知道以前的三十多年,全是发昏;然而须十分小心。不然,那赵家的狗,何以看我两眼呢?

我怕得有理。

二

今天全没月光,我知道不妙。早上小心出门,赵贵翁的眼色便怪:似乎怕我,似乎想害我。还有七八个人,交头接耳的议论我,又怕我看见。一路上的人,都是如此。其中最凶的一个人,张着嘴,对我笑了一笑;我便从头直冷到脚跟,晓得他们布置,都已妥当了。

我可不怕,仍旧走我的路。前面一伙小孩子,也在那里议论我;眼色也同赵贵翁一样,脸色也都铁青。我想我同小孩子有什么仇,他也这样。忍不住大声说,"你告诉我!"他们可就跑了。

我想:我同赵贵翁有什么仇,同路上的人又

英汉对照
English-Chinese
中国文学宝库
Gems of Chinese Literature
现代文学系列
Modern Literature

grudge the people on the road can have against me. I can think of nothing except that twenty years ago I trod on Mr Gu Jiu's[①] account sheets for many years past, and Mr Gu was very displeased. Although Mr Zhao does not know him, he must have heard talk of this and decided to avenge him, so he is conspiring with the people on the road against me. But then what of the children? At that time they were not yet born, so why should they have eyed me so strangely today, as if they were afraid of me, as if they wanted to murder me? This really frightens me, it is so bewildering and upsetting.

I know. They must have learnt this from their parents!

3

I can't sleep at night. Everything requires careful consideration if one is to understand it.

Those people — some of them have been pilloried by the magistrate, some slapped in the face by the local gentry, some have had their wives taken away by bailiffs, some have had their parents driven to death by creditors; yet they never looked as frightened and as fierce then as they did yesterday.

The most extraordinary thing was that woman on the street yesterday who was spanking her son and saying, "Little devil! I'd like to bite several mouthfuls out of you to work off my feelings!" Yet

---

① Gu Jiu means "Ancient Times." Lu Xun had in mind the long history of feudal oppression in China.

有什么仇；只有廿年以前，把古久先生的陈年流水簿子①，踹了一脚，古久先生很不高兴。赵贵翁虽然不认识他，一定也听到风声，代抱不平；约定路上的人，同我作冤对。但是小孩子呢？那时候，他们还没有出世，何以今天也睁着怪眼睛，似乎怕我，似乎想害我。这真教我怕，教我纳罕而且伤心。

我明白了。这是他们娘老子教的！

三

晚上总是睡不着。凡事须得研究，才会明白。

他们——也有给知县打枷过的，也有给绅士掌过嘴的，也有衙役占了他妻子的，也有老子娘被债主逼死的；他们那时候的脸色，全没有昨天这么怕，也没有这么凶。

最奇怪的是昨天街上的那个女人，打他儿子，嘴里说道，"老子呀！我要咬你几口才出

---

① 古久先生的陈年流水簿子：这是比喻我国封建主义统治的长久历史。

all the time she was looking at me. I gave a start, unable to control myself; then all those green-faced, long-toothed people began to laugh derisively. Old Chen hurried forward and dragged me home.

He dragged me home. The folk at home all pretended not to know me; they had the same look in their eyes as all the others. When I went into the study, they locked the door outside as if cooping up a chicken or a duck. This incident left me even more bewildered.

A few days ago a tenant of ours from Wolf Cub Village came to report the failure of the crops, and told my elder brother that a notorious character in their village had been beaten to death; then some people had taken out his heart and liver, fried them in oil and eaten them, as a means of increasing their courage. When I interrupted, the tenant and my brother both stared at me. Only today have I realized that they had exactly the same look in their eyes as those people outside.

Just to think of it sets me shivering from the crown of my head to the soles of my feet.

They eat human beings, so they may eat me.

I see that woman's "bite several mouthfuls out of you," the laughter of those green-faced, long-toothed people and the tenant's story the other day are obviously secret signs. I realize all the poison in their speech, all the daggers in their laughter. Their teeth are white and glistening: they are all man-eaters.

It seems to me, although I am not a bad man, ever since I trod on Mr Gu's accounts it has been touch-and-go. They seem to have secrets which I cannot guess, and once they are angry they will

气!"他眼睛却看着我。我出了一惊,遮掩不住;那青面獠牙的一伙人,便都哄笑起来。陈老五赶上前,硬把我拖回家中了。

拖我回家,家里的人都装作不认识我;他们的眼色,也全同别人一样。进了书房,便反扣上门,宛然是关了一只鸡鸭。这一件事,越教我猜不出底细。

前几天,狼子村的佃户来告荒,对我大哥说,他们村里的一个大恶人,给大家打死了;几个人便挖出他的心肝来,用油煎炒了吃,可以壮壮胆子。我插了一句嘴,佃户和大哥便都看我几眼。今天才晓得他们的眼光,全同外面的那伙人一模一样。

想起来,我从顶上直冷到脚跟。

他们会吃人,就未必不会吃我。

你看那女人"咬你几口"的话,和一伙青面獠牙人的笑,和前天佃户的话,明明是暗号。我看出他话中全是毒,笑中全是刀。他们的牙齿,全是白厉厉的排着,这就是吃人的家伙。

照我自己想,虽然不是恶人,自从踹了古家的簿子,可就难说了。他们似乎别有心思,我全猜不出。况且他们一翻脸,便说人是恶人。我

英汉对照
English-Chinese
中国文学宝库
Gems of Chinese Literature
现代文学系列
Modern Literature

call anyone a bad character. I remember when my elder brother taught me to write compositions, no matter how good a man was, if I produced arguments to the contrary he would mark that passage to show approval; while if I excused evil-doers, he would say: "Good for you, that shows originality." How can I possibly guess their secret thoughts — especially when they are ready to eat people?

Everything requires careful consideration if one is to understand it. In ancient times, as I recollect, people often ate human beings, but I am rather hazy about it. I tried to look this up, but my history has no chronology, and scrawled all over each page are the words: "Virtue and Morality." Since I could not sleep anyway, I read hard half the night, until I began to see words between the lines, the whole book being filled with the two words — "Eat people."

All these words written in the book, all the words spoken by our tenant, gaze at me strangely with an enigmatic smile.

I too am a human being, and they want to eat me!

4

In the morning I sat quietly for some time. Old Chen brought lunch in: one bowl of vegetables, one bowl of steamed fish. The eyes of the fish were white and hard, and its mouth was open just like those people who want to eat human beings. After a few mouthfuls I could not tell whether the slippery morsels were fish or human flesh, so I brought it all up.

I said, "Old Chen, tell my brother that I am feeling quite

还记得大哥教我做论，无论怎样好人，翻他几句，他便打上几个圈；原谅坏人几句，他便说"翻天妙手，与众不同"。我那里猜得到他们的心思，究竟怎样；况且是要吃的时候。

凡事总须研究，才会明白。古来时常吃人，我也还记得，可是不甚清楚。我翻开历史一查，这历史没有年代，歪歪斜斜的每叶上都写着"仁义道德"几个字。我横竖睡不着，仔细看了半夜，才从字缝里看出字来，满本都写着两个字是"吃人"！

书上写着这许多字，佃户说了这许多话，却都笑吟吟的睁着怪眼睛看我。

我也是人，他们想要吃我了！

四

早上，我静坐了一会。陈老五送进饭来，一碗菜，一碗蒸鱼；这鱼的眼睛，白而且硬，张着嘴，同那一伙想吃人的人一样。吃了几筷，滑溜溜的不知是鱼是人，便把他兜肚连肠的吐出。

我说"老五，对大哥说，我闷得慌，想到园里

英汉对照
English-Chinese
中国文学宝库
Gems of Chinese Literature
现代文学系列
Modern Literature

suffocated, and want to have a stroll in the garden." Old Chen said nothing but went out, and presently he came back and opened the gate.

I did not move, watching to see how they would treat me, knowing that they certainly would not let me go. Sure enough! My elder brother came slowly out, leading an old man. There was a murderous gleam in his eyes, and fearing that I would see it he lowered his head, stealing glances at me from the side of his spectacles.

"You seem to be very well today," said my brother.

"Yes," said I.

"I have invited Mr He here today," said my brother, "to examine you."

"All right," said I. But actually I know quite well that this old man was the executioner in disguise! He was simply using the pretext of feeling my pulse to see how fat I was; for by so doing he would be given a share of my flesh. Still I was not afraid. Although I do not eat men, my courage is greater than theirs. I held out my two fists, watching what he would do. The old man sat down, closed his eyes, fumbled for some time and remained still for some time; then he opened his shifty eyes and said, "Don't let your imagination run away with you. Rest quietly for a few days, and you will be all right."

Don't let your imagination run away with you! Rest quietly for a few days! When I have grown fat, naturally they will have mor to eat; but what good will it do me, or how can it be "all right". All these people wanting to eat human flesh and at the same time stealthily trying to keep up appearances, not daring to act

走走。"老五不答应,走了;停一会,可就来开了门。

我也不动,研究他们如何摆布我;知道他们一定不肯放松。果然!我大哥引了一个老头子,慢慢走来;他满眼凶光,怕我看出,只是低头向着地,从眼镜横边暗暗看我。大哥说,"今天你仿佛很好。"我说"是的。"大哥说,"今天请何先生来,给你诊一诊。"我说"可以!"其实我岂不知道这老头子是刽子手扮的!无非借了看脉这名目,揣一揣肥瘠:因这功劳,也分一片肉吃。我也不怕;虽然不吃人,胆子却比他们还壮。伸出两个拳头,看他如何下手。老头子坐着,闭了眼睛,摸了好一会,呆了好一会;便张开他鬼眼睛说,"不要乱想。静静的养几天,就好了。"

不要乱想,静静的养!养肥了,他们是自然可以多吃;我有什么好处,怎么会"好了"?他们这群人,又想吃人,又是鬼鬼祟祟,想法子遮掩,

promptly, really made me nearly die of laughter. I could not help roaring with laughter, I felt so amused. I knew that in this laughter were courage and integrity. Both the old man and my brother turned pale, awed by my courage and integrity.

But just because I am brave they are the more eager to eat me, in order to acquire some of my courage. The old man went out of the gate, but before he had gone far he said to my brother in a low voice, "To be eaten at once!" And my brother nodded. So you are in it too! This stupendous discovery, although it came as a shock, is yet no more than I had expected: the accomplice in eating me is my elder brother!

The eater of human flesh is my elder brother!

I am the younger brother of an eater of human flesh!

I myself will be eaten by others, but none the less I am the younger brother of an eater of human flesh!

5

These few days I have been thinking again: suppose that old man were not an executioner in disguise, but a real doctor; he would be none the less an eater of human flesh. In that book on herbs, written by his predecessor Li Shizhen,① it is clearly stated that human flesh can be boiled and eaten; so can he still say that he does not eat humans?

---

① A famous pharmacologist (1518-1593), author of *Ben-cao-gang-mu*, the *Materia Medica*.

不敢直捷下手,真要令我笑死。我忍不住,便放声大笑起来,十分快活。自己晓得这笑声里面,有的是义勇和正气。老头子和大哥,都失了色,被我这勇气正气镇压住了。

但是我有勇气,他们便越想吃我,沾光一点这勇气。老头子跨出门,走不多远,便低声对大哥说道,"赶紧吃罢!"大哥点点头。原来也有你!这一件大发见,虽似意外,也在意中:合伙吃我的人,便是我的哥哥!

吃人的是我哥哥!

我是吃人的人的兄弟!

我自己被人吃了,可仍然是吃人的人的兄弟!

五

这几天是退一步想:假使那老头子不是刽子手扮的,真是医生,也仍然是吃人的人。他们的祖师李时珍做的"本草什么"① 上,明明写着人肉可以煎吃;他还能说自己不吃人么?

---

① "本草什么":指明代李时珍的药物学著作《本草纲目》。该书曾经提到唐代陈藏器《本草拾遗》中以人肉医治痨病的记载,并表示了异议。这里说李时珍的书"明明写着人肉可以煎吃",当是"狂人"的"记中语误"。

英汉对照
English-Chinese
中国文学宝库
Gems of Chinese Literature
现代文学系列
Modern Literature

As for my elder brother, I have also good reason to suspect him. When he was teaching me, he said with his own lips, "People exchange their sons to eat."[①] And once, in discussing a bad man, he said that not only did he deserve to be killed, he should "have his flesh eaten and his hide slept on."[②] I was still young then, and my heart beat faster for some time. And he was not at all surprised by the story about eating a man's heart and liver that our tenant from Wolf Cub Village told us the other day, but kept nodding his head. He is evidently just as cruel as before. Since it is possible to "exchange sons to eat," then anything can be exchanged, anyone can be eaten. In the past I simply listened to his explanations, and let it go at that; now I know that when he was explaining to me, not only was there human oil at the corner of his lips, but his whole heart was set on eating men.

6

Pitch dark. I don't know whether it is day or night. The Zhao family dog has started barking again.

The fierceness of a lion, the timidity of a rabbit, the craftiness of a fox...

7

I know their way; they are not willing to kill anyone outright,

---

① These are quotations from the old classic, *Zuo Zhuan*.
② These are quotations from the old classic, *Zuo Zhuan*.

至于我家大哥,也毫不冤枉他。他对我讲书的时候,亲口说过可以"易子而食"①;又一回偶然议论起一个不好的人,他便说不但该杀,还当"食肉寝皮"②。我那时年纪还小,心跳了好半天。前天狼子村佃户来说吃心肝的事,他也毫不奇怪,不住的点头。可见心思是同从前一样狠。既然可以"易子而食",便什么都易得,什么人都吃得。我从前单听他讲道理,也胡涂过去;现在晓得他讲道理的时候,不但唇边还抹着人油,而且心里满装着吃人的意思。

六

黑漆漆的,不知是日是夜。赵家的狗又叫起来了。

狮子似的凶心,兔子的怯弱,狐狸的狡猾,……

七

我晓得他们的方法,直捷杀了,是不肯的,

---

① "易子而食":语见《左传》宣公十五年,是宋将华元对楚将子反叙说宋国都城被楚军围困时的惨状:"敝邑易子而食,析骸而爨。"

② "食肉寝皮":语出《左传》襄公二十一年,晋国州绰对齐庄公说:"然二子者,譬于禽兽,臣食其肉而寝处其皮矣。"按"二子"指齐国的殖绰和郭最,他们曾被州绰俘虏过。

英汉对照
English-Chinese
中国文学宝库
Gems of Chinese Literature
现代文学系列
Modern Literature

nor do they dare, for fear of the consequences. So they have all banded together and set traps everywhere, to force me to kill myself. Just look at the behaviour of the men and women in the street a few days ago, and my elder brother's attitude these last few days, it is quite obvious. What they like best is for a man to take off his belt, and hang himself from a beam; for then they can enjoy their heart's desire without being blamed for murder. Naturally that sets them roaring with morbid laughter. On the other hand, if a man is frightened or worried to death, although that makes him rather thin, they still nod in approval.

They will only eat dead flesh! I remember reading somewhere of a hideous beast, with an ugly look in its eye, called "hyena" which often eats dead flesh. Even the largest bones it grinds into fragments and swallows: the mere thought of this is enough to terrify one. Hyenas are related to wolves, and wolves belong to the canine species. The other day the dog in the Zhao house looked at me several times; obviously it is in the plot too and has become their accomplice. The old man's eyes were cast down, but how could that deceive me!

The most deplorable is my elder brother. He is also a man, so why is he not afraid, why is he plotting with others to eat me? Is it that when one is used to it he no longer thinks it a crime? Or is it that he has hardened his heart to do something he knows is wrong?

In cursing man-eaters, I shall start with my brother, and in dissuading man-eaters, I shall start with him too.

8

Actually, such arguments should have convinced them long

而且也不敢,怕有祸祟。所以他们大家连络,布满了罗网,逼我自戕。试看前几天街上男女的样子,和这几天我大哥的作为,便足可悟出八九分了。最好是解下腰带,挂在梁上,自己紧紧勒死;他们没有杀人的罪名,又偿了心愿,自然都欢天喜地的发出一种呜呜咽咽的笑声。否则惊吓忧愁死了,虽则略瘦,也还可以首肯几下。

他们是只会吃死肉的!——记得什么书上说,有一种东西,叫"海乙那"① 的,眼光和样子都很难看;时常吃死肉,连极大的骨头,都细细嚼烂,咽下肚子去,想起来也教人害怕。"海乙那"是狼的亲眷,狼是狗的本家。前天赵家的狗,看我几眼,可见他也同谋,早已接洽。老头子眼看着地,岂能瞒得我过。

最可怜的是我的大哥,他也是人,何以毫不害怕;而且合伙吃我呢?还是历来惯了,不以为非呢?还是丧了良心,明知故犯呢?

我诅咒吃人的人,先从他起头;要劝转吃人的人,也先从他下手。

八

其实这种道理,到了现在,他们也该早已懂

---

① "海乙那":英语 Hyena 的音译,即鬣狗(又名土狼),一种食肉兽,常跟在狮虎等猛兽之后,以它们吃剩的兽类的残尸为食。

ago...

Suddenly someone came in. He was only about twenty years old and I did not see his features very clearly. His face was wreathed in smiles, and when he nodded to me his smile did not seem genuine. Then I asked him: "Is it right to eat human beings?"

Still smiling, he replied, "When there is no famine how can one eat human beings?"

I realized at once, he was one of them; but still I summoned up courage to repeat my question:

"Is it right?"

"What makes you ask such a thing? You really are... fond of a joke... It is very fine today."

"It is fine, and the moon is very bright. But I want to ask you: Is it right?"

He looked disconcerted, and muttered: "No..."

"No? Then why do they still do it?"

"What are you talking about?"

"What am I talking about? They are eating men now in Wolf Cub Village, and you can see it written all over the books, in fresh red ink."

His expression changed, and he grew ghastly pale. "It may be so," he said, staring at me. "It has always been like that..."

"Is it right because it has always been like that?"

"I refuse to discuss these things with you. Anyway, you shouldn't talk about it. Whoever talks about it is in the wrong!"

I leapt up and opened my eyes wide, but the man had vanished. I was soaked with perspiration. He was much younger than my

得,……

忽然来了一个人;年纪不过二十左右,相貌是不很看得清楚,满面笑容,对了我点头,他的笑也不像真笑。我便问他,"吃人的事,对么?"他仍然笑着说,"不是荒年,怎么会吃人。"我立刻就晓得,他也是一伙,喜欢吃人的;便自勇气百倍,偏要问他。

"对么?"

"这等事问他什么。你真会……说笑话。……今天天气很好。"

天气是好,月色也很亮了。可是我要问你,"对么?"

他不以为然了。含含胡胡的答道,"不……"

"不对?他们何以竟吃?!"

"没有的事……"

"没有的事?狼子村现吃;还有书上都写着,通红斩新!"

他便变了脸,铁一般青。睁着眼说,"有许有的,这是从来如此……"

"从来如此,便对么?"

"我不同你讲这些道理;总之你不该说,你说便是你错!"

我直跳起来,张开眼,这人便不见了。全身出了一大片汗。他的年纪,比我大哥小得远,居

英汉对照
English-Chinese
中国文学宝库
Gems of Chinese Literature
现代文学系列
Modern Literature

elder brother, but even so he was in it. He must have been taught by his parents. And I am afraid he has already taught his son: that is why even the children look at me so fiercely.

9

Wanting to eat men, at the same time afraid of being eaten themselves, they all look at each other with the deepest suspicion...

How comfortable life would be for them if they could get rid of such obsessions and go to work, walk, eat and sleep at ease. They have only this one step to take. And yet fathers and sons, husbands and wives, brothers, friends, teachers and students, sworn enemies and even strangers have all joined in this conspiracy, discouraging and preventing each other from taking this step.

10

Early this morning I went to look for my elder brother. He was standing outside the hall door looking at the sky, when I walked up behind him, stood between him and the door, and with exceptional poise and politeness said to him:

"Brother, I have something to say to you."

"Well, what is it?" said he, quickly turning towards me and nodding.

"It is very little, but I find it difficult to say. Brother, probably all primitive people ate a little human flesh to begin with. Later, because their outlook changed, some of them stopped, and

然也是一伙；这一定是他娘老子先教的。还怕已经教给他儿子了；所以连小孩子，也都恶狠狠的看我。

九

自己想吃人，又怕被别人吃了，都用着疑心极深的眼光，面面相觑。……

去了这心思，放心做事走路吃饭睡觉，何等舒服。这只是一条门槛，一个关头。他们可是父子兄弟夫妇朋友师生仇敌和各不相识的人，都结成一伙，互相劝勉，互相牵掣，死也不肯跨过这一步。

十

大清早，去寻我大哥；他立在堂门外看天，我便走到他背后，拦住门，格外沉静，格外和气的对他说，

"大哥，我有话告诉你。"

"你说就是，"他赶紧回过脸来，点点头。

"我只有几句话，可是说不出来。大哥，大约当初野蛮的人，都吃过一点人。后来因为心

英汉对照
English-Chinese
中国文学宝库
Gems of Chinese Literature
现代文学系列
Modern Literature

because they tried to be good they changed into humans, changed into real human beings. But some are still eating — just like reptiles: some have changed into fish, birds, monkeys and finally humans; but some do not try to be good, and remain reptiles still. When those who eat men compare themselves with those who do not, how ashamed they must be. Probably much more ashamed than the reptiles before the monkeys.

"In ancient times Yi Ya boiled his son for Nüe and Zhou to eat, that is the old story.① But actually since the creation of heaven and earth by Pan Gu men have been eating each other, from the time of Yi Ya's son to the time of Xu Xilin,② and from the time of Xu Xilin down to the man caught in Wolf Cub Village. Last year they executed a criminal in the city, and a consumptive soaked a piece of bread in his blood and sucked it.③

"They want to eat me, and of course you can do nothing about it single-handed; but why should you join them? As man-eaters they are capable of anything. If they eat me, they can eat you as well; members of the same group can still eat each other. But if you will just change your ways immediately, then everyone will have peace. Although this has been going on since time immemorial, today we

---

① According to ancient records, Yi Ya cooked his son and presented him to Duke Huan of Qi who reigned from 685 to 643 B C. Nie and Zhou were tyrants of an earlier age. The madman has made a mistake here.

② A revolutionary at the end of the Qing Dynasty (1644-1911), Xu Xilin was executed in 1907 for assassinating a Manchu official. His heart and liver were eaten.

③ It was believed that human blood cured consumption. Thus after the execution of a criminal, the executioner would sell steamed bread dipped in blood.

思不同，有的不吃人了，一味要好，便变了人，变了真的人。有的却还吃，——也同虫子一样，有的变了鱼鸟猴子，一直变到人。有的不要好，至今还是虫子。这吃人的人比不吃人的人，何等惭愧。怕比虫子的惭愧猴子，还差得很远很远。

"易牙① 蒸了他儿子，给桀纣吃，还是一直从前的事。谁晓得从盘古开辟天地以后，一直吃到易牙的儿子；从易牙的儿子，一直吃到徐锡林②；从徐锡林，又一直吃到狼子村捉住的人。去年城里杀了犯人，还有一个生痨病的人，用馒头蘸血舐。

"他们要吃我，你一个人，原也无法可想；然而又何必去入伙。吃人的人，什么事做不出；他们会吃我，也会吃你，一伙里面，也会自吃。但只要转一步，只要立刻改了，也就人人太平。虽

---

① 易牙：春秋时齐国人，善于调味。据《管子·小称》："夫易牙以调和事公（按指齐桓公），公曰'惟蒸婴儿之未尝'，于是蒸其首子而献之公。"桀、纣各为我国夏朝和商朝的最后一代君主，易牙和他们不是同时代人。这里说的"易牙蒸了他儿子，给桀纣吃"，也是"狂人""语颇错杂无伦次"的表现。

② 徐锡林：隐指徐锡麟（1873—1907），字伯荪，浙江绍兴人，清末革命团体光复会的重要成员。一九〇七年与秋瑾准备在浙、皖两省同时起义，七月六日，他以安徽巡警处会办兼巡警学堂监督身份为掩护，乘学堂举行毕业典礼之机刺死安徽巡抚恩铭，率领学生攻占军械局，弹尽被捕，当日惨遭杀害，心肝被恩铭的卫队挖出炒食。

27

could make a special effort to be good, and say this can't be done! I'm sure you can say so, brother. The other day when the tenant wanted the rent reduced, you said it couldn't be done."

At first he only smiled cynically, then a murderous gleam came into his eyes, and when I spoke of their secret his face turned pale. Outside the gate stood a group of people, including Mr Zhao and his dog, all craning their necks and trying to edge themselves into the room. I could not see all their faces, for they seemed to be masked in cloths; some of them looked pale and ghastly still, concealing their laughter. I knew they were one band, all eaters of human flesh. But I also knew that they did not all think alike by any means. Some of them thought that since it had always been so, men should be eaten. Some of them knew that they should not eat men, but still wanted to; and they were afraid people might disclose their secret; thus when they heard me they became angry, but they still smiled their cynical, tight-lipped smile.

Suddenly my brother looked furious, and shouted in a loud voice:

"Get out of here, all of you! What is the point of looking at a madman?"

Then I realized part of their cunning. They would never be willing to change their stand, and their plans were all laid; they had stigmatized me as a madman. In future when I was eaten, not only would there be no trouble, but people would probably be grateful to them. When our tenant spoke of the villagers eating a bad character, it was exactly the same device. This is their old trick.

Old Chen came in too, in a great temper, but they could not

然从来如此,我们今天也可以格外要好,说是不能! 大哥,我相信你能说,前天佃户要减租,你说过不能。"

当初,他还只是冷笑,随后眼光便凶狠起来,一到说破他们的隐情,那就满脸都变成青色了。大门外立着一伙人,赵贵翁和他的狗,也在里面,都探头探脑的挨进来。有的是看不出面貌,似乎用布蒙着;有的是仍旧青面獠牙,抿着嘴笑。我认识他们是一伙,都是吃人的人。可是也晓得他们心思很不一样,一种是以为从来如此,应该吃的;一种是知道不该吃,可是仍然要吃,又怕别人说破他,所以听了我的话,越发气愤不过,可是抿着嘴冷笑。

这时候,大哥也忽然显出凶相,高声喝道,"都出去! 疯子有什么好看!"

这时候,我又懂得一件他们的巧妙了。他们岂但不肯改,而且早已布置;预备下一个疯子的名目罩上我。将来吃了,不但太平无事,怕还会有人见情。佃户说的大家吃了一个恶人,正是这方法。这是他们的老谱!

陈老五也气愤愤的直走进来。如何按得住

英汉对照
English-Chinese
中国文学宝库
Gems of Chinese Literature
现代文学系列
Modern Literature

stop my mouth, I had to speak to those people:

"You should change, change from the bottom of your hearts!" I said. "You must know that in future there will be no place for man-eaters in the world.

"If you don't change, you may all be eaten by each other. Although so many are born, they will be wiped out by the real men, just like wolves killed by the hunters. Just like reptiles!"

Old Chen drove everybody away. My brother had disappeared. Old Chen advised me to go back to my room. The room was pitch dark. The beams and rafters shook above my head. After shaking for some time they grew larger. They piled on top of me.

The weight was so great, I could not move. They meant that I should die. I knew that the weight was false, so I struggled out, covered in perspiration. But I had to say:

"You should change at once, change from the bottom of your hearts! You must know that in future there will be no place for man-eaters in the world..."

11

The sun does not shine, the door is not opened, every day two meals.

I took up my chopsticks, then thought of my elder brother; I know now how my little sister died: it was all through him. My sister was only five at the time. I can still remember how lovable and pathetic she looked. Mother cried and cried, but he begged her not to cry, probably because he had eaten my sister himself, and

我的口,我偏要对这伙人说,

"你们可以改了,从真心改起!要晓得将来容不得吃人的人,活在世上。

"你们要不改,自己也会吃尽。即使生得多,也会给真的人除灭了,同猎人打完狼子一样!——同虫子一样!"

那一伙人,都被陈老五赶走了。大哥也不知那里去了。陈老五劝我回屋子里去。屋里面全是黑沉沉的。横梁和椽子都在头上发抖;抖了一会,就大起来,堆在我身上。

万分沉重,动弹不得;他的意思是要我死。我晓得他的沉重是假的,便挣扎出来,出了一身汗。可是偏要说,

"你们立刻改了,从真心改起!你们要晓得将来是容不得吃人的人,……"

十一

太阳也不出,门也不开,日日是两顿饭。

我捏起筷子,便想起我大哥;晓得妹子死掉的缘故,也全在他。那时我妹子才五岁,可爱可怜的样子,还在眼前。母亲哭个不住,他却劝母亲不要哭;大约因为自己吃了,哭起来不免有点

英汉对照
English-Chinese
中国文学宝库
Gems of Chinese Literature
现代文学系列
Modern Literature

so her crying made him feel ashamed. If he had any sense of shame...

My sister was eaten by my brother, but I don't know whether mother realized it or not.

I think mother must have known, but when she was crying she did not say so outright, probably because she thought it proper too. I remember when I was four or five years old, sitting in the cool of the hall, my brother told me that if a man's parents were ill he should cut off a piece of his flesh and boil it for them, if he wanted to be considered a good son; and mother did not contradict him. If one piece could be eaten, obviously so could the whole. And yet just to think of the mourning then still makes my heart bleed; that is the extraordinary thing about it!

12

I can't bear to think of it.

I have only just realized that I have been living all these years in a place where for four thousand years they have been eating human flesh. My brother had just taken over the charge of the house when our sister died, and he may well have used her flesh in our rice and dishes, making us eat it unwittingly.

It is possible that I ate several pieces of my sister's flesh unwittingly, and now it is my turn...

How can a man like myself, after four thousand years of man-eating history — even though I knew nothing about it at first — ever hope to face real men?

过意不去。如果还能过意不去,……

妹子是被大哥吃了,母亲知道没有,我可不得而知。

母亲想也知道;不过哭的时候,却并没有说明,大约也以为应当的了。记得我四五岁时,坐在堂前乘凉,大哥说爷娘生病,做儿子的须割下一片肉来,煮熟了请他吃,①才算好人;母亲也没有说不行。一片吃得,整个的自然也吃得。但是那天的哭法,现在想起来,实在还教人伤心,这真是奇极的事!

十二

不能想了。

四千年来时时吃人的地方,今天才明白,我也在其中混了多年;大哥正管着家务,妹子恰恰死了,他未必不和在饭菜里,暗暗给我们吃。

我未必无意之中,不吃了我妹子的几片肉,现在也轮到我自己,……

有了四千年吃人履历的我,当初虽然不知道,现在明白,难见真的人!

---

① 即所谓"割股疗亲",割取自己的股肉煎药,以医治父母的重病。《宋史·选举志一》:"上以孝取人,则勇者割股,怯者庐墓。"

英汉对照
English-Chinese
中国文学宝库
Gems of Chinese Literature
现代文学系列
Modern Literature

13

Perhaps there are still children who have not eaten men?
Save the children...

April 1918

十三

没有吃过人的孩子,或者还有?

救救孩子……

一九一八年四月。

Kong Yiji

The layout of Luzhen's taverns is unique. In each, facing you as you enter, is a bar in the shape of a carpenter's square where hot water is kept ready for warming rice wine. When men come off work at midday and in the evening they spend four coppers on a bowl of wine — or so they did twenty years ago; now it costs ten — and drink this warm, standing by the bar, taking it easy. Another copper will buy a plate of salted bamboo shoots or peas flavoured with aniseed to go with the wine, while a dozen will buy a meat dish; but most of the customers here belong to the short-coated class, few of whom can afford this. As for those in long gowns, they go into the inner room to order wine and dishes and sit drinking at their leisure.

At the age of twelve I started work as a pot-boy in Prosperity Tavern at the edge of the town. The boss put me to work in the outer room, saying that I looked too much of a fool to serve long-gowned customers. The short-coated customers there were easier to deal with, it is true, but among them were quite a few pernickety ones who insisted on watching for themselves while the yellow wine was ladled from the keg, looked for water at the bottom of the winepot, and personally inspected the pot's immersion into the hot water. Under such strict surveillance, diluting the wine was very hard indeed. Thus it did not take my boss many days to decide that this job too was beyond me. Luckily I had been recommended by somebody influential, so my boss

孔乙己①

鲁镇的酒店的格局,是和别处不同的:都是当街一个曲尺形的大柜台,柜里面预备着热水,可以随时温酒。做工的人,傍午傍晚散了工,每每花四文铜钱,买一碗酒,——这是二十多年前的事,现在每碗要涨到十文,——靠柜外站着,热热的喝了休息;倘肯多花一文,便可以买一碟盐煮笋,或者茴香豆,做下酒物了,如果出到十几文,那就能买一样荤菜,但这些顾客,多是短衣帮,大抵没有这样阔绰。只有穿长衫的,才踱进店里隔壁的房子里,要酒要菜,慢慢地坐喝。

我从十二岁起,便在镇口的咸亨酒店里当伙计,掌柜说,样子太傻,怕侍候不了长衫主顾,就在外面做点事罢。外面的短衣主顾,虽然容易说话,但唠唠叨叨缠夹不清的也很不少。他们往往要亲眼看着黄酒从坛子里舀出,看过壶子底里有水没有,又亲看将壶子放在热水里,然后放心:在这严重监督之下,羼水也很为难。所以过了几天,掌柜又说我干不了这事。幸亏荐

---

① 本篇最初发表于一九一九年四月《新青年》第六卷第四号。

Kong Yiji

could not sack me. Instead I was transferred to the dull task of simply warming wine.

After that I stood all day behind the bar attending to my duties. Although I was satisfactory at this post, I found it somewhat boring and monotonous. Our boss was a grim-faced man, nor were the customers much pleasanter, which made the atmosphere quite gloomy. The only times when there was any laughter were when Kong Yiji came to the tavern. That is why I remember him.

Kong Yiji was the only long-gowned customer who used to drink his wine standing. A big, pallid man whose wrinkled face often bore scars, he had a large, unkempt and grizzled beard. And although he wore a long gown it was dirty and tattered. It had not by the look of it been washed or mended for ten years or more. He used so many archaisms in his speech that half of it was barely intelligible. And as his surname was Kong, he was given the nickname Kong Yiji from Kong Yi Ji, the first three characters in the old-fashioned children's copybook. Whenever he came in, everyone there would look at him and chuckle. And someone was sure to call out:

"Kong Yiji! What are those fresh scars on your face?"

Ignoring this, he would lay nine coppers on the bar and order two bowls of heated wine with a dish of aniseed-peas. Then someone else would bawl:

"You must have been stealing again!"

"Why sully a man's good name for no reason at all?" Kong Yiji would ask, raising his eyebrows.

"Good name? Why, the day before yesterday you were trussed up and beaten for stealing books from the He family. I saw you!"

头的情面大,辞退不得,便改为专管温酒的一种无聊职务了。

我从此便整天的站在柜台里,专管我的职务。虽然没有什么失职,但总觉有些单调,有些无聊。掌柜是一副凶脸孔,主顾也没有好声气,教人活泼不得;只有孔乙己到店,才可以笑几声,所以至今还记得。

孔乙己是站着喝酒而穿长衫的唯一的人。他身材很高大;青白脸色,皱纹间时常夹些伤痕;一部乱蓬蓬的花白的胡子。穿的虽然是长衫,可是又脏又破,似乎十多年没有补,也没有洗。他对人说话,总是满口之乎者也,教人半懂不懂的。因为他姓孔,别人便从描红纸① 上的"上大人孔乙己"这半懂不懂的话里,替他取下一个绰号,叫作孔乙己。孔乙己到店,所有喝酒的人便都看着他笑,有的叫道,"孔乙己,你脸上又添上新伤疤了!"他不回答,对柜里说,"温两碗酒,要一碟茴香豆。"便排出九文大钱。他们又故意的高声嚷道,"你一定又偷了人家的东西了!"孔乙己睁大眼睛说,"你怎么这样凭空污人清白……""什么清白?我前天亲眼见你偷了

---

① 描红纸:一种印有红色楷字,供儿童摹写毛笔字用的字帖。

英汉对照
English-Chinese
中国文学宝库
Gems of Chinese Literature
现代文学系列
Modern Literature

At that Kong Yiji would flush, the veins on his forehead standing out as he protested, "Taking books can't be counted as stealing... Taking books... for a scholar... can't be counted as stealing." Then followed such quotations from the classics as "A gentleman keeps his integrity even in poverty," together with a spate of archaisms which soon had everybody roaring with laughter, enlivening the whole tavern.

From the gossip that I heard, it seemed that Kong Yiji had studied the classics but never passed the official examinations and, not knowing any way to make a living, he had grown steadily poorer until he was almost reduced to beggary. Luckily he was a good calligrapher and could find enough copying work to fill his rice-bowl. But unfortunately he had his failings too: laziness and a love of tippling. So after a few days he would disappear, taking with him books, paper, brushes and inkstone. And after this had happened several times, people stopped employing him as a copyist. Then all he could do was resort to occasional pilfering. In our tavern, though, he was a model customer who never failed to pay up. Sometimes, it is true, when he had no ready money, his name would be chalked up on our tallyboard; but in less than a month he invariably settled the bill, and the name Kong Yiji would be wiped off the board again.

After Kong Yiji had drunk half a bowl of wine, his flushed cheeks would stop burning. But then someone would ask:

"Kong Yiji, can you really read?"

When he glanced back as if such a question were not worth answering, they would continue: "How is it you never passed even the lowest official examination?"

何家的书,吊着打。"孔乙己便涨红了脸,额上的青筋条条绽出,争辩道,"窃书不能算偷……窃书!……读书人的事,能算偷么?"接连便是难懂的话,什么"君子固穷"①,什么"者乎"之类,引得众人都哄笑起来:店内外充满了快活的空气。

听人家背地里谈论,孔乙己原来也读过书,但终于没有进学②,又不会营生;于是愈过愈穷,弄到将要讨饭了。幸而写得一笔好字,便替人家钞钞书,换一碗饭吃。可惜他又有一样坏脾气,便是好喝懒做。坐不到几天,便连人和书籍纸张笔砚,一齐失踪。如是几次,叫他钞书的人也没有了。孔乙己没有法,便免不了偶然做些偷窃的事。但他在我们店里,品行却比别人都好,就是从不拖欠;虽然间或没有现钱,暂时记在粉板上,但不出一月,定然还清,从粉板上拭去了孔乙己的名字。

孔乙己喝过半碗酒,涨红的脸色渐渐复了原,旁人便又问道,"孔乙己,你当真认识字么?"孔乙己看着问他的人,显出不屑置辩的神气。他们便接着说道,"你怎的连半个秀才也捞不到

---

① "君子固穷":语见《论语·卫灵公》。"固穷"即"固守其穷",不以穷困而改变操守的意思。

② 进学:明清科举制度,童生经过县考初试,府考复试,再参加由学政主持的院考(道考),考取的列名府、县学籍,叫进学,也就成了秀才。又规定每三年举行一次乡试(省一级考试),由秀才或监生应考,取中的就是举人。

At once a grey tinge would overspread Kong Yiji's dejected, discomfited face, and he would mumble more of those unintelligible archaisms. Then everyone there would laugh heartily again, enlivening the whole tavern.

At such times I could join in the laughter with no danger of a dressing-down from my boss. In fact he always put such questions to Kong Yiji himself, to raise a laugh. Knowing that it was no use talking to the men, Kong Yiji would chat with us boys. Once he asked me:

"Have you had any schooling?"

When I nodded curtly he said, "Well then, I'll test you. How do you write the '*hui*'[①] as in aniseed-peas?"

Who did this beggar think he was, testing me! I turned away and ignored him. After waiting for some time he said earnestly:

"You can't write it, eh? I'll show you. Mind you remember. You ought to remember such characters, because you'll need them to write up your accounts when you have a shop of your own."

It seemed to me that I was still very far from having a shop of my own; in addition to which, our boss never entered aniseed-peas in his account-book. Half amused and half exasperated, I drawled: "I don't need you to show me. Isn't it the *hui* written with the element for grass?"

Kong Yiji's face lit up. Tapping two long finger-nails on the bar, he nodded. "Quite correct!" he said. "There are four different ways of writing *hui*. Do you know them?"

But with my patience exhausted, I scowled and moved away. Kong

---

① A Chinese character meaning "aniseed."

呢?"孔乙己立刻显出颓唐不安模样,脸上笼上了一层灰色,嘴里说些话;这回可是全是之乎者也之类,一些不懂了。在这时候,众人也都哄笑起来:店内外充满了快活的空气。

在这些时候,我可以附和着笑,掌柜是决不责备的。而且掌柜见了孔乙己,也每每这样问他,引人发笑。孔乙己自己知道不能和他们谈天,便只好向孩子说话。有一回对我说道,"你读过书么?"我略略点一点头。他说,"读过书,……我便考你一考。茴香豆的茴字,怎样写的?"我想,讨饭一样的人,也配考我么?便回过脸去,不再理会。孔乙己等了许久,很恳切的说道,"不能写罢?……我教给你,记着!这些字应该记着。将来做掌柜的时候,写账要用。"我暗想我和掌柜的等级还很远呢,而且我们掌柜也从不将茴香豆上账;又好笑,又不耐烦,懒懒的答他道,"谁要你教,不是草头底下一个来回的回字么?"孔乙己显出极高兴的样子,将两个指头的长指甲敲着柜台,点头说,"对呀对呀!……回字有四样写法,你知道么?"我愈不耐烦

英汉对照
English-Chinese
中国文学宝库
Gems of Chinese Literature
现代文学系列
Modern Literature

Yiji had dipped his finger in wine to trace the characters on the bar. When he saw my utter indifference his face fell and he sighed.

Sometimes children in the neighbourhood, hearing laughter, came in to join in the fun and surrounded Kong Yiji. Then he would give them aniseed-peas, one apiece. After eating the peas the children would still hang round, their eyes fixed on the dish. Growing flustered, he would cover it with his hand and bending forward from the waist would say: "There aren't many left, not many at all." Straightening up to look at the peas again, he would shake his head and reiterate: "Not many, I do assure you. Not many, nay, not many at all." Then the children would scamper off, shouting with laughter.

That was how Kong Yiji contributed to our enjoyment, but we got along all right without him too.

One day, shortly before the Mid-Autumn Festival, at least I think it was, my boss, who was slowly making out his accounts, took down the tallyboard. "Kong Yiji hasn't shown up for a long time," he remarked suddenly. "He still owes nineteen coppers." That made me realize how long it was since we had seen him.

"How could he?" rejoined one of the customers. "His legs were broken in that last beating up."

"Ah!" said my boss.

"He'd been stealing again. This time he was fool enough to steal from Mr Ding, the provincial-grade scholar. As if anybody could get away with that!"

"So what happened?"

"What happened? First he wrote a confession, then he was beaten. The beating lasted nearly all night, and they broke both his legs."

了,努着嘴走远。孔乙己刚用指甲蘸了酒,想在柜上写字,见我毫不热心,便又叹一口气,显出极惋惜的样子。

有几回,邻舍孩子听得笑声,也赶热闹,围住了孔乙己。他便给他们茴香豆吃,一人一颗。孩子吃完豆,仍然不散,眼睛都望着碟子。孔乙己着了慌,伸开五指将碟子罩住,弯腰下去说道,"不多了,我已经不多了。"直起身又看一看豆,自己摇头说,"不多不多!多乎哉?不多也。"① 于是这一群孩子都在笑声里走散了。

孔乙己是这样的使人快活,可是没有他,别人也便这么过。

有一天,大约是中秋前的两三天,掌柜正在慢慢的结账,取下粉板,忽然说,"孔乙己长久没有来了。还欠十九个钱呢!"我才觉得他的确长久没有来了。一个喝酒的人说道,"他怎么会来?……他打折了腿了。"掌柜说,"哦!""他总仍旧是偷。这一回,是自己发昏,竟偷到丁举人家里去了。他家的东西,偷得的么?""后来怎么样?""怎么样?先写服辩②,后来是打,打了大

---

① "多乎哉?不多也":语见《论语·子罕》:"大宰问于子贡曰:'夫子圣者与?何其多能也!'子贡曰:'固天纵之将圣,又多能也。'子闻之,曰:'大宰知我乎?吾少也贱,故多能鄙事。君子多乎哉?不多也。'"这里与原意无关。

② 服辩:又作伏辩,即认罪书。

英汉对照
English-Chinese
中国文学宝库
Gems of Chinese Literature
现代文学系列
Modern Literature

"And then?"

"Well, his legs were broken."

"Yes, but after?"

"After?... Who knows? He may be dead."

My boss asked no further questions but went on slowly making up his accounts.

After the Mid-Autumn Festival the wind grew daily colder as winter approached, and even though I spent all my time by the stove I had to wear a padded jacket. One afternoon, when the tavern was deserted, as I sat with my eyes closed I heard the words:

"Warm a bowl of wine."

It was said in a low but familiar voice. I opened my eyes. There was no one to be seen. I stood up to look out. There below the bar, facing the door, sat Kong Yiji. His face was thin and grimy — he looked a wreck. He had on a ragged lined jacket and was squatting cross-legged on a mat which was attached to his shoulders by a straw rope. When he saw me he repeated:

"Warm a bowl of wine."

At this point my boss leaned over the bar to ask: "Is that Kong Yiji? You still owe nineteen coppers."

"That... I'll settle next time." He looked up dejectedly. "Here's cash. Give me some good wine."

My boss, just as in the past, chuckled and said:

"Kong Yiji, you've been stealing again!"

But instead of a stout denial, the answer simply was:

"Don't joke with me."

"Joke? How did your legs get broken if you hadn't been stealing?"

半夜,再打折了腿。""后来呢?""后来打折了腿了。""打折了怎样呢?""怎样?……谁晓得?许是死了。"掌柜也不再问,仍然慢慢的算他的账。

中秋过后,秋风是一天凉比一天,看看将近初冬;我整天的靠着火,也须穿上棉袄了。一天的下半天,没有一个顾客,我正合了眼坐着。忽然间听得一个声音,"温一碗酒。"这声音虽然极低,却很耳熟。看时又全没有人。站起来向外一望,那孔乙己便在柜台下对了门槛坐着。他脸上黑而且瘦,已经不成样子;穿一件破夹袄,盘着两腿,下面垫一个蒲包,用草绳在肩上挂住;见了我,又说道,"温一碗酒。"掌柜也伸出头去,一面说,"孔乙己么?你还欠十九个钱呢!"孔乙己很颓唐的仰面答道,"这……下回还清罢。这一回是现钱,酒要好。"掌柜仍然同平常一样,笑着对他说,"孔乙己,你又偷了东西了!"但他这回却不十分分辩,单说了一句"不要取笑!""取笑?要是不偷,怎么会打断腿?"孔乙己

英汉对照
English-Chinese
中国文学宝库
Gems of Chinese Literature
现代文学系列
Modern Literature

"I fell," whispered Kong Yiji. "Broke them in a fall." His eyes pleaded with the boss to let the matter drop. By now several people had gathered round, and they all laughed with the boss. I warmed the wine, carried it over, and set it on the threshold. He produced four coppers from his ragged coat pocket, and as he placed them in my hand I saw that his own hands were covered with mud — he must have crawled there on them. Presently he finished the wine and, in taunts and laughter, slowly pushed himself off with his hands.

A long time went by after that without our seeing Kong Yiji again. At the end of the year, when the boss took down the tallyboard he said: "Kong Yiji still owes nineteen coppers." At the Dragon-Boat Festival the next year he said the same thing again. But when the Mid-Autumn Festival arrived he was silent on the subject, and another New Year came round without our seeing any more of Kong Yiji.

Nor have I ever seen him since — probably Kong Yiji really is dead.

March 1919

低声说道,"跌断,跌,跌……"他的眼色,很像恳求掌柜,不要再提。此时已经聚集了几个人,便和掌柜都笑了。我温了酒,端出去,放在门槛上。他从破衣袋里摸出四文大钱,放在我手里,见他满手是泥,原来他便用这手走来的。不一会,他喝完酒,便又在旁人的说笑声中,坐着用这手慢慢走去了。

自此以后,又长久没有看见孔乙己。到了年关,掌柜取下粉板说,"孔乙己还欠十九个钱呢!"到第二年的端午,又说"孔乙己还欠十九个钱呢!"到中秋可是没有说,再到年关也没有看见他。

我到现在终于没有见——大约孔乙己的确死了。

一九一九年三月。①

---

① 据本篇发表时的作者《附记》,本文当作于一九一八年冬天。按本书各篇最初发表时都未署写作日期,现在篇末的日期为作者在编集时所补记。

英汉对照
English-Chinese
中国文学宝库
Gems of Chinese Literature
现代文学系列
Modern Literature

Medicine

I

It was autumn, in the small hours of the morning. The moon had gone down, but the sun had not yet risen, and the sky appeared a sheet of darkening blue. Apart from night-prowlers, all was asleep. Old Shuan suddenly sat up in bed. He struck a match and lit the grease-covered oil-lamp, which shed a ghostly light over the two rooms of the tea-house.

"Are you going, now, Dad?" queried an old woman's voice. And from the small inner room a fit of coughing was heard.

"H'm."

Old Shuan listened as he fastened his clothes, then stretching out his hand said, "Let's have it."

After some fumbling under the pillow his wife produced a packet of silver dollars which she handed over. Old Shuan pocketed it nervously, patted his pocket twice, then lighting a paper lantern and blowing out the lamp went into the inner room. A rustling was heard, and then more coughing. When all was quiet again, Old Shuan called softly: "Son!... Don't you get up!... Your mother will see to the shop."

Receiving no answer, Old Shuan assumed his son must be sound

药①

一

秋天的后半夜,月亮下去了,太阳还没有出,只剩下一片乌蓝的天;除了夜游的东西,什么都睡着。华老栓忽然坐起身,擦着火柴,点上遍身油腻的灯盏,茶馆的两间屋子里,便弥满了青白的光。

"小栓的爹,你就去么?"是一个老女人的声音。里边的小屋子里,也发出一阵咳嗽。

"唔。"老栓一面听,一面应,一面扣上衣服;伸手过去说,"你给我罢。"

华大妈在枕头底下掏了半天,掏出一包洋钱②,交给老栓,老栓接了,抖抖的装入衣袋,又在外面按了两下;便点上灯笼,吹熄灯盏,走向里屋子去了。那屋子里面,正在窸窸窣窣的响,

---

① 本篇最初发表于一九一九年五月《新青年》第六卷第五号。按篇中人物夏瑜隐喻清末女革命党人秋瑾。秋瑾在徐锡麟被害后不久,也于一九〇七年七月十五日遭清政府杀害,就义的地点在绍兴城内的轩亭口,街旁有一牌楼,匾上题有"古轩亭口"四字。

② 洋钱:指银元。银元最初是从外国流入我国的,所以俗称洋钱;我国自清代后期开始自铸银元,但民间仍沿用这个旧称。

Medicine

asleep again; so he went out into the street. In the darkness nothing could be seen but the grey roadway. Then lantern light fell on his pacing feet. Here and there he came across dogs, but none of them barked. It was much colder than indoors, yet Old Shuan's spirits rose, as if he had grown suddenly younger and possessed some miraculous life-giving power. He had lengthened his stride. And the road became increasingly clear, the sky increasingly bright.

Absorbed in his walking, Old Shuan was startled when he saw the crossroads lying distinctly ahead of him. He walked back a few steps to stand under the eaves of a shop, in front of its closed door. After some time he began to feel chilly.

"Uh, an old chap."

"Seems rather cheerful..."

Old Shuan started again and, opening his eyes, saw several men passing. One of them even turned back to look at him, and although he could not see him clearly, the man's eyes shone with a lustful light, like a famished person's at the sight of food. Looking at his lantern, Old Shuan saw it had gone out. He patted his pocket — the hard packet was still there. Then he looked round and saw many strange people, in twos and threes, wandering about like lost souls. However, when he gazed steadily at them, he could not see anything else strange about them.

Presently he saw some soldiers strolling around. The large white circles on their uniforms, both in front and behind, were clear even at a distance; and as they drew nearer, the dark red border could be seen too. The next second, with a trampling of feet, a

接着便是一通咳嗽。老栓候他平静下去,才低低的叫道,"小栓……你不要起来。……店么?你娘会安排的。"

老栓听得儿子不再说话,料他安心睡了;便出了门,走到街上。街上黑沉沉的一无所有,只有一条灰白的路,看得分明。灯光照着他的两脚,一前一后的走。有时也遇到几只狗,可是一只也没有叫。天气比屋子里冷得多了;老栓倒觉爽快,仿佛一旦变了少年,得了神通,有给人生命的本领似的,跨步格外高远。而且路也愈走愈分明,天也愈走愈亮了。

老栓正在专心走路,忽然吃了一惊,远远里看见一条丁字街,明明白白横着。他便退了几步,寻到一家关着门的铺子,蹩进檐下,靠门立住了。好一会,身上觉得有些发冷。

"哼,老头子。"

"倒高兴……。"

老栓又吃一惊,睁眼看时,几个人从他面前过去了。一个还回头看他,样子不甚分明,但很像久饿的人见了食物一般,眼里闪出一种攫取的光。老栓看看灯笼,已经熄了。按一按衣袋,硬硬的还在。仰起头两面一望,只见许多古怪的人,三三两两,鬼似的在那里徘徊;定睛再看,却也看不出什么别的奇怪。

没有多久,又见几个兵,在那边走动;衣服前后的一个大白圆圈,远地里也看得清楚,走过面前的,并且看出号衣① 上暗红色的镶边。——

① 号衣:指清朝士兵的军衣,前后胸都缀有一块圆形白布,上有"兵"或"勇"字样。

Medicine

crowd rushed past. Thereupon the small groups which had arrived earlier suddenly converged and surged forward. Just before the crossroads, they came to a sudden stop and grouped themselves in a semi-circle.

Old Shuan looked in that direction too, but could only see people's backs. Craning their necks as far as they would go, they looked like so many ducks, held and lifted by some invisible hand. For a moment all was still; then a sound was heard, and a stir swept through the onlookers. There was a rumble as they pushed back, sweeping past Old Shuan and nearly knocking him down.

"Hey! Give me the cash, and I'll give you the goods!" A man clad entirely in black stood before him, his eyes like daggers, making Old Shuan shrink to half his normal size. This man was thrusting one huge extended hand towards him, while in the other he held a roll of steamed bread, from which crimson drops were dripping to the ground.

Hurriedly Old Shuan fumbled for his dollars, and trembling he was about to hand them over, but he dared not take the object. The other grew impatient, and shouted: "What are you afraid of? Why not take it?" When Old Shuan still hesitated, the man in black snatched his lantern and tore off its paper shade to wrap up the roll. This package he thrust into Old Shuan's hand, at the same time seizing the silver and giving it a cursory feel. Then he turned away, muttering, "Old fool..."

"Whose sickness is this for?" Old Shuan seemed to hear someone ask; but he made no reply. His whole mind was on the

阵脚步声响,一眨眼,已经拥过了一大簇人。那三三两两的人,也忽然合作一堆,潮一般向前赶;将到丁字街口,便突然立住,簇成一个半圆。

老栓也向那边看,却只见一堆人的后背;颈项都伸得很长,仿佛许多鸭,被无形的手捏住了的,向上提着。静了一会,似乎有点声音,便又动摇起来,轰的一声,都向后退;一直散到老栓立着的地方,几乎将他挤倒了。

"喂!一手交钱,一手交货!"一个浑身黑色的人,站在老栓面前,眼光正像两把刀,刺得老栓缩小了一半。那人一只大手,向他摊着;一只手却撮着一个鲜红的馒头①,那红的还是一点一点的往下滴。

老栓慌忙摸出洋钱,抖抖的想交给他,却又不敢去接他的东西。那人便焦急起来,嚷道,"怕什么?怎的不拿!"老栓还踌躇着;黑的人便抢过灯笼,一把扯下纸罩,裹了馒头,塞与老栓;一手抓过洋钱,捏一捏,转身去了。嘴里哼着说,"这老东西……。"

"这给谁治病的呀?"老栓也似乎听得有人问他,但他并不答应;他的精神,现在只在一个

---

① 鲜红的馒头:即蘸有人血的馒头。旧时迷信,以为人血可以医治肺痨,刽子手便借此骗取钱财。

package, which he carried as carefully as if it were the sole heir to an ancient house. Nothing else mattered now. He was about to transplant this new life to his own home, and reap much happiness. The sun too had risen, lighting up the broad highway before him, which led straight home, and the worn tablet behind him at the crossroads with its faded gold inscription: "Ancient Pavilion."

II

When Old Shuan reached home, the shop had been cleaned, and the rows of tea-tables were shining brightly; but no customers had arrived. Only his son was sitting at a table by the wall, eating. Beads of sweat stood out on his forehead, his lined jacket was sticking to his spine, and his shoulder blades stuck out so sharply, an inverted V seemed stamped there. At this sight, Old Shuan's brow, which had been clear, contracted again. His wife hurried in from the kitchen, with expectant eyes and a tremor to her lips.

"Get it?"

"Yes."

They went together into the kitchen, and conferred for a time. Then the old woman went out, to return shortly with a dried lotus leaf which she spread on the table. Old Shuan unwrapped the crimson stained roll from the lantern paper and transferred it to the lotus leaf. Little Shuan had finished his meal, but his mother exclaimed hastily:

"Sit still, Little Shuan! Don't come over here."

Mending the fire in the stove, Old Shuan put the green package

包上,仿佛抱着一个十世单传的婴儿,别的事情,都已置之度外了。他现在要将这包里的新的生命,移植到他家里,收获许多幸福。太阳也出来了;在他面前,显出一条大道,直到他家中,后面也照见丁字街头破匾上"古□亭口"这四个黯淡的金字。

二

老栓走到家,店面早经收拾干净,一排一排的茶桌,滑溜溜的发光。但是没有客人;只有小栓坐在里排的桌前吃饭,大粒的汗,从额上滚下,夹袄也帖住了脊心,两块肩胛骨高高凸出,印成一个阳文的"八"字。老栓见这样子,不免皱一皱展开的眉心。他的女人,从灶下急急走出,睁着眼睛,嘴唇有些发抖。

"得了么?"

"得了。"

两个人一齐走进灶下,商量了一会;华大妈便出去了,不多时,拿着一片老荷叶回来,摊在桌上。老栓也打开灯笼罩,用荷叶重新包了那红的馒头。小栓也吃完饭,他的母亲慌忙说:

"小栓——你坐着,不要到这里来。"

一面整顿了灶火,老栓便把一个碧绿的包,

and the red and white lantern paper into the stove together. A redblack flame flared up, and a strange odour permeated the shop.

"Smells good! What are you eating?" The hunchback had arrived. He was one of those who spend all their time in tea-shops, the first to come in the morning and the last to leave. Now he had just stumbled to a corner table facing the street, and sat down. But no one answered his question.

"Puffed rice gruel?"

Still no reply. Old Shuan hurried out to brew tea for him.

"Come here, Little Shuan!" His mother called him into the inner room, set a stool in the middle, and sat the child down. Then, bringing him a round black object on a plate, she said gently:

"Eat it up... then you'll be better."

Little Shuan picked up the black object and looked at it. He had the oddest feeling, as if he were holding his own life in his hands. Presently he split it carefully open. From within the charred crust a jet of white vapour escaped, then scattered, leaving only two halves of a white flour steamed roll. Soon it was all eaten, the flavour completely forgotten, only the empty plate left. His father and mother were standing one on each side of him, their eyes apparently pouring something into him and at the same time extracting something. His small heart began to beat faster, and, putting his hands to his chest, he began to cough again.

"Have a sleep; then you'll be all right," said his mother.

Obediently, Little Shuan coughed himself to sleep. The woman waited till his breathing was regular, then covered him lightly with a much patched quilt.

一个红红白白的破灯笼,一同塞在灶里;一阵红黑的火焰过去时,店屋里散满了一种奇怪的香味。

"好香!你们吃什么点心呀?"这是驼背五少爷到了。这人每天总在茶馆里过日,来得最早,去得最迟,此时恰恰蹩到临街的壁角的桌边,便坐下问话,然而没有人答应他。"炒米粥么?"仍然没有人应。老栓匆匆走出,给他泡上茶。

"小栓进来罢!"华大妈叫小栓进了里面的屋子,中间放好一条凳,小栓坐了。他的母亲端过一碟乌黑的圆东西,轻轻说:

"吃下去罢,——病便好了。"

小栓撮起这黑东西,看了一会,似乎拿着自己的性命一般,心里说不出的奇怪。十分小心的拗开了,焦皮里面窜出一道白气,白气散了,是两半个白面的馒头。——不多工夫,已经全在肚里了,却全忘了什么味;面前只剩下一张空盘。他的旁边,一面立着他的父亲,一面立着他的母亲,两人的眼光,都仿佛要在他身里注进什么又要取出什么似的;便禁不住心跳起来,按着胸膛,又是一阵咳嗽。

"睡一会罢,——便好了。"

小栓依他母亲的话,咳着睡了。华大妈候他喘气平静,才轻轻的给他盖上了满幅补钉的夹被。

英汉对照
English-Chinese
中国文学宝库
Gems of Chinese Literature
现代文学系列
Modern Literature

III

The shop was crowded, and Old Shuan was busy, carrying a big copper kettle to make tea for one customer after another. But there were dark circles under his eyes.

"Aren't you well, Old Shuan?... What's wrong with you?" asked one greybeard.

"Nothing."

"Nothing?... No, I suppose from your smile, there couldn't be..." The old man corrected himself.

"It's just that Old Shuan's busy," said the hunchback. "If his son..." But before he could finish, a heavy-jowled man burst in. He had over his shoulders a dark brown shirt, unbuttoned and fastened carelessly by a broad dark brown girdle at his waist. As soon as he entered, he shouted to Old Shuan:

"Has he taken it? Any better? Luck's with you, Old Shuan. What luck! If not for my hearing of things so quickly..."

Holding the kettle in one hand, the other straight by his side in an attitude of respect, Old Shuan listened with a smile. In fact, all present were listening respectfully. The old woman, dark circles under her eyes, too, came out smiling with a bowl containing tea leaves and an added olive, over which Old Shuan poured boiling water for the newcomer.

"This is a guaranteed cure! Not like other things!" declared the heavy-jowled man. "Just think, brought back warm, and eaten warm!"

三

店里坐着许多人,老栓也忙了,提着大铜壶,一趟一趟的给客人冲茶;两个眼眶,都围着一圈黑线。

"老栓,你有些不舒服么?——你生病么?"一个花白胡子的人说。

"没有。"

"没有?——我想笑嘻嘻的,原也不像……"花白胡子便取消了自己的话。

"老栓只是忙。要是他的儿子……"驼背五少爷话还未完,突然闯进了一个满脸横肉的人,披一件玄色布衫,散着纽扣,用很宽的玄色腰带,胡乱捆在腰间。刚进门,便对老栓嚷道:

"吃了么?好了么?老栓,就是运气了你!你运气,要不是我信息灵……。"

老栓一手提了茶壶,一手恭恭敬敬的垂着;笑嘻嘻的听。满座的人,也都恭恭敬敬的听。华大妈也黑着眼眶,笑嘻嘻的送出茶碗茶叶来,加上一个橄榄,老栓便去冲了水。

"这是包好!这是与众不同的。你想,趁热的拿来,趁热吃下。"横肉的人只是嚷。

英汉对照
English-Chinese
中国文学宝库
Gems of Chinese Literature
现代文学系列
Modern Literature

"Yes indeed, we couldn't have managed it without Uncle Kang's help." The old woman thanked him very warmly.

"A guaranteed cure! Eaten warm like this. A roll dipped in human blood like this can cure any consumption!"

The old woman seemed a little disconcerted by the word "consumption," and turned a shade paler; however, she forced a smile again at once and found some pretext to leave. Meanwhile the man in brown was indiscreet enough to go on talking at the top of his voice until the child in the inner room was woken and started coughing.

"So you've had such a stroke of luck for your Little Shuan! Of course his sickness will be cured completely. No wonder Old Shuan keeps smiling." As he spoke, the greybeard walked up to the man in brown, and lowered his voice to ask:

"Mr Kang, I heard the criminal executed today came from the Xia family. Who was it? And why was he executed?"

"Who? Son of Widow Xia, of course! Young rascal!"

Seeing how they were all hanging on his words, Mr Kang's spirits rose even higher. His jowls quivered, and he made his voice as loud as he could.

"The rogue didn't want to live, simply didn't want to! There was nothing in it for me this time. Even the clothes stripped from him were taken by Red-eye, the jailer. Our Old Shuan was the luckiest, and after him Third Uncle Xia. The latter pocketed the whole reward — twenty-five taels of bright silver — and didn't have to spend a cent!"

Little Shuan walked slowly out of the inner room, his hands to

药

"真的呢,要没有康大叔照顾,怎么会这样……"华大妈也很感激的谢他。

"包好,包好!这样的趁热吃下。这样的人血馒头,什么痨病都包好!"

华大妈听到"痨病"这两个字,变了一点脸色,似乎有些不高兴;但又立刻堆上笑,搭赸着走开了。这康大叔却没有觉察,仍然提高了喉咙只是嚷,嚷得里面睡着的小栓也合伙咳嗽起来。

"原来你家小栓碰到了这样的好运气。这病自然一定全好;怪不得老栓整天的笑着呢。"花白胡子一面说,一面走到康大叔面前,低声下气的问道,"康大叔——听说今天结果的一个犯人,便是夏家的孩子,那是谁的孩子?究竟是什么事?"

"谁的?不就是夏四奶奶的儿子么?那个小家伙!"康大叔见众人都耸起耳朵听他,便格外高兴,横肉块块饱绽,越发大声说,"这小东西不要命,不要就是了。我可是这一回一点没有得到好处;连剥下来的衣服,都给管牢的红眼睛阿义拿去了。——第一要算我们的栓叔运气;第二是夏三爷赏了二十五两雪白的银子,独自落腰包,一文不花。"

小栓慢慢的从小屋子走出,两手按了胸口,

英汉对照
English-Chinese
中国文学宝库
Gems of Chinese Literature
现代文学系列
Modern Literature

63

his chest, coughing repeatedly. He went to the kitchen, filled a bowl with cold rice, added hot water to it, and sitting down started to eat. His mother, hovering over him, asked softly:

"Do you feel better, son? Still as hungry as ever?"

"A guaranteed cure!" Kang glanced at the child, then turned back to address the company. "Third Uncle Xia is really smart. If he hadn't informed, even his family would have been executed, and their property confiscated. But instead? Silver! That young rogue was a real scoundrel! He even tried to incite the jailer to revolt!"

"No! The idea of it!" A man in his twenties, sitting in the back row, expressed indignation.

"You know, Red-eye went to sound him out, but he started chatting with him. He said the great Manchu empire belongs to us. Just think: is that kind of talk rational? Red-eye knew he had only an old mother at home, but had never imagined he was so poor. He couldn't squeeze anything out of him; he was already good and angry, and then the young fool would 'scratch the tiger's head,' so he gave him a couple of slaps."

"Red-eye is a good boxer. Those slaps must have hurt!" The hunchback in the corner by the wall exulted.

"The rotter was not afraid of being beaten. He even said how sorry he was."

"Nothing to be sorry about in beating a wretch like that," said Greybeard.

Kang looked at him superciliously and said disdainfully: "You misunderstood. The way he said it, he was sorry for Red-eye."

不住的咳嗽;走到灶下,盛出一碗冷饭,泡上热水,坐下便吃。华大妈跟着他走,轻轻的问道,"小栓,你好些么?——你仍旧只是肚饿?……"

"包好,包好!"康大叔瞥了小栓一眼,仍然回过脸,对众人说,"夏三爷真是乖角儿,要是他不先告官,连他满门抄斩。现在怎样?银子!——这小东西也真不成东西!关在牢里,还要劝牢头造反。"

"阿呀,那还了得。"坐在后排的一个二十多岁的人,很现出气愤模样。

"你要晓得红眼睛阿义是去盘盘底细的,他却和他攀谈了。他说:这大清的天下是我们大家的。你想:这是人话么?红眼睛原知道他家里只有一个老娘,可是没有料到他竟会那么穷,榨不出一点油水,已经气破肚皮了。他还要老虎头上搔痒,便给他两个嘴巴!"

"义哥是一手好拳棒,这两下,一定够他受用了。"壁角的驼背忽然高兴起来。

"他这贱骨头打不怕,还要说可怜可怜哩。"

花白胡子的人说,"打了这种东西,有什么可怜呢?"

康大叔显出看他不上的样子,冷笑着说,"你没有听清我的话;看他神气,是说阿义可怜哩!"

英汉对照
English-Chinese
中国文学宝库
Gems of Chinese Literature
现代文学系列
Modern Literature

His listeners' eyes took on a glazed look, and no one spoke. Little Shuan had finished his rice and was perspiring profusely, his head steaming.

"Sorry for Red-eye — crazy! He must have been crazy!" said Greybeard, as if suddenly he saw light.

"He must have been crazy!" echoed the man in his twenties.

Once more the customers began to show animation, and conversation was resumed. Under cover of the noise, the child was seized by a paroxysm of coughing. Kang went up to him, clapped him on the shoulder, and said:

"A guaranteed cure! Don't cough like that, Little Shuan! A guaranteed cure!"

"Crazy!" agreed the hunchback, nodding his head.

IV

Originally, the land adjacent to the city wall outside the West Gate had been public land. The zigzag path slanting across it, trodden out by passers-by seeking a short cut, had become a natural boundary line. Left of the path, executed criminals or those who had died of neglect in prison were buried. Right of the path were paupers' graves. The series of grave mounds on both sides looked like the rolls laid out for a rich man's birthday.

The Qingming Festival that year was unusually cold. Willows were only beginning to put forth shoots no larger than grains of rice. Shortly after daybreak, Old Shuan's wife brought four dishes and a bowl of rice to set before a new grave in the right section,

听着的人的眼光,忽然有些板滞;话也停顿了。小栓已经吃完饭,吃得满身流汗,头上都冒出蒸气来。

"阿义可怜——疯话,简直是发了疯了。"花白胡子恍然大悟似的说。

"发了疯了。"二十多岁的人也恍然大悟的说。

店里的坐客,便又现出活气,谈笑起来。小栓也趁着热闹,拼命咳嗽;康大叔走上前,拍他肩膀说:

"包好!小栓——你不要这么咳。包好!"

"疯了。"驼背五少爷点着头说。

四

西关外靠着城根的地面,本是一块官地;中间歪歪斜斜一条细路,是贪走便道的人,用鞋底造成的,但却成了自然的界限。路的左边,都埋着死刑和瘐毙的人,右边是穷人的丛冢。两面都已埋到层层叠叠,宛然阔人家里祝寿时候的馒头。

这一年的清明,分外寒冷;杨柳才吐出半粒米大的新芽。天明未久,华大妈已在右边的一坐新坟前面,排出四碟菜,一碗饭,哭了一场。

英汉对照
English-Chinese
中国文学宝库
Gems of Chinese Literature
现代文学系列
Modern Literature

and wailed before it. When she had burned paper money she sat on the ground in a stupor as if waiting for something; but for what, she herself did not know. A breeze sprang up and stirred her short hair, which was certainly whiter than in the previous year.

Another woman came down the path, grey-haired and in rags. She was carrying an old, round, red-lacquered basket, with a string of paper money hanging from it; and she walked haltingly. When she saw Old Shuan's wife sitting on the ground watching her, she hesitated, and a flush of shame spread over her pale face. However, she summoned up courage to cross over to a grave in the left section, where she set down her basket.

That grave was directly opposite Little Shuan's, separated only by the path. As she watched the other woman set out four dishes and a bowl of rice, then stand up to wail and burn paper money. Old Shuan's wife thought: "It must be her son in that grave too." The older woman took a few aimless steps and stared vacantly around, then suddenly she began to tremble and stagger backward in a daze.

Fearing sorrow might send her out of her mind, Old Shuan's wife got up and stepped across the path, to say quietly: "Don't grieve, let's go home."

The other nodded, but her eyes were still fixed, and she muttered: "Look! What's that?"

Looking where she pointed, Old Shuan's wife saw that the grave in front had not yet been overgrown with grass. Ugly patches of soil still showed. But when she looked carefully, she was surprised to see at the top of the mound a wreath of red and white flowers.

化过纸①,呆呆的坐在地上;仿佛等候什么似的,但自己也说不出等候什么。微风起来,吹动他短发,确乎比去年白得多了。

小路上又来了一个女人,也是半白头发,褴褛的衣裙;提一个破旧的朱漆圆篮,外挂一串纸锭,三步一歇的走。忽然见华大妈坐在地上看他,便有些踌躇,惨白的脸上,现出些羞愧的颜色;但终于硬着头皮,走到左边的一坐坟前,放下了篮子。

那坟与小栓的坟,一字儿排着,中间只隔一条小路。华大妈看他排好四碟菜,一碗饭,立着哭了一通,化过纸锭;心里暗暗地想,"这坟里的也是儿子了。"那老女人徘徊观望了一回,忽然手脚有些发抖,跄跄踉踉退下几步,瞪着眼只是发怔。

华大妈见这样子,生怕他伤心到快要发狂了;便忍不住立起身,跨过小路,低声对他说,"你这位老奶奶不要伤心了, 我们还是回去罢。"

那人点一点头,眼睛仍然向上瞪着;也低声吃吃的说道,"你看,——看这是什么呢?"

华大妈跟了他指头看去,眼光便到了前面的坟,这坟上草根还没有全合,露出一块一块的黄土,煞是难看。再往上仔细看时,却不觉也吃一惊;——分明有一圈红白的花,围着那尖圆的坟顶。

---

① 化过纸:纸指纸钱,一种迷信用品,旧俗认为把它火化后可供死者在"阴间"使用。下文说的"纸锭",是用纸或锡箔折成的元宝。

英汉对照
English-Chinese
中国文学宝库
Gems of Chinese Literature
现代文学系列
Modern Literature

Both of them suffered from failing eyesight, yet they could see these red and white flowers clearly. There were not many, but they were placed in a circle; and although not very fresh, were neatly set out. Little Shuan's mother looked round and found her own son's grave, like most of the rest, dotted with only a few little, pale flowers shivering in the cold. Suddenly she had a sense of futility and stopped feeling curious about the wreath.

Meantime the old woman had gone up to the grave to look more closely. "They have no roots," she said to herself. "They can't have grown here. Who could have been here? Children don't come here to play, and none of our relatives have ever been here. What could have happened?" She puzzled over it, until suddenly her tears began to fall, and she cried aloud:

"Yu, my son, they all wronged you, and you do not forget. Is your grief still so great that today you worked this wonder to let me know?"

She looked all around, but could see only a crow perched on a leafless bough. "I know," she continued. "They murdered you. But a day of reckoning will come, Heaven will see to it. Close your eyes in peace... If you are really here, and can hear me, make that crow fly on to your grave as a sign."

The breeze had long since dropped, and the dry grass stood stiff and straight as copper wires. A faint, tremulous sound vibrated in the air, then faded and died away. All around was deadly still. They stood in the dry grass, looking up at the crow; and the crow, on the rigid bough of the tree, its head drawn in, stood immobile as iron.

他们的眼睛都已老花多年了,但望这红白的花,却还能明白看见。花也不很多,圆圆的排成一个圈,不很精神,倒也整齐。华大妈忙看他儿子和别人的坟,却只有不怕冷的几点青白小花,零星开着;便觉得心里忽然感到一种不足和空虚,不愿意根究。那老女人又走近几步,细看了一遍,自言自语的说,"这没有根,不像自己开的。——这地方有谁来呢?孩子不会来玩;——亲戚本家早不来了。——这是怎么一回事呢?"他想了又想,忽又流下泪来,大声说道:

"瑜儿,他们都冤枉了你,你还是忘不了,伤心不过,今天特意显点灵,要我知道么?"他四面一看,只见一只乌鸦,站在一株没有叶的树上,便接着说,"我知道了。——瑜儿,可怜他们坑了你,他们将来总有报应,天都知道;你闭了眼睛就是了。——你如果真在这里,听到我的话,——便教这乌鸦飞上你的坟顶,给我看罢。"

微风早经停息了;枯草支支直立,有如铜丝。一丝发抖的声音,在空气中愈颤愈细,细到没有,周围便都是死一般静。两人站在枯草丛里,仰面看那乌鸦;那乌鸦也在笔直的树枝间,缩着头,铁铸一般站着。

英汉对照
English-Chinese
中国文学宝库
Gems of Chinese Literature
现代文学系列
Modern Literature

Time passed. More people, young and old, came to visit the graves.

Old Shuan's wife felt somehow as if a load had been lifted from her mind and, wanting to leave, she urged the other:

"Let's go."

The old woman sighed, and listlessly picked up the rice and dishes. After a moment's hesitation she started slowly off, still muttering to herself:

"What could it mean?"

They had not gone thirty paces when they heard a loud caw behind them. Startled, they looked round and saw the crow stretch wings, brace itself to take off, then fly like an arrow towards the far horizon.

April 1919

许多的工夫过去了；上坟的人渐渐增多，几个老的小的，在土坟间出没。

华大妈不知怎的，似乎卸下了一挑重担，便想到要走；一面劝着说，"我们还是回去罢。"

那老女人叹一口气，无精打采的收起饭菜；又迟疑了一刻，终于慢慢地走了。嘴里自言自语的说，"这是怎么一回事呢？……"

他们走不上二三十步远，忽听得背后"哑——"的一声大叫；两个人都竦然的回过头，只见那乌鸦张开两翅，一挫身，直向着远处的天空，箭也似的飞去了。

一九一九年四月。

英汉对照
English-Chinese
中国文学宝库
Gems of Chinese Literature
现代文学系列
Modern Literature

The True Story of Ah Q

CHAPTER 1

Introduction

For several years now I have been meaning to write the true story of Ah Q. But while wanting to write I was in some trepidation too, which goes to show that I am not one of those who achieve glory by writing; for an immortal pen has always been required to record the deeds of an immortal man, the man becoming known to posterity through the writing and the writing known to posterity through the man — until finally it is not clear which is making which known. But in the end, as though possessed by some fiend, I always came back to the idea of writing the story of Ah Q.

And yet no sooner had I taken up my pen than I became conscious of tremendous difficulties in writing this far-from-immortal work. The first was the question of what to call it. Confucius said, "If the name is not correct, the words will not ring true"; and this axiom should be most scrupulously observed. There are many types of biography: official biographies, autobiographies, unauthorized biographies, legends, supplementary biographies, family histories, sketches... But unfortunately none of these suited my purpose.

阿 Q 正传[①]

第一章 序

我要给阿 Q 做正传,已经不止一两年了。但一面要做,一面又往回想,这足见我不是一个"立言"的人,因为从来不朽之笔,须传不朽之人,于是人以文传,文以人传——究竟谁靠谁传,渐渐的不甚了然起来,而终于归结到传阿 Q,仿佛思想里有鬼似的。

然而要做这一篇速朽的文章,才下笔,便感到万分的困难了。第一是文章的名目。孔子曰,"名不正则言不顺"。这原是应该极注意的。传的名目很繁多:列传,自传,内传,外传,别传,家传,小传……,而可惜都不合。"列传"么,这

---

① 本篇最初分章发表于北京《晨报副刊》,自一九二一年十二月四日起至一九二二年二月十二日止,每周或隔周刊登一次,署名巴人。

英汉对照
English-Chinese
中国文学宝库
Gems of Chinese Literature
现代文学系列
Modern Literature

"Official biography?" This account will obviously not be included with those of many eminent people in some authentic history. "Autobiography?" But I am obviously not Ah Q. If I were to call this an "unauthorized biography," then where is his "authenticated biography?" The use of "legend" is impossible because Ah Q was no legendary figure. "Supplementary biography?" But no president has ever ordered the National Historical Institute to write a "standard life" of Ah Q. It is true that although there are no "lives of gamblers" in authentic English history, the well-known author Conan Doyle nevertheless wrote *Rodney Stone*;[1] but while this is permissible for a well-known author it is not permissible for such as I. Then there is "family history"; but I do not know whether I belong to the same family as Ah Q or not, nor have his children or grandchildren ever entrusted me with such a task. If I were to use "sketch," it might be objected that Ah Q has no "complete account." In short, this is really a "life," but since I write in vulgar vein using the language of hucksters and pedlars, I dare not presume to give it so high-sounding a title. So I will take as my title the last two words of a stock phrase of the novelists, who are not reckoned among the Three Cults and Nine Schools,[2] "Enough of this digression, and back to the true story"; and if this is reminiscent of the *True Story of Calligraphy* [3] of the ancients, it cannot be helped.

The second difficulty confronting me was that a biography of this

---

[1] In Chinese this title was translated as *Supplementary Biographies of the Gamblers*.

[2] The Three cults were Confucianism, Buddhism, and Taoism. The Nine Schools included the Confucian, Taoist, Legalist, Moist, and other schools.

[3] A book by Feng Wu of the Qing Dynasty(1644 – 1911).

一篇并非和许多阔人排在"正史"里;"自传"么,我又并非就是阿Q。说是"外传","内传"在那里呢?倘用"内传",阿Q又决不是神仙。"别传"呢,阿Q实在未曾有大总统上谕宣付国史馆立"本传"——虽说英国正史上并无"博徒列传",而文豪迭更司也做过《博徒别传》这一部书,但文豪则可,在我辈却不可的。其次是"家传",则我既不知与阿Q是否同宗,也未曾受他子孙的拜托;或"小传",则阿Q又更无别的"大传"了。总而言之,这一篇也便是"本传",但从我的文章着想,因为文体卑下,是"引车卖浆者流"所用的话,所以不敢僭称,便从不入三教九流的小说家所谓"闲话休题言归正传"这一句套话里,取出"正传"两个字来,作为名目,即使与古人所撰《书法正传》的"正传"字面上很相混,也顾不得了。

第二,立传的通例,开首大抵该是"某,字

The True Story of Ah Q

type should start off something like this: "So-and-so, whose other name was so-and-so, was a native of such-and-such a place"; but I don't really know what Ah Q's surname was. Once, he seemed to be named Zhao, but the next day there was some confusion about the matter again. This was after Mr Zhao's son had passed the county examination and, to the sound of gongs, his success was announced in the village. Ah Q, who had just drunk two bowls of yellow wine, began to prance about declaring that this reflected credit on him too, since he belonged to the same clan as Mr Zhao and by an exact reckoning was three generations senior to the successful candidate. At the time several bystanders even began to stand slightly in awe of Ah Q. But the next day the bailiff summoned him to Mr Zhao's house. The old gentleman set eyes on him, his face turning crimson with fury, and roared:

"Ah Q, you miserable wretch! Did you say I belonged to the same clan as you?"

Ah Q made no reply.

The more he looked at Ah Q the angrier Mr Zhao became. Advancing menacingly a few steps he said, "How dare you talk such nonsense! How could I have such a relative as you? Is your surname Zhao?"

Ah Q made no reply and was about to step back, when Mr Zhao darted forward and gave him a slap on the face.

"How could you be a Zhao? Are you worthy of the name Zhao?"

Ah Q made no attempt to defend his right to the name Zhao but rubbing his left cheek went out with the bailiff from whom, once outside, he had to listen to another torrent of abuse. He then by way of

某,某地人也",而我并不知道阿Q姓什么。有一回,他似乎是姓赵,但第二日便模糊了。那是赵太爷的儿子进了秀才的时候,锣声镗镗的报到村里来,阿Q正喝了两碗黄酒,便手舞足蹈的说,这于他也很光采,因为他和赵太爷原来是本家,细细的排起来他还比秀才长三辈呢。其时几个旁听人倒也肃然的有些起敬了。那知道第二天,地保便叫阿Q到赵太爷家里去;太爷一见,满脸溅朱,喝道:

"阿Q,你这浑小子!你说我是你的本家么?"

阿Q不开口。

赵太爷愈看愈生气了,抢进几步说:"你敢胡说!我怎么会有你这样的本家?你姓赵么?"

阿Q不开口,想往后退了;赵太爷跳过去,给了他一个嘴巴。

"你怎么会姓赵!——你那里配姓赵!"

阿Q并没有抗辩他确凿姓赵,只用手摸着左颊,和地保退出去了;外面又被地保训斥了一

英汉对照
English-Chinese
中国文学宝库
Gems of Chinese Literature
现代文学系列
Modern Literature

atonement paid him two hundred cash. All who heard this said Ah Q was a great fool to ask for a beating like that. Even if his surname were Zhao — which wasn't likely — he should have known better than to boast like that when there was a Mr Zhao living in the village. After this no further mention was made of Ah Q's ancestry, thus I still have no idea what his surname really was.

The third difficulty I encountered in writing this work was that I don't know how Ah Q's personal name should be written either. During his lifetime everybody called him Ah Quei, but after his death not a soul mentioned Ah Quei again; for he was obviously not one of those whose name is "preserved on bamboo tablets and silk."① If there is any question of preserving his name, this essay must be the first attempt at doing so. Hence I am confronted with this difficulty at the outset. I have given the question careful thought. Ah Quei — would that be the "Quei" meaning fragrant osmanthus or the "Quei" meaning nobility? If his other name had been Moon Pavilion, or if he had celebrated his birthday in the month of the Moon Festival, then it would certainly be the "Quei" for fragrant osmanthus.② But since he had no other name — or if he had, no one knew it — and since he never sent out invitations on his birthday to secure complimentary verses, it would be arbitrary to write Ah Quei (fragrant osmanthus). Again, if he had had an elder or younger brother called Ah Fu

---

① A phrase used before paper was invented when bamboo and silk served as writing material in China.

② The fragrant osmanthus blooms in the month of the Moon Festival. And according to Chinese folklore, the shadow on the moon is an osmanthus tree.

番,谢了地保二百文酒钱。知道的人都说阿Q太荒唐,自己去招打;他大约未必姓赵,即使真姓赵,有赵太爷在这里,也不该如此胡说的。此后便再没有人提起他的氏族来,所以我终于不知道阿Q究竟什么姓。

第三,我又不知道阿Q的名字是怎么写的。他活着的时候,人都叫他阿Quei,死了以后,便没有一个人再叫阿Quei了,那里还会有"著之竹帛"的事。若论"著之竹帛",这篇文章要算第一次,所以先遇着了这第一个难关。我曾经仔细想:阿Quei,阿桂还是阿贵呢?倘使他号叫月亭,或者在八月间做过生日,那一定是阿桂了。而他既没有号——也许有号,只是没有人知道他,——又未尝散过生日征文的帖子:写作阿桂,是武断的。又倘若他有一位老兄或

英汉对照
English-Chinese
中国文学宝库
Gems of Chinese Literature
现代文学系列
Modern Literature

(prosperity), then he would certainly be called Ah Quei (nobility). But he was all on his own; thus there is no justification for writing Ah Quei (nobility). All the other, unusual characters with the sound *Quei* are even less suitable. I once put this question to Mr Zhao's son, the successful county candidate, but even such a learned man as he was baffled by it. According to him, however, the reason why this name could not be traced was that Chen Duxiu had brought out the magazine *New Youth* advocating the use of the Western alphabet, hence the national culture was going to the dogs. As a last resort, I asked someone from my native place to go and look up the legal documents recording Ah Q's case, but after eight months he sent me a letter saying that there was no name anything like Ah Quei in those records. Although uncertain whether this was the truth or whether my friend had simply done nothing, after failing to trace the name this way I could think of no other means of finding it. Since I am afraid the new system of phonetics has not yet come into common use, there is nothing for it but to use the Western alphabet, writing the name according to the English spelling as Ah Quei and abbreviating it to Ah Q. This approximates to blindly following *New Youth*, and I am thoroughly ashamed of myself; but since even such a learned man as Mr Zhao's son could not solve my problem, what else can I do?

My fourth difficulty was with Ah Q's place of origin. If his surname were Zhao, then according to the old custom which still prevails of classifying people by their district, one might look up the

令弟叫阿富,那一定是阿贵了;而他又只是一个人;写作阿贵,也没有佐证的。其余音 Quei 的偏僻字样,更加凑不上了。先前,我也曾问过赵太爷的儿子茂才先生,谁料博雅如此公,竟也茫然,但据结论说,是因为陈独秀办了《新青年》提倡洋字,所以国粹沦亡,无可查考了。我的最后的手段,只有托一个同乡去查阿 Q 犯事的案卷,八个月之后才有回信,说案卷里并无与阿 Quei 的声音相近的人。我虽不知道是真没有,还是没有查,然而也再没有别的方法了。生怕注音字母还未通行,只好用了"洋字",照英国流行的拼法写他为阿 Quei,略作阿 Q。这近于盲从《新青年》,自己也很抱歉,但茂才公尚且不知,我还有什么好办法呢。

　　第四,是阿 Q 的籍贯了。倘他姓赵,则据现在好称郡望的老例,可以照《郡名百家姓》上

英汉对照
English-Chinese
中国文学宝库
Gems of Chinese Literature
现代文学系列
Modern Literature

commentary in the *Hundred Surnames*[1] and find "Native of Tianshui in Gansu." But unfortunately this surname is open to question, with the result that Ah Q's place of origin must also remain uncertain. Although he lived for the most part in Weizhuang, he often stayed in other places, so that it would be wrong to call him a native of Weizhuang. It would, in fact, amount to a distortion of history.

The only thing that consoles me is the fact that the character "Ah" is absolutely correct. This is definitely not the result of false analogy, and is well able to stand the test of scholarly criticism. As for the other problems, it is not for such unlearned people as myself to solve them, and I can only hope that disciples of Dr Hu Shi, who has such "a passion for history and research," may be able in future to throw new light on them. I am afraid, however, that by that time my "True Story of Ah Q" will have long since passed into oblivion.

The foregoing may be considered as an introduction.

CHAPTER 2

A Brief Account of Ah Q's Victories

In addition to the uncertainty regarding Ah Q's surname, given name, and place of origin, there is even some uncertainty

---

[1] A school primer in which surnames were written into verse.

的注解,说是"陇西天水人也",但可惜这姓是不甚可靠的,因此籍贯也就有些决不定。他虽然多住未庄,然而也常常宿在别处,不能说是"未庄人",即使说是"未庄人也",也仍然有乖史法的。

我所聊以自慰的,是还有一个"阿"字非常正确,绝无附会假借的缺点,颇可以就正于通人。至于其余,却都非浅学所能穿凿,只希望有"历史癖与考据癖"的胡适之先生的门人们,将来或者能寻出许多新端绪来,但是我这《阿Q正传》到那时却又怕早经消灭了。

以上可以算是序。

第二章　优胜记略

阿Q不独是姓名籍贯有些渺茫,连他先前

The True Story of Ah Q

regarding his "background." This is because the people of Weizhuang only made use of his services or treated him as a laughing-stock, without ever paying the slightest attention to his "background." Ah Q himself remained silent on this subject, except that when quarrelling with someone he might glare at him and say, "We used to be much better off than you! Who do you think you are?"

Ah Q had no family but lived in the Tutelary God's Temple at Weizhuang. He had no regular work either, being simply an odd-job man for others: when there was wheat to be cut he would cut it, when there was rice to be hulled he would hull it, when there was a boat to be punted he would punt it. If the work lasted for any length of time he might stay in the house of his temporary employer, but as soon as it was finished he would leave. Thus whenever people had work to be done they would remember Ah Q, but what they remembered was his service and not his "background." By the time the job was done even Ah Q himself was out of their minds, to say nothing of his "background." Once indeed an old man remarked, "What a great worker Ah Q is!" Ah Q, bare-backed scrawny and sluggard, was standing before him at the time, and others could not tell whether the remark was serious or derisive, but Ah Q was overjoyed.

Ah Q, again, had a very high opinion of himself. He looked down on all the inhabitants of Weizhuang, thinking even the two young "scholars" not worth a smile, though most young scholars were likely to pass the official examinations. Mr Zhao and Mr Qian were held in great respect by the villagers, for in addition to being rich they were both the fathers of young scholars. Ah Q alone

的"行状"也渺茫。因为未庄的人们之于阿Q,只要他帮忙,只拿他玩笑,从来没有留心他的"行状"的。而阿Q自己也不说,独有和别人口角的时候,间或瞪着眼睛道:

"我们先前——比你阔的多啦!你算是什么东西!"

阿Q没有家,住在未庄的土谷祠里;也没有固定的职业,只给人家做短工,割麦便割麦,舂米便舂米,撑船便撑船。工作略长久时,他也或住在临时主人的家里,但一完就走了。所以,人们忙碌的时候,也还记起阿Q来,然而记起的是做工,并不是"行状";一闲空,连阿Q都早忘却,更不必说"行状"了。只是有一回,有一个老头子颂扬说:"阿Q真能做!"这时阿Q赤着膊,懒洋洋的瘦伶仃的正在他面前,别人也摸不着这话是真心还是讥笑,然而阿Q很喜欢。

阿Q又很自尊,所有未庄的居民,全不在他眼睛里,甚而至于对于两位"文童"也有以为不值一笑的神情。夫文童者,将来恐怕要变秀才者也;赵太爷钱太爷大受居民的尊敬,除有钱之外,就因为都是文童的爹爹,而阿Q在精神

英汉对照
English-Chinese
中国文学宝库
Gems of Chinese Literature
现代文学系列
Modern Literature

showed them no exceptional deference, thinking to himself, "My sons may be much greater."

Moreover, after Ah Q had been to town several times he naturally became even more conceited, although at the same time he had the greatest contempt for townspeople. For instance, a bench made of a wooden plank three feet by three inches the Weizhuang villagers called a "long bench." Ah Q called it a "long bench" too; but the townspeople called it a "straight bench," and he thought, "This is wrong. Ridiculous!" Again, when they fried large-headed fish in oil the Weizhuang villagers all added shallots sliced half an inch thick, whereas the townspeople added finely shredded shallots, and he thought, "This is wrong too. Ridiculous!" But the Weizhuang villagers were really ignorant rustics who had never seen fish fried in town!

Ah Q who "used to be much better off," who was a man of the world and a "worker," would have been almost the perfect man had it not been for a few unfortunate physical blemishes. The most annoying were some patches on his scalp where at some uncertain date shiny ringworm scars had appeared. Although these were on his own head, apparently Ah Q did not consider them as altogether honourable, for he refrained from using the word "ringworm" or any words that sounded anything like it. Later he improved on this, making "bright" and "light" forbidden words, while later still even "lamp" and "candle" were taboo. Whenever this taboo was disregarded, whether intentionally or not, Ah Q would fly into a rage, his ringworm scars turning scarlet. He would look over the offender, and if it were someone weak in repartee he would curse

上独不表格外的崇奉,他想:我的儿子会阔得多啦!加以进了几回城,阿Q自然更自负,然而他又很鄙薄城里人,譬如用三尺长三寸宽的木板做成的凳子,未庄叫"长凳",他也叫"长凳",城里人却叫"条凳",他想:这是错的,可笑!油煎大头鱼,未庄都加上半寸长的葱叶,城里却加上切细的葱丝,他想:这也是错的,可笑!然而未庄人真是不见世面的可笑的乡下人呵,他们没有见过城里的煎鱼!

阿Q"先前阔",见识高,而且"真能做",本来几乎是一个"完人"了,但可惜他体质上还有一些缺点。最恼人的是在他头皮上,颇有几处不知起于何时的癞疮疤。这虽然也在他身上,而看阿Q的意思,倒也似乎以为不足贵的,因为他讳说"癞"以及一切近于"赖"的音,后来推而广之,"光"也讳,"亮"也讳,再后来,连"灯""烛"都讳了。一犯讳,不问有心与无心,阿Q便全疤通红的发起怒来,估量了对手,口讷的他

英汉对照
English-Chinese
中国文学宝库
Gems of Chinese Literature
现代文学系列
Modern Literature

him, while if it were a poor fighter he would hit him. Yet, curiously enough, it was usually Ah Q who was worsted in these encounters, until finally he adopted new tactics, contenting himself in general with a furious glare.

It so happened, however, that after Ah Q had taken to using this furious glare, the idlers in Weizhuang grew even more fond of making jokes at his expense. As soon as they saw him they would pretend to give a start and say:

"Look! It's lighting up."

Ah Q rising to the bait as usual would glare in fury.

"So there is a paraffin lamp here," they would continue, unafraid.

Ah Q could do nothing but rack his brains for some retort. "You don't even deserve..." At this juncture it seemed as if the bald patches on his scalp were noble and honourable, not just ordinary ringworm scars. However, as we said above, Ah Q was a man of the world: he knew at once that he had nearly broken the "taboo" and refrained from saying any more.

If the idlers were still not satisfied but continued to pester him, they would in the end come to blows. Then only after Ah Q had to all appearances been defeated, had his brownish queue pulled and his head bumped against the wall four or five times, would the idlers walk away, satisfied at having won. And Ah Q would stand there for a second thinking to himself, "It's as if I were beaten by my son. What is the world coming to nowadays..." Thereupon he too would walk away, satisfied at having won.

Whatever Ah Q thought he was sure to tell people later; thus

便骂,气力小的他便打;然而不知怎么一回事,总还是阿Q吃亏的时候多。于是他渐渐的变换了方针,大抵改为怒目而视了。

谁知道阿Q采用怒目主义之后,未庄的闲人们便愈喜欢玩笑他。一见面,他们便假作吃惊的说:

"哙,亮起来了。"

阿Q照例的发了怒,他怒目而视了。

"原来有保险灯在这里!"他们并不怕。

阿Q没有法,只得另外想出报复的话来:

"你还不配……"这时候,又仿佛在他头上的是一种高尚的光荣的癞头疮,并非平常的癞头疮;但上文说过,阿Q是有见识的,他立刻知道和"犯忌"有点抵触,便不再往底下说。

闲人还不完,只撩他,于是终而至于打。阿Q在形式上打败了,被人揪住黄辫子,在壁上碰了四五个响头,闲人这才心满意足的得胜的走了,阿Q站了一刻,心里想,"我总算被儿子打了,现在的世界真不像样……"于是也心满意足的得胜的走了。

阿Q想在心里的,后来每每说出口来,所

almost all who made fun of Ah Q knew that he had this means of winning a psychological victory. So after this anyone who pulled or twisted his brown queue would forestall him by saying: "Ah Q, this is not a son beating his father, it is a man beating a beast. Let's hear you say it: A man beating a beast!"

Then Ah Q, clutching at the root of his queue, his head on one side, would say: "Beating an insect — how about that? I am an insect — now will you let me go?"

But although he was an insect the idlers would not let him go until they had knocked his head five or six times against something nearby, according to their custom, after which they would walk away satisfied that they had won, confident that this time Ah Q was done for. In less than ten seconds, however, Ah Q would walk away also satisfied that he had won, thinking that he was the "Number One self-belittler," and that after subtracting "self-belittler" what remained was "Number One." Was not the highest successful candidate in the official examination also "Number One?" "And who do you think you are?"

After employing such cunning devices to get even with his enemies, Ah Q would make his way cheerfully to the tavern to drink a few bowls of wine, joke with the others again, quarrel with them again, come off victorious again, and return cheerfully to the Tutelary God's Temple, there to fall asleep as soon as his head touched the pillow. If he had money he would gamble. A group of men would squat on the ground, Ah Q sandwiched in their midst, his face streaming with sweat; and his voice would shout the loudest: "Four hundred on the Green Dragon!"

以凡有和阿Q玩笑的人们,几乎全知道他有这一种精神上的胜利法,此后每逢揪住他黄辫子的时候,人就先一着对他说:

"阿Q,这不是儿子打老子,是人打畜生。自己说:人打畜生!"

阿Q两只手都捏住了自己的辫根,歪着头,说道:

"打虫豸,好不好?我是虫豸——还不放么?"

但虽然是虫豸,闲人也并不放,仍旧在就近什么地方给他碰了五六个响头,这才心满意足的得胜的走了,他以为阿Q这回可遭了瘟。然而不到十秒钟,阿Q也心满意足的得胜的走了,他觉得他是第一个能够自轻自贱的人,除了"自轻自贱"不算外,余下的就是"第一个"。状元不也是"第一个"么?"你算是什么东西"呢!?

阿Q以如是等等妙法克服怨敌之后,便愉快的跑到酒店里喝几碗酒,又和别人调笑一通,口角一通,又得了胜,愉快的回到土谷祠,放倒头睡着了。假使有钱,他便去押牌宝,一堆人蹲在地面上,阿Q即汗流满面的夹在这中间;声音他最响:

"青龙四百!"

英汉对照
English-Chinese
中国文学宝库
Gems of Chinese Literature
现代文学系列
Modern Literature

"Hey — open there!"

The stake-holder, his face streaming with sweat too, would open the box and chant: "Heavenly Gate! — Nothing for the Corner!... No stakes on Popularity Passage! Pass over Ah Q's coppers!"

"The Passage — one hundred — one hundred and fifty."

To the tune of this chanting, Ah Q's money would gradually vanish into the pockets of other sweating players. Finally he would be forced to squeeze his way out of the crowd and watch from the back, taking a vicarious interest in the game until it broke up, when he would return reluctantly to the Tutelary God's Temple. The next day he would go to work with swollen eyes.

However, the truth of the proverb "Misfortune may prove a blessing in disguise" was shown when Ah Q was unfortunate enough to win and almost suffered defeat in the end.

This was the evening of the Festival of the Gods in Weizhuang. According to custom there was an opera; and close to the stage, also according to custom, were numerous gambling tables. The drums and gongs of the opera sounded miles away to Ah Q who had ears only for the stake-holder's chant. He staked successfully again and again, his coppers turning into silver coins, his silver coins into dollars, and his dollars mounting up. In his excitement he cried out. "Two dollars on Heavenly Gate!"

He never knew who started the fight, nor for what reason. Curses, blows, and footsteps formed a confused medley of sound in his head, and by the time he clambered to his feet the gambling tables had vanished and so had the gamblers. Several parts of his body

"咳～～开～～啦!"桩家揭开盒子盖,也是汗流满面的唱。"天门啦～～～角回啦～～～!人和穿堂空在那里啦～～～!阿Q的铜钱拿过来!～～～"

"穿堂一百——一百五十!"

阿Q的钱便在这样的歌吟之下,渐渐的输入别个汗流满面的人物的腰间。他终于只好挤出堆外,站在后面看,替别人着急,一直到散场,然后恋恋的回到土谷祠,第二天,肿着眼睛去工作。

但真所谓"塞翁失马安知非福"罢,阿Q不幸而赢了一回,他倒几乎失败了。

这是未庄赛神的晚上。这晚上照例有一台戏,戏台左近,也照例有许多的赌摊。做戏的锣鼓,在阿Q耳朵里仿佛在十里之外;他只听得桩家的歌唱了。他赢而又赢,铜钱变成角洋,角洋变成大洋,大洋又成了叠。他兴高采烈得非常:

"天门两块!"

他不知道谁和谁为什么打起架来了。骂声打声脚步声,昏头昏脑的一大阵,他才爬起来,赌摊不见了,人们也不见了,身上有几处很似乎

英汉对照
English-Chinese
中国文学宝库
Gems of Chinese Literature
现代文学系列
Modern Literature

seemed to be aching as if he had been kicked and knocked about, while a number of people were looking at him in astonishment. Feeling as if something were amiss he walked back to the Tutelary God's Temple, and by the time he had calmed down he realized that his pile of dollars had gone. Since most of the people who ran gambling tables at the Festival were not natives of Weizhuang, where could he look for the culprits?

So white and glittering a pile of silver! All of it his... but now it had disappeared. Even to consider this tantamount to being robbed by his son did not comfort him. To consider himself as an insect did not comfort him either. This time he really tasted something of the bitterness of defeat.

But presently he changed defeat into victory. Raising his right hand he slapped his own face hard, twice, so that it tingled with pain. After this slapping his heart felt lighter, for it seemed as if the one who had given the slap was himself, the one slapped some other self, and soon it was just as if he had beaten someone else — in spite of the fact that his face was still tingling. He lay down satisfied that he had gained the victory.

Soon he was asleep.

CHAPTER 3

A Further Account of Ah Q's Victories

Although Ah Q was always gaining victories, it was only after he was favoured with a slap in the face by Mr Zhao that he became

有些痛,似乎也挨了几拳几脚似的,几个人诧异的对他看。他如有所失的走进土谷祠,定一定神,知道他的一堆洋钱不见了。赶赛会的赌摊多不是本村人,还到那里去寻根柢呢?

很白很亮的一堆洋钱!而且是他的——现在不见了!说是算被儿子拿去了罢,总还是忽忽不乐;说自己是虫豸罢,也还是忽忽不乐;他这回才有些感到失败的苦痛了。

但他立刻转败为胜了。他擎起右手,用力的在自己脸上连打了两个嘴巴,热剌剌的有些痛;打完之后,便心平气和起来,似乎打的是自己,被打的是别一个自己,不久也就仿佛是自己打了别个一般,——虽然还有些热剌剌,——心满意足的得胜的躺下了。

他睡着了。

第三章　续优胜记略

然而阿Q虽然常优胜,却直待蒙赵太爷打他嘴巴之后,这才出了名。

英汉对照
English-Chinese
中国文学宝库
Gems of Chinese Literature
现代文学系列
Modern Literature

famous.

After paying the bailiff two hundred cash he lay down angrily. Then he said to himself, "What is the world coming to nowadays, with sons beating their fathers..." And then the thought of the prestige of Mr Zhao, who was now his son, gradually raised his spirits. He scrambled up and made his way to the tavern singing *The Young Widow at Her Husband's Grave*.① At that time he did feel that Mr Zhao was a cut above most people.

After this incident, strange to relate, it was true that everybody seemed to pay him unusual respect. He probably attributed this to the fact that he was Mr Zhao's father, but actually such was not the case. In Weizhuang, as a rule, if the seventh child hit the eighth child or Li So-and-so hit Zhang So-and-so, it was not taken seriously. A beating had to be connected with some important personage like Mr Zhao before the villagers thought it worth talking about. But once they thought it worth talking about, since the beater was famous the one beaten enjoyed some of his reflected fame. As for the fault being Ah Q's, that was naturally taken for granted, the reason being that Mr Zhao could do no wrong. But if Ah Q were wrong, why did everybody seem to treat him with unusual respect? This is difficult to explain. We may put forward the hypothesis that it was because Ah Q had said he belonged to the same family as Mr Zhao; thus, although he had been beaten, people were still afraid there might be some truth in his assertion and therefore thought it safer to treat him more respectfully. Or,

---

① A local opera popular in Shaoxing.

他付过地保二百文酒钱,愤愤的躺下了,后来想:"现在的世界太不成话,儿子打老子……"于是忽而想到赵太爷的威风,而现在是他的儿子了,便自己也渐渐的得意起来,爬起身,唱着《小孤孀上坟》到酒店去。这时候,他又觉得赵太爷高人一等了。

说也奇怪,从此之后,果然大家也仿佛格外尊敬他。这在阿Q,或者以为因为他是赵太爷的父亲,而其实也不然。未庄通例,倘如阿七打阿八,或者李四打张三,向来本不算一件事,必须与一位名人如赵太爷者相关,这才载上他们的口碑。一上口碑,则打的既有名,被打的也就托庇有了名。至于错在阿Q,那自然是不必说。所以者何?就因为赵太爷是不会错的。但他既然错,为什么大家又仿佛格外尊敬他呢?这可难解,穿凿起来说,或者因为阿Q说是赵太爷的本家,虽然挨了打,大家也还怕有些真,总不

英汉对照
English-Chinese
中国文学宝库
Gems of Chinese Literature
现代文学系列
Modern Literature

alternatively, it may have been like the case of the sacrificial beef in the Confucian temple: although the beef was in the same category as the pork and mutton, being of animal origin just as they were, later Confucians did not dare touch it since the sage had enjoyed it.

After this Ah Q prospered for several years.

One spring day, when he was walking along in a state of happy intoxication, he saw Whiskers Wang sitting stripped to the waist in the sunlight at the foot of a wall, catching lice; and at this sight his own body began to itch. Since Whiskers Wang was scabby and bewhiskered, everybody called him "Ringworm Whiskers Wang." Although Ah Q omitted the word "Ringworm," he had the greatest contempt for the man. To Ah Q, while scabs were nothing to take exception to, such hairy cheeks were really too outlandish and could excite nothing but scorn. So Ah Q sat down by his side. Had it been any other idler, Ah Q would never have dared sit down so casually; but what had he to fear by the side of Whiskers Wang? In fact, his willingness to sit down was doing the fellow an honour.

Ah Q took off his tattered lined jacket and turned it inside out; but either because he had washed it recently or because he was too clumsy, a long search yielded only three or four lice. He saw that Whiskers Wang, on the other hand, was catching first one and then another in swift succession, cracking them between his teeth with a popping sound.

Ah Q felt first disappointed, then resentful: the despicable Whiskers Wang had so many, he himself so few — what a great loss of face! He longed to find one or two big ones, but there were

如尊敬一些稳当。否则,也如孔庙里的太牢一般,虽然与猪羊一样,同是畜生,但既经圣人下箸,先儒们便不敢妄动了。

阿Q此后倒得意了许多年。

有一年的春天,他醉醺醺的在街上走,在墙根的日光下,看见王胡在那里赤着膊捉虱子,他忽然觉得身上也痒起来了。这王胡,又癞又胡,别人都叫他王癞胡,阿Q却删去了一个癞字,然而非常渺视他。阿Q的意思,以为癞是不足为奇的,只有这一部络腮胡子,实在太新奇,令人看不上眼。他于是并排坐下去了。倘是别的闲人们,阿Q本不敢大意坐下去。但这王胡旁边,他有什么怕呢?老实说:他肯坐下去,简直还是抬举他。

阿Q也脱下破夹袄来,翻检了一回,不知道因为新洗呢还是因为粗心,许多工夫,只捉到三四个。他看那王胡,却是一个又一个,两个又三个,只放在嘴里毕毕剥剥的响。

阿Q最初是失望,后来却不平了:看不上眼的王胡尚且那么多,自己倒反这样少,这是怎样的大失体统的事呵!他很想寻一两个大的,

none, and when at last he managed to catch a middle-sized one, stuffed it fiercely between his thick lips and bit hard, the resultant pop was again inferior to the noise made by Whiskers Wang.

All Ah Q's ringworm patches turned scarlet. He flung his jacket on the ground, spat, and swore, "Hairy worm!"

"Mangy dog, who are you calling names?" Whiskers Wang looked up contemptuously.

Although the relative respect accorded him in recent years had increased Ah Q's pride, he was still rather timid when confronted by those loafers accustomed to fighting. But today he was feeling exceptionally pugnacious. How dare a hairy-cheeked creature like this insult him?

"If the cap fits wear it," he retorted, standing up and putting his hands on his hips.

"Are your bones itching?" demanded Whiskers Wang, standing up too and draping his jacket over his shoulders.

Thinking that the fellow meant to run away, Ah Q lunged forward to punch him. But before his fist reached the target, his opponent seized him and gave him a tug which sent him staggering. Then Whiskers Wang seized his queue and started dragging him towards the wall to knock his head in the time-honoured manner.

"'A gentleman uses his tongue but not his hands!'" protested Ah Q, his head on one side.

Apparently Whiskers Wang was no gentleman, for without paying the slightest attention to what Ah Q said he knocked his head against the wall five times in succession, then with a great push shoved him two yards away, after which he walked off in triumph.

然而竟没有,好容易才捉到一个中的,恨恨的塞在厚嘴唇里,狠命一咬,劈的一声,又不及王胡响。

他癞疮疤块块通红了,将衣服摔在地上,吐一口唾沫,说:

"这毛虫!"

"癞皮狗,你骂谁?"王胡轻蔑的抬起眼来说。

阿Q近来虽然比较的受人尊敬,自己也更高傲些,但和那些打惯的闲人们见面还胆怯,独有这回却非常武勇了。这样满脸胡子的东西,也敢出言无状么?

"谁认便骂谁!"他站起来,两手叉在腰间说。

"你的骨头痒了么?"王胡也站起来,披上衣服说。

阿Q以为他要逃了,抢进去就是一拳。这拳头还未达到身上,已经被他抓住了,只一拉,阿Q跄跄踉踉的跌进去,立刻又被王胡扭住了辫子,要拉到墙上照例去碰头。

"'君子动口不动手'!"阿Q歪着头说。

王胡似乎不是君子,并不理会,一连给他碰了五下,又用力的一推,至于阿Q跌出六尺多远,这才满足的去了。

英汉对照
English-Chinese
中国文学宝库
Gems of Chinese Literature
现代文学系列
Modern Literature

As far as Ah Q could remember, this was the first humiliation of his life, because he had always scoffed at Whiskers Wang on account of his ugly bewhiskered cheeks, but had never been scoffed at, much less beaten by him. And now, contrary to all expectations, Whiskers Wang had beaten him. Could it really be true, as they said in the market-place: "The Emperor has abolished the official examinations, so that scholars who have passed them are no longer in demand?" This must have undermined the Zhao family's prestige. Was this why people were treating him contemptuously too?

Ah Q stood there irresolutely.

From the distance approached another of Ah Q's enemies. This was Mr Qian's eldest son whom Ah Q thoroughly despised. After studying in a foreign-style school in the city, it seemed he had gone to Japan. When he came home half a year later his legs were straight[①] and his queue had disappeared. His mother wept bitterly a dozen times, and his wife tried three times to jump into the well. Later his mother told everyone, "His queue was cut off by some scoundrel when he was drunk. By rights he ought to be a big official, but now he'll have to wait till it's grown again." Ah Q, however, did not believe this, and insisted on calling him a "Bogus Foreign Devil" or "Traitor in Foreign Pay." At sight of him he would start cursing under his breath.

What Ah Q despised and detested most in him was his false queue. When it came to having a false queue, a man could scarcely be considered human; and the fact that his wife had not attempted to jump

---

① The stiff-legged stride of many foreigners led some Chinese to believe that their knees had no joints.

在阿Q的记忆上,这大约要算是生平第一件的屈辱,因为王胡以络腮胡子的缺点,向来只被他奚落,从没有奚落他,更不必说动手了。而他现在竟动手,很意外,难道真如市上所说,皇帝已经停了考,不要秀才和举人了,因此赵家减了威风,因此他们也便小觑了他么?

阿Q无可适从的站着。

远远的走来了一个人,他的对头又到了。这也是阿Q最厌恶的一个人,就是钱太爷的大儿子。他先前跑上城里去进洋学堂,不知怎么又跑到东洋去了,半年之后他回到家里来,腿也直了,辫子也不见了,他的母亲大哭了十几场,他的老婆跳了三回井。后来,他的母亲到处说,"这辫子是被坏人灌醉了酒剪去的。本来可以做大官,现在只好等留长再说了。"然而阿Q不肯信,偏称他"假洋鬼子",也叫作"里通外国的人",一见他,一定在肚子里暗暗的咒骂。

阿Q尤其"深恶而痛绝之"的,是他的一条假辫子。辫子而至于假,就是没有了做人的资

into the well a fourth time showed that she was not a good woman either.

Now this "Bogus Foreign Devil" was approaching.

"Baldhead! Ass..." In the past Ah Q had just cursed under his breath, inaudibly; but today, because he was in a rage and itching for revenge, the words slipped out involuntarily.

Unfortunately this Baldhead was carrying a shiny brown cane which looked to Ah Q like the "staff carried by a mourner." With great strides he bore down on Ah Q who, guessing at once that a beating was in the offing, hastily flexed his muscles and hunched his shoulders in anticipation. Sure enough. Thwack! Something struck him on the head.

"I meant him!" explained Ah Q, pointing to a nearby child. Thwack! Thwack! Thwack!

As far as Ah Q could remember, this was the second humiliation of his life. Fortunately after the thwacking stopped it seemed to him that the matter was closed, and he even felt somewhat relieved. Moreover, the precious "ability to forget" handed down by his ancestors stood him in good stead. He walked slowly away and by the time he approached the tavern door he was quite cheerful again.

Just then, however, a small nun from the Convent of Quiet Self-Improvement came walking towards him. The sight of a nun always made Ah Q swear; how much more so, then after these humiliations? When he recalled what had happened, his anger flared up again.

"I couldn't think what made my luck so bad today — so it's meeting you that did it!" he fumed to himself.

Going towards her he spat noisily. "Ugh!... Pah!"

格;他的老婆不跳第四回井,也不是好女人。

这"假洋鬼子"近来了。

"秃儿。驴……"阿Q历来本只在肚子里骂,没有出过声,这回因为正气忿,因为要报仇,便不由的轻轻的说出来了。

不料这秃儿却拿着一支黄漆的棍子——就是阿Q所谓哭丧棒——大踏步走了过来。阿Q在这刹那,便知道大约要打了,赶紧抽紧筋骨,耸了肩膀等候着,果然,拍的一声,似乎确凿打在自己头上了。

"我说他!"阿Q指着近旁的一个孩子,分辩说。

拍!拍拍!

在阿Q的记忆上,这大约要算是生平第二件的屈辱。幸而拍拍的响了之后,于他倒似乎完结了一件事,反而觉得轻松些,而且"忘却"这一件祖传的宝贝也发生了效力,他慢慢的走,将到酒店门口,早已有些高兴了。

但对面走来了静修庵里的小尼姑。阿Q便在平时,看见伊也一定要唾骂,而况在屈辱之后呢?他于是发生了回忆,又发生了敌忾了。

"我不知道我今天为什么这样晦气,原来就因为见了你!"他想。

他迎上去,大声的吐一口唾沫:

"咳,呸!"

英汉对照
English-Chinese
中国文学宝库
Gems of Chinese Literature
现代文学系列
Modern Literature

The small nun paid not the least attention but walked on with lowered head. Ah Q stepped up to her and shot out a hand to rub her newly shaved scalp, then with a guffaw cried, "Baldhead! Go back quick, your monk's waiting for you..."

"Who are you pawing?..." demanded the nun, flushing all over her face as she quickened her pace.

The men in the tavern roared with laughter. This appreciation of his feat added to Ah Q's elation.

"If the monk paws you, why can't I?" He pinched her cheek.

Again the men in the tavern roared with laughter. More bucked than ever, and eager to please his admirers, Ah Q pinched her hard again before letting her go.

This encounter had made him forget Whiskers Wang and the Bogus Foreign Devil, as if all the day's bad luck had been avenged. And strange to relate, even more completely relaxed than after the thwacking, he felt as light as if he were walking on air.

"Ah Q, may you die sonless!" wailed the little nun already some distance away.

Ah Q roared with delighted laughter.

The men in the tavern joined in, with only a shade less gusto in their laughter.

CHAPTER 4

The Tragedy of Love

There are said to be some victors who take no pleasure in a

小尼姑全不睬,低了头只是走。阿Q走近伊身旁,突然伸出手去摩着伊新剃的头皮,呆笑着,说:

"秃儿!快回去,和尚等着你……"

"你怎么动手动脚……"尼姑满脸通红的说,一面赶快走。

酒店里的人大笑了。阿Q看见自己的勋业得了赏识,便愈加兴高采烈起来:

"和尚动得,我动不得?"他扭住伊的面颊。

酒店里的人大笑了。阿Q更得意,而且为满足那些赏鉴家起见,再用力的一拧,才放手。

他这一战,早忘却了王胡,也忘却了假洋鬼子,似乎对于今天的一切"晦气"都报了仇;而且奇怪,又仿佛全身比拍拍的响了之后更轻松,飘飘然的似乎要飞去了。

"这断子绝孙的阿Q!"远远地听得小尼姑的带哭的声音。

"哈哈哈!"阿Q十分得意的笑。

"哈哈哈!"酒店里的人也九分得意的笑。

第四章　恋爱的悲剧

有人说:有些胜利者,愿意敌手如虎,如鹰,

英汉对照
English-Chinese
中国文学宝库
Gems of Chinese Literature
现代文学系列
Modern Literature

victory unless their opponents are as fierce as tigers or eagles: in the case of foes as timid as sheep or chickens they find their triumph empty. There are other victors who, having carried all before them, with the enemy slain or surrendered, utterly cowed, realize that now no foe, no rival, no friend is left — none but themselves, supreme, lonely, lost, and forlorn. Then they find their triumph a tragedy. But not so our hero: he was always exultant. This may be a proof of the moral supremacy of China over the rest of the world.

Look at Ah Q, elated as if he were walking on air!

This victory was not without strange consequences, though. For after walking on air for quite a time he floated into the Tutelary God's Temple, where he would normally have started snoring as soon as he lay down. This evening, however, he found it very hard to close his eyes, being struck by something odd about his thumb and first finger, which seemed to be smoother than usual. It is impossible to say whether something soft and smooth on the little nun's face had stuck to his fingers, or whether his fingers had been rubbed smooth against her cheek.

"Ah Q, may you die sonless!"

These words sounded again in Ah Q's ears, and he thought, "Quite right, I should take a wife; for if a man dies sonless he has no one to sacrifice a bowl of rice to his spirit... I ought to have a wife." As the saying goes, "There are three forms of unfilial conduct, of which the worst is to have no descendants,"[1] and it is one

---

[1] A quotation from Mencius (372-289 B C).

他才感得胜利的欢喜;假使如羊,如小鸡,他便反觉得胜利的无聊。又有些胜利者,当克服一切之后,看见死的死了,降的降了,"臣诚惶诚恐死罪死罪",他于是没有了敌人,没有了对手,没有了朋友,只有自己在上,一个,孤另另,凄凉,寂寞,便反而感到了胜利的悲哀。然而我们的阿Q却没有这样乏,他是永远得意的:这或者也是中国精神文明冠于全球的一个证据了。

看哪,他飘飘然的似乎要飞去了!

然而这一次的胜利,却又使他有些异样。他飘飘然的飞了大半天,飘进土谷祠,照例应该躺下便打鼾。谁知道这一晚,他很不容易合眼,他觉得自己的大拇指和第二指有点古怪:仿佛比平常滑腻些。不知道是小尼姑的脸上有一点滑腻的东西粘在他指上,还是他的指头在小尼姑脸上磨得滑腻了?……

"断子绝孙的阿Q!"

阿Q的耳朵里又听到这句话。他想:不错,应该有一个女人,断子绝孙便没有人供一碗饭,……应该有一个女人。夫"不孝有三无后为

英汉对照
English-Chinese
中国文学宝库
Gems of Chinese Literature
现代文学系列
Modern Literature

of the tragedies of life that "spirits without descendants go hungry."① Thus his view was absolutely in accordance with the teachings of the saints and sages, and it is indeed a pity that later he should have run amok.

"Woman, woman!..." he thought.

"... The monk paws... Woman, woman!... Woman!" he thought again.

We shall never know when Ah Q finally fell asleep that evening. After this, however, he probably always found his fingers rather soft and smooth, and always remained a little light-headed. "Woman..." he kept thinking.

From this we can see that woman is a menace to mankind.

The majority of Chinese men could become saints and sages, were it not for the unfortunate fact that they are ruined by women. The Shang Dynasty was destroyed by Da Ji, the Zhou Dynasty was undermined by Bao Si; as for the Qin Dynasty, although there is no historical evidence to that effect, if we assume that it fell on account of some woman we shall probably not be far wrong. And it is a fact that Dong Zhuo's death was caused by Diao Chan.②

Ah Q, too, was a man of strict morals to begin with. Although we do not know whether he was guided by some good teacher, he had always shown himself most scrupulous in observing "strict

---

① A quotation from the old classic *Zuo Zhuan*.

② Da Ji, in the twelfth century B C, was the concubine of the last king of the Shang Dynasty. Bao Si, in the eighth century B C, was the concubine of the last king of the Western Zhou Dynasty. Diao Chan was the concubine of Dong Zhuo, a powerful warlord at the end of the Han Dynasty.

大",而"若敖之鬼馁而",也是一件人生的大哀,所以他那思想,其实是样样合于圣经贤传的,只可惜后来有些"不能收其放心"了。

"女人,女人!……"他想。

"……和尚动得……女人,女人!……女人!"他又想。

我们不能知道这晚上阿Q在什么时候才打鼾。但大约他从此总觉得指头有些滑腻,所以他从此总有些飘飘然;"女……"他想。

即此一端,我们便可以知道女人是害人的东西。

中国的男人,本来大半都可以做圣贤,可惜全被女人毁掉了。商是妲己闹亡的;周是褒姒弄坏的;秦……虽然史无明文,我们也假定他因为女人,大约未必十分错;而董卓可是的确给貂蝉害死了。

阿Q本来也是正人,我们虽然不知道他曾蒙什么明师指授过,但他对于"男女之大防"却

英汉对照
English-Chinese
中国文学宝库
Gems of Chinese Literature
现代文学系列
Modern Literature

segregation of the sexes," and was righteous enough to denounce such heretics as the little nun and the Bogus Foreign Devil. His view was, "All nuns must carry on in secret with monks. If a woman walks alone on the street, she must want to seduce men. When a man and a woman talk together, it must be to arrange a secret rendezvous." In order to correct such people, he would glare furiously, pass loud, cutting remarks, or, if the place were deserted, throw a small stone from behind.

Who could tell that close on thirty, when a man should "stand firm,"① he would lose his head like this over a little nun? Such light-headedness, according to the classical canons, is most reprehensible; thus women certainly are hateful creatures. For if the little nun's face had not been soft and smooth, Ah Q would not have been bewitched by her; nor would this have happened if the little nun's face had been covered by a cloth. Five or six years before, when watching an open-air opera, he had pinched the leg of a woman in the audience; but because it was separated from him by the cloth of her trousers he had not had this light-headed feeling afterwards. The little nun had not covered her face, however, and this is another proof of the odiousness of the heretic.

"Woman..." thought Ah Q.

He kept a close watch on those women who he believed must "want to seduce men," but they did not smile at him. He listened very carefully to those women who talked to him, but not one of

---

① Confucius said that at thirty he "stood firm." The phrase was later used to indicate that a man was thirty years old.

历来非常严;也很有排斥异端——如小尼姑及假洋鬼子之类——的正气。他的学说是:凡尼姑,一定与和尚私通;一个女人在外面走,一定想引诱野男人;一男一女在那里讲话,一定要有勾当了。为惩治他们起见,所以他往往怒目而视,或者大声说几句"诛心"话,或者在冷僻处,便从后面掷一块小石头。

谁知道他将到"而立"之年,竟被小尼姑害得飘飘然了。这飘飘然的精神,在礼教上是不应该有的,——所以女人真可恶,假使小尼姑的脸上不滑腻,阿Q便不至于被蛊,又假使小尼姑的脸上盖一层布,阿Q便也不至于被蛊了,——他五六年前,曾在戏台下的人丛中拧过一个女人的大腿,但因为隔一层裤,所以此后并不飘飘然,——而小尼姑并不然,这也足见异端之可恶。

"女……"阿Q想。

他对于以为"一定想引诱野男人"的女人,时常留心看,然而伊并不对他笑。他对于和他讲话的女人,也时常留心听,然而伊又并不提起

英汉对照
English-Chinese
中国文学宝库
Gems of Chinese Literature
现代文学系列
Modern Literature

them mentioned anything relevant to a secret rendezvous. Ah! This was simply another example of the odiousness of women: they all assumed a false modesty.

One day when Ah Q was grinding rice in Mr Zhao's house, he sat down in the kitchen after supper to smoke a pipe. If it had been anyone else's house, he could have gone home after supper, but they dined early in the Zhao family. Although it was the rule that you must not light a lamp but go to bed after eating, there were occasional exceptions to the rule. Before Mr Zhao's son passed the county examination he was allowed to light a lamp to study the examination essays, and when Ah Q went to do odd jobs he was allowed to light a lamp to grind rice. Because of this latter exception to the rule, Ah Q still sat in the kitchen smoking before going on with his work.

When Amah Wu, the only maidservant in the Zhao household, had finished washing the dishes, she sat down on the long bench too and started chatting to Ah Q:

"Our mistress hasn't eaten anything for two days, because the master wants to get a concubine..."

"Woman... Amah Wu... this little widow," thought Ah Q.

"Our young mistress is going to have a baby in the eighth month..."

"Woman..." thought Ah Q.

He put down his pipe and stood up.

"Our young mistress — " Amah Wu chattered on.

"Sleep with me!" Ah Q suddenly rushed forward and threw himself at her feet.

关于什么勾当的话来。哦,这也是女人可恶之一节:伊们全都要装"假正经"的。

这一天,阿Q在赵太爷家里舂了一天米,吃过晚饭,便坐在厨房里吸旱烟。倘在别家,吃过晚饭本可以回去的了,但赵府上晚饭早,虽说定例不准掌灯,一吃完便睡觉,然而偶然也有一些例外:其一,是赵大爷未进秀才的时候,准其点灯读文章;其二,便是阿Q来做短工的时候,准其点灯舂米。因为这一条例外,所以阿Q在动手舂米之前,还坐在厨房里吸旱烟。

吴妈,是赵太爷家里唯一的女仆,洗完了碗碟,也就在长凳上坐下了,而且和阿Q谈闲天:

"太太两天没有吃饭哩,因为老爷要买一个小的……"

"女人……吴妈……这小孤孀……"阿Q想。

"我们的少奶奶是八月里要生孩子了……"

"女人……"阿Q想。

阿Q放下烟管,站了起来。

"我们的少奶奶……"吴妈还唠叨说。

"我和你困觉,我和你困觉!"阿Q忽然抢上去,对伊跪下了。

英汉对照
English-Chinese
中国文学宝库
Gems of Chinese Literature
现代文学系列
Modern Literature

There was a moment of absolute silence.

"*Aiya*!" Dumbfounded for an instant, Amah Wu suddenly began to tremble, then rushed out shrieking and could soon be heard wailing.

Ah Q kneeling opposite the wall was dumbfounded too. He grasped the empty bench with both hands and stood up slowly, dimly aware that something was wrong. In fact, by this time he was in rather a nervous state himself. In a flurry, he stuck his pipe into his belt and decided to go back to grind rice. But — Bang! — a heavy blow landed on his head, and he spun round to see the successful county candidate standing before him brandishing a big bamboo pole.

"How dare you... you..."

The big bamboo pole came down across Ah Q's shoulders. When he put up both hands to protect his head, the blow landed on his knuckles, causing him considerable pain. As he escaped through the kitchen door it seemed as if his back also received a blow.

"Turtle's egg!" shouted the successful candidate, cursing him in mandarin from behind.

Ah Q fled to the hulling-floor where he stood alone, his knuckles still aching and still remembering that "Turtle's egg!" because it was an expression never used by the Weizhuang villagers but only by the rich who had seen something of official life. This made it the more alarming, the more impressive. By now, however, all thought of "Woman..." had flown. After this cursing and beating it seemed as if something were done with, and quite light-heartedly he began to grind rice again. Soon this made him hot, and he

一刹时中很寂然。

"阿呀!"吴妈楞了一息,突然发抖,大叫着往外跑,且跑且嚷,似乎后来带哭了。

阿Q对了墙壁跪着也发楞,于是两手扶着空板凳,慢慢的站起来,仿佛觉得有些糟。他这时确也有些忐忑了,慌张的将烟管插在裤带上,就想去舂米。蓬的一声,头上着了很粗的一下,他急忙回转身去,那秀才便拿了一支大竹杠站在他面前。

"你反了……你这……"

大竹杠又向他劈下来了。阿Q两手去抱头,拍的正打在指节上,这可很有一些痛。他冲出厨房门,仿佛背上又着了一下似的。

"忘八蛋!"秀才在后面用了官话这样骂。

阿Q奔入舂米场,一个人站着,还觉得指头痛,还记得"忘八蛋",因为这话是未庄的乡下人从来不用,专是见过官府的阔人用的,所以格外怕,而印象也格外深。但此时,他那"女……"的思想却也没有了。而且打骂之后,似乎一件事也已经收束,倒反觉得一无挂碍似的,便动手去舂米。舂了一会,他热起来了,又歇了手脱衣服。

英汉对照
English-Chinese
中国文学宝库
Gems of Chinese Literature
现代文学系列
Modern Literature

stopped to take off his shirt.

While taking off his shirt he heard an uproar outside, and since Ah Q was all for excitement he went out in search of the sound. Step by step he traced it into Mr Zhao's inner courtyard. Although it was dusk he could see many people there: all the Zhao family including the mistress who had not eaten for two days. In addition, their neighbour Mrs Zou was there, as well as their relatives Zhao Baiyan and Zhao Sichen.

The young mistress was leading Amah Wu out of the servants' quarters, saying:

"Come outside... don't stay brooding in your own room."

"Everybody knows you are a good woman," put in Mrs Zou from the side. "You mustn't think of committing suicide."

Amah Wu merely wailed, muttering something unintelligible.

"This is interesting," thought Ah Q. "What mischief can this little widow be up to?" Wanting to find out, he was approaching Zhao Sichen when suddenly he caught sight of Mr Zhao's eldest son rushing towards him with, what was worse, the big bamboo pole in his hand. The sight of this big bamboo pole reminded him that he had been beaten by it, and he realized that apparently he was connected in some way with all this excitement. He turned and ran, hoping to escape to the hulling-floor, not foreseeing that the bamboo pole would cut off his retreat. When it did, he turned and ran in the other direction, leaving without further ado by the back gate. Soon he was back in the Tutelary God's Temple.

After Ah Q had been sitting down for a time, he broke out in gooseflesh and felt cold, because although it was spring the nights

脱下衣服的时候,他听得外面很热闹,阿Q生平本来最爱看热闹,便即寻声走出去了。寻声渐渐的寻到赵太爷的内院里,虽然在昏黄中,却辨得出许多人,赵府一家连两日不吃饭的太太也在内,还有间壁的邹七嫂,真正本家的赵白眼,赵司晨。

少奶奶正拖着吴妈走出下房来,一面说:"你到外面来,……不要躲在自己房里想……"

"谁不知道你正经,……短见是万万寻不得的。"邹七嫂也从旁说。

吴妈只是哭,夹些话,却不甚听得分明。

阿Q想:"哼,有趣,这小孤孀不知道闹着什么玩意儿了?"他想打听,走近赵司晨的身边。这时他猛然间看见赵大爷向他奔来,而且手里捏着一支大竹杠。他看见这一支大竹杠,便猛然间悟到自己曾经被打,和这一场热闹似乎有点相关。他翻身便走,想逃回春米场,不图这支竹杠阻了他的去路,于是他又翻身便走,自然而然的走出后门,不多工夫,已在土谷祠内了。

阿Q坐了一会,皮肤有些起粟,他觉得冷了,因为虽在春季,而夜间颇有余寒,尚不宜于

were still chilly and not suited to bare backs. He remembered that he had left his shirt in the Zhaos' house but was afraid that if he went to fetch it he might get another taste of the successful candidate's bamboo pole.

Then the bailiff came in.

"Curse you, Ah Q!" said the bailiff. "So you can't even keep your hands off the Zhaos' servants, you rebel! You've made me lose my sleep, damn it!..."

Under this torrent of abuse Ah Q naturally had nothing to say. Finally, since it was night-time, he had to pay the bailiff double: four hundred cash. Because he happened to have no ready money by him, he gave his felt hat as security, and agreed to the following five terms:

1. The next morning Ah Q must take a pair of red candles, weighing one pound each, and a bundle of incense sticks to the Zhao family to atone for his misdeeds.

2. Ah Q must pay for the Taoist priests whom the Zhao family had called to exorcize evil spirits.

3. Ah Q must never again set foot in the Zhao household.

4. If anything unfortunate should happen to Amah Wu, Ah Q must be held responsible.

5. Ah Q must not go back for his wages or shirt.

Ah Q naturally agreed to everything, but unfortunately he had no ready money. Luckily it was already spring, so it was possible to do without his padded quilt which he pawned for two thousand cash to comply with the terms stipulated. After kowtowing with bare back he still had a few cash left, but instead of redeeming his felt

赤膊,他也记得布衫留在赵家,但倘若去取,又深怕秀才的竹杠。然而地保进来了。

"阿Q,你的妈妈的!你连赵家的用人都调戏起来,简直是造反。害得我晚上没有觉睡,你的妈妈的!……"

如是云云的教训了一通,阿Q自然没有话。临末,因为在晚上,应该送地保加倍酒钱四百文,阿Q正没有现钱,便用一顶毡帽做抵押,并且订定了五条件:

一 明天用红烛——要一斤重的——一对,香一封,到赵府上去赔罪。

二 赵府上请道士被除缢鬼,费用由阿Q负担。

三 阿Q从此不准踏进赵府的门槛。

四 吴妈此后倘有不测,惟阿Q是问。

五 阿Q不准再去索取工钱和布衫。

阿Q自然都答应了,可惜没有钱。幸而已经春天,棉被可以无用,便质了二千大钱,履行条约。赤膊磕头之后,居然还剩几文,他也不再

hat from the bailiff, he spent them all on drink.

Actually, the Zhao family burned neither the incense nor the candles. Instead, they put them aside for the mistress to worship Buddha. Most of the ragged shirt was made into diapers for the baby which was born to the young mistress in the eighth month, while the tattered remainder was used by Amah Wu to make shoesoles.

CHAPTER 5

The Problem of Making a Living

After Ah Q had kowtowed and complied with the Zhao family's terms, he went back as usual to the Tutelary God's Temple. The sun had gone down, and he began to feel that something was wrong. Careful thought led him to the conclusion that this was probably because his back was bare. Remembering that he still had a ragged lined jacket, he put it on and lay down, and when he opened his eyes again the sun was already shining on the top of the west wall. He sat up, saying, "Curse it..."

After getting up he loafed about the streets as usual, until he began to feel that something else was wrong, though this was not to be compared to the physical discomfort of a bare back. Apparently, from that day onwards all the women in Weizhuang fought shy of Ah Q: whenever they saw him coming they took refuge indoors. In fact, even Mrs Zou who was nearing fifty retreated in confusion with the rest, calling her eleven-year-old daughter to go inside. This struck Ah Q as very strange. "The bitches!" he thought. "All

赎毡帽,统统喝了酒了。但赵家也并不烧香点烛,因为太太拜佛的时候可以用,留着了。那破布衫是大半做了少奶奶八月间生下来的孩子的衬尿布,那小半破烂的便都做了吴妈的鞋底。

第五章　生计问题

阿Q礼毕之后,仍旧回到土谷祠,太阳下去了,渐渐觉得世上有些古怪。他仔细一想,终于省悟过来:其原因盖在自己的赤膊。他记得破夹袄还在,便披在身上,躺倒了,待张开眼睛,原来太阳又已经照在西墙上头了。他坐起身,一面说道,"妈妈的……"

他起来之后,也仍旧在街上逛,虽然不比赤膊之有切肤之痛,却又渐渐的觉得世上有些古怪。仿佛从这一天起,未庄的女人们忽然都怕了羞,伊们一见阿Q走来,便个个躲进门里去。甚而至于将近五十岁的邹七嫂,也跟着别人乱钻,而且将十一岁的女儿都叫进去了。阿Q很以为奇,而且想:"这些东西忽然都学起小

英汉对照
English-Chinese
中国文学宝库
Gems of Chinese Literature
现代文学系列
Modern Literature

of a sudden they're behaving like young ladies..."

A good many days later, however, he felt even more forcibly that something was wrong. First, the tavern refused him credit; secondly, the old man in charge of the Tutelary God's Temple made some uncalled-for remarks, as if he wanted Ah Q to leave; and thirdly, for many days — how many exactly he could not remember — not a soul had come to hire him. To be refused credit in the tavern he could put up with; if the old man kept urging him to leave, he could just ignore his complaints; but when no one came to hire him he had to go hungry, and this was really a "cursed" state to be in.

When Ah Q could stand it no longer he went to his former employers' homes to find out what was the matter — it was only Mr Zhao's threshold that he was not allowed to cross. But he met with a strange reception. The one to appear was always a man looking thoroughly annoyed who waved him away as if he were a beggar, saying:

"There's nothing for you, get out!"

Ah Q found it more and more extraordinary. "These people always needed help in the past," he thought. "They can't suddenly have nothing to be done. This looks fishy." After making careful inquiries he found out that when they had any odd jobs they all called in Young D. Now this Young D was a thin and weakly pauper, even lower in Ah Q's eyes than Whiskers Wang. Who could have thought that this low fellow would steal his living from him? So this time Ah Q's indignation was greater than usual, and going on his way, fuming, he suddenly raised his arm and sang. "Steel

姐模样来了。这娼妇们……"

但他更觉得世上有些古怪,却是许多日以后的事。其一,酒店不肯赊欠了;其二,管土谷祠的老头子说些废话,似乎叫他走;其三,他虽然记不清多少日,但确乎有许多日,没有一个人来叫他做短工。酒店不赊,熬着也罢了;老头子催他走,噜苏一通也就算了;只是没有人来叫他做短工,却使阿Q肚子饿:这委实是一件非常"妈妈的"的事情。

阿Q忍不下去了,他只好到老主顾的家里去探问,——但独不许踏进赵府的门槛,——然而情形也异样:一定走出一个男人来,现了十分烦厌的相貌,像回复乞丐一般的摇手道:

"没有没有!你出去!"

阿Q愈觉得稀奇了。他想,这些人家向来少不了要帮忙,不至于现在忽然都无事,这总该有些蹊跷在里面了。他留心打听,才知道他们有事都去叫小Don。这小D,是一个穷小子,又瘦又乏,在阿Q的眼睛里,位置是在王胡之下的,谁料这小子竟谋了他的饭碗去。所以阿Q这一气,更与平常不同,当气愤愤的走着的时候,忽然将手一扬,唱道:

英汉对照
English-Chinese
中国文学宝库
Gems of Chinese Literature
现代文学系列
Modern Literature

mace in hand I shall trounce you..."①

A few days later he did indeed meet Young D in front of Mr Qian's house. "When two foes meet, there is no mistaking each other." As Ah Q advanced upon him, Young D stood his ground.

"Beast!" spluttered Ah Q, glaring.

"I'm an insect — will that do?..." rejoined Young D.

Such modesty only enraged Ah Q even more, but since he had no steel mace in his hand all he could do was rush forward to grab at Young D's queue. Young D, protecting his own queue with one hand, grabbed at Ah Q's with the other, whereupon Ah Q also used his free hand to protect his own queue. In the past Ah Q had never considered Young D worth taking seriously, but owing to his recent privations he was now as thin and weak as his opponent, so that they presented a spectacle of evenly matched antagonists, four hands clutching at two heads, both men bending at the waist, casting a blue, rainbow-shaped shadow on the Qian family's white wall for over half an hour.

"All right! All right!" exclaimed some of the onlookers, probably by way of mediation.

"Good, good!" exclaimed others, but whether to mediate, applaud the fighters, or spur them on to further efforts, was not certain.

The two combatants turned deaf ears to them all, however. If Ah Q advanced three paces, Young D would recoil three paces, and

---

① A line from *The Battle of the Dragon and the Tiger*, an opera popular in Shaoxing.

"我手执钢鞭将你打!……"

几天之后,他竟在钱府的照壁前遇见了小D。"仇人相见分外眼明",阿Q便迎上去,小D也站住了。

"畜生!"阿Q怒目而视的说,嘴角上飞出唾沫来。

"我是虫豸,好么?……"小D说。

这谦逊反使阿Q更加愤怒起来,但他手里没有钢鞭,于是只得扑上去,伸手去拔小D的辫子。小D一手护住了自己的辫根,一手也来拔阿Q的辫子,阿Q便也将空着的一只手护住了自己的辫根。从先前的阿Q看来,小D本来是不足齿数的,但他近来挨了饿,又瘦又乏已经不下于小D,所以便成了势均力敌的现象,四只手拔着两颗头,都弯了腰,在钱家粉墙上映出一个蓝色的虹形,至于半点钟之久了。

"好了,好了!"看的人们说,大约是解劝的。

"好,好!"看的人们说,不知道是解劝,是颂扬,还是煽动。

然而他们都不听。阿Q进三步,小D便退

英汉对照
English-Chinese
中国文学宝库
Gems of Chinese Literature
现代文学系列
Modern Literature

129

there they would stand. If Young D advanced three paces, Ah Q would recoil three paces, and there they would stand again. After about half an hour — Weizhuang had few clocks, so it is difficult to tell the time; it may have been twenty minutes — when steam was rising from their heads and sweat pouring down their cheeks, Ah Q let fall his hands, and in the same second Young D's hands fell too. They straightened up simultaneously and stepped back simultaneously, pushing their way out through the crowd.

"Just you wait, curse you!..." called Ah Q over his shoulder.

"Curse you! Just you wait..." echoed Young D, also over his shoulder.

This epic struggle had apparently ended in neither victory nor defeat, and it is not known whether the spectators were satisfied or not, for none of them expressed any opinion. But still not a soul came to hire Ah Q for odd jobs.

One warm day, when a balmy breeze seemed to give some foretaste of summer, Ah Q actually felt cold; but he could put up with this — his greatest worry was an empty stomach. His cotton quilt, felt hat, and shirt had long since disappeared, and after that he had sold his padded jacket. Now nothing was left but his trousers, and these of course he could not take off. He had a ragged lined jacket, it was true; but this was certainly worthless, unless he gave it away to be made into shoe-soles. He had long been dreaming of finding some money on the road, but hitherto he had not come across any; he had also been hoping he might suddenly discover some money in his tumble-down room, and had frantically ransacked it, but the room was quite, quite empty. Then he made

三步,都站着;小 D 进三步,阿 Q 便退三步,又都站着。大约半点钟,——未庄少有自鸣钟,所以很难说,或者二十分,——他们的头发里便都冒烟,额上便都流汗,阿 Q 的手放松了,在同一瞬间,小 D 的手也正放松了,同时直起,同时退开,都挤出人丛去。

"记着罢,妈妈的……"阿 Q 回过头去说。

"妈妈的,记着罢……"小 D 也回过头来说。

这一场"龙虎斗"似乎并无胜败,也不知道看的人可满足,都没有发什么议论,而阿 Q 却仍然没有人来叫他做短工。

有一日很温和,微风拂拂的颇有些夏意了,阿 Q 却觉得寒冷起来,但这还可担当,第一倒是肚子饿。棉被,毡帽,布衫,早已没有了,其次就卖了棉袄;现在有裤子,却万不可脱的;有破夹袄,又除了送人做鞋底之外,决定卖不出钱。他早想在路上拾得一注钱,但至今还没有见;他想在自己的破屋里忽然寻到一注钱,慌张的四顾,但屋内是空虚而且了然。于是他决计出门

英汉对照
English-Chinese
中国文学宝库
Gems of Chinese Literature
现代文学系列
Modern Literature

up his mind to go out in search of food.

As he walked along the road "in search of food" he saw the familiar tavern and the familiar steamed bread, but he passed them by without pausing for a second, without even hankering after them. It was not these he was looking for, although what exactly he was looking for he did not know himself.

Since Weizhuang was not a big place, he soon left it behind. Most of the country outside the village consisted of paddy fields, green as far as the eye could see with the tender shoots of young rice, dotted here and there with round black, moving objects — peasants cultivating their fields. But blind to the delights of country life, Ah Q simply went on his way, for he knew instinctively that this was far removed from his "search for food." Finally, however, he came to the walls of the Convent of Quiet Self-Improvement.

The convent too was surrounded by paddy fields, its white walls standing out sharply in the fresh green, and inside the low earthen wall at the back was a vegetable garden. Ah Q hesitated for a time, looking around him. Since there was no one in sight he scrambled on to the low wall, holding on to some milkwort. The mud wall started crumbling, and Ah Q shook with fear; however, by clutching at the branch of a mulberry tree he managed to jump over it. Within was a wild profusion of vegetation, but no sign of yellow wine, steamed bread, or anything edible. A clump of bamboos by the west wall had put forth many young shoots, but unfortunately these were not cooked. There was also rape which had long since gone to seed, mustard already about to flower, and some

求食去了。

他在路上走着要"求食",看见熟识的酒店,看见熟识的馒头,但他都走过了,不但没有暂停,而且并不想要。他所求的不是这类东西了;他求的是什么东西,他自己不知道。

未庄本不是大村镇,不多时便走尽了。村外多是水田,满眼是新秧的嫩绿,夹着几个圆形的活动的黑点,便是耕田的农夫。阿Q并不赏鉴这田家乐,却只是走,因为他直觉的知道这与他的"求食"之道是很辽远的。但他终于走到静修庵的墙外了。

庵周围也是水田,粉墙突出在新绿里,后面的低土墙里是菜园。阿Q迟疑了一会,四面一看,并没有人。他便爬上这矮墙去,扯着何首乌藤,但泥土仍然簌簌的掉,阿Q的脚也索索的抖;终于攀着桑树枝,跳到里面了。里面真是郁郁葱葱,但似乎并没有黄酒馒头,以及此外可吃的之类。靠西墙是竹丛,下面许多笋,只可惜都是并未煮熟的,还有油菜早经结子,芥菜已将开

英汉对照
English-Chinese
中国文学宝库
Gems of Chinese Literature
现代文学系列
Modern Literature

133

tough old cabbages.

Resentful as a scholar who has failed the examinations, Ah Q walked slowly towards the gate of the garden. Suddenly, however, he gave a start of joy, for what did he see there but a patch of turnips! He knelt down and had just begun pulling when a round head appeared from behind the gate, only to be promptly withdrawn. This was no other than the little nun. Now though Ah Q had always had the greatest contempt for such people as little nuns, there are times when "discretion is the better part of valour." He hastily pulled up four turnips, tore off the leaves, and stuffed them under his jacket. By this time an old nun had already come out.

"May Buddha preserve us, Ah Q! How dare you climb into our garden to steal turnips!... Mercy on us, what a wicked thing to do! *Aiya*, Buddha preserve us!..."

"When did I ever climb into your garden and steal turnips?" retorted Ah Q as he started off, keeping his eyes on her.

"Now — aren't you?" The old nun pointed at the bulge in his jacket.

"Are these yours? Will they answer when you call? You..."

Leaving his sentence unfinished, Ah Q took to his heels as fast as he could, followed by a huge fat black dog. Originally this dog had been at the front gate, and how it reached the back garden was a mystery. With a snarl the black dog gave chase and was just about to bite Ah Q's leg when most opportunely a turnip fell from his jacket, and the dog, taken by surprise, stopped for a second. During this time Ah Q scrambled up the mulberry tree, scaled the

花,小白菜也很老了。

阿Q仿佛文童落第似的觉得很冤屈,他慢慢走近园门去,忽而非常惊喜了,这分明是一畦老萝卜。他于是蹲下便拔,而门口突然伸出一个很圆的头来,又即缩回去了,这分明是小尼姑。小尼姑之流是阿Q本来视若草芥的,但世事须"退一步想",所以他便赶紧拔起四个萝卜,拧下青叶,兜在大襟里。然而老尼姑已经出来了。

"阿弥陀佛,阿Q,你怎么跳进园里来偷萝卜⋯⋯阿呀,罪过呵,阿唷,阿弥陀佛!⋯⋯"

"我什么时候跳进你的园里来偷萝卜?"阿Q且看且走的说。

"现在⋯⋯这不是?"老尼姑指着他的衣兜。

"这是你的?你能叫得他答应你么?你⋯⋯"

阿Q没有说完话,拔步便跑;追来的是一匹很肥大的黑狗。这本来在前门的,不知怎的到后园来了。黑狗哼而且追,已经要咬着阿Q的腿,幸而从衣兜里落下一个萝卜来,那狗给一吓,略略一停,阿Q已经爬上桑树,跨到土墙,

英汉对照
English-Chinese
中国文学宝库
Gems of Chinese Literature
现代文学系列
Modern Literature

mud wall, and fell, turnips and all, outside the convent. He left the black dog still barking by the mulberry tree, and the old nun saying her prayers.

Fearing that the nun would let the black dog out again, Ah Q gathered together his turnips and ran, picking up a few small stones as he went. But the black dog did not reappear. Ah Q threw away the stones and walked on, eating as he went, thinking to himself: "There is nothing to be had here: better go to town..."

By the time the third turnip was finished he had made up his mind to go to town.

CHAPTER 6

Form Resurgence to Decline

Weizhuang did not see Ah Q again till just after the Moon Festival that year. Everybody was surprised to hear of his return, and this made them think back and wonder where he had been all that time. In the past Ah Q had usually taken great pleasure in announcing his few visits to town; but since he had not done so this time, his going had passed unnoticed. He may have told the old man in charge of the Tutelary God's Temple, but according to the custom of Weizhuang only a trip to town by Mr Zhao, Mr Qian, or the successful county candidate counted as important. Even the Bogus Foreign Devil's going was not talked about, much less Ah Q's. This would explain why the old man had not spread the news for him, with the result that the villagers remained in the dark.

连人和萝卜都滚出墙外面了。只剩着黑狗还在对着桑树嗥,老尼姑念着佛。

阿Q怕尼姑又放出黑狗来,拾起萝卜便走,沿路又检了几块小石头,但黑狗却并不再出现。阿Q于是抛了石块,一面走一面吃,而且想道,这里也没有什么东西寻,不如进城去……

待三个萝卜吃完时,他已经打定了进城的主意了。

第六章　从中兴到末路

在未庄再看见阿Q出现的时候,是刚过了这年的中秋。人们都惊异,说是阿Q回来了,于是又回上去想道,他先前那里去了呢?阿Q前几回的上城,大抵早就兴高采烈的对人说,但这一次却并不,所以也没有一个人留心到。他或者也曾告诉过管土谷祠的老头子,然而未庄老例,只有赵太爷钱太爷和秀才大爷上城才算一件事。假洋鬼子尚且不足数,何况是阿Q:因此老头子也就不替他宣传,而未庄的社会上也就无从知道了。

英汉对照
English-Chinese
中国文学宝库
Gems of Chinese Literature
现代文学系列
Modern Literature

Ah Q's return this time was very different from before, and in fact quite enough to occasion astonishment. The day was growing dark when he showed up, bleary-eyed, at the tavern door, walked up to the counter, and tossed down on it a handful of silver and coppers produced from his belt. "Cash!" he announced. "Bring the wine!" He was wearing a new lined jacket and at his waist hung a large purse, the great weight of which caused his belt to sag in a sharp curve.

It was the custom in Weizhuang that anyone in any way unusual should be treated with respect rather than disregarded, and now, although they knew quite well that this was Ah Q, still he was very different from the Ah Q in the ragged coat. The ancients say, "A scholar who has been away three days must be looked at with new eyes." So the waiter, tavern-keeper, customers, and passersby all quite naturally expressed a kind of suspicion mingled with respect. The tavern-keeper started off by nodding, following this up with the words:

"So you're back, Ah Q!"

"Yes, I'm back."

"Made a pretty packet, eh?... Where...?"

"I've been in town."

By the next day this piece of news had spread through Weizhuang. And since everybody wanted to hear the success story of this Ah Q of the ready money and the new lined jacket, in the tavern, tea-house, and under the temple eaves, the villagers gradually ferreted out the news. The result was that they began to treat Ah Q with a new deference.

但阿Q这回的回来,却与先前大不同,确乎很值得惊异。天色将黑,他睡眼蒙胧的在酒店门前出现了,他走近柜台,从腰间伸出手来,满把是银的和铜的,在柜上一扔说,"现钱!打酒来!"穿的是新夹袄,看去腰间还挂着一个大搭连,沉钿钿的将裤带坠成了很弯很弯的弧线。未庄老例,看见略有些醒目的人物,是与其慢也宁敬的,现在虽然明知道是阿Q,但因为和破夹袄的阿Q有些两样了,古人云,"士别三日便当刮目相待",所以堂倌,掌柜,酒客,路人,便自然显出一种疑而且敬的形态来。掌柜既先之以点头,又继之以谈话:

"嚄,阿Q,你回来了!"

"回来了。"

"发财发财,你是——在……"

"上城去了!"

这一件新闻,第二天便传遍了全未庄。人人都愿意知道现钱和新夹袄的阿Q的中兴史,所以在酒店里,茶馆里,庙檐下,便渐渐的探听出来了。这结果,是阿Q得了新敬畏。

According to Ah Q, he had been a servant in the house of a successful provincial candidate. This part of the story filled all who heard it with awe. This successful provincial candidate was named Bai, but because he was the only successful provincial candidate in the whole town there was no need to use his surname: Whenever one spoke of the successful provincial candidate, he meant him. And this was so not only in Weizhuang, for almost everyone within a radius of thirty miles imagined his name to be Mr Successful Provincial Candidate. To have worked in the household of such a man naturally called for respect; but according to Ah Q's further statements, he was unwilling to go on working there because this successful candidate was really too much of a "turtle's egg." This part of the story made all who heard it sigh, but with a sense of pleasure, because it showed that Ah Q was unworthy to work in the household of such a man, yet not to work there was a pity.

According to Ah Q, his return was also due to his dissatisfaction with the townspeople because they called a long bench a straight bench, used shredded shallots to fry fish, and — a defect he had recently discovered — the women did not sway in a very satisfactory manner as they walked. However, the town had its good points too; for instance, in Weizhuang everyone played with thirty-two bamboo counters and only the Bogus Foreign Devil could play mahjong, but in town even the street urchins excelled at mahjong. You had only to place the Bogus Foreign Devil in the hands of these teenage rascals for him straightway to become like "a small devil before the King of Hell". This part of the story made all who heard it blush.

据阿Q说,他是在举人老爷家里帮忙。这一节,听的人都肃然了。这老爷本姓白,但因为合城里只有他一个举人,所以不必再冠姓,说起举人来就是他。这也不独在未庄是如此,便是一百里方圆之内也都如此,人们几乎多以为他的姓名就叫举人老爷的了。在这人的府上帮忙,那当然是可敬的。但据阿Q又说,他却不高兴再帮忙了,因为这举人老爷实在太"妈妈的"了。这一节,听的人都叹息而且快意,因为阿Q本不配在举人老爷家里帮忙,而不帮忙是可惜的。

据阿Q说,他的回来,似乎也由于不满意城里人,这就在他们将长凳称为条凳,而且煎鱼用葱丝,加以最近观察所得的缺点,是女人的走路也扭得不很好。然而也偶有大可佩服的地方,即如未庄的乡下人不过打三十二张的竹牌,只有假洋鬼子能够叉"麻酱",城里却连小乌龟子都叉得精熟的。什么假洋鬼子,只要放在城里的十几岁的小乌龟子的手里,也就立刻是"小鬼见阎王"。这一节,听的人都赧然了。

"Have you seen an execution?" asked Ah Q. "Ah, that's a fine sight... When they execute the revolutionaries... Ah, that's a fine sight, a fine sight..." He shook his head, sending his spittle flying on to the face of Zhao Sichen who was standing opposite him. This part of the story made all his audience tremble. Then with a glance around, he suddenly raised his right hand and dropped it on the neck of Whiskers Wang who, craning forward, was listening with rapt attention.

"Off with his head!" shouted Ah Q.

Whiskers Wang gave a start, and jerked back his head as fast as lightning or a spark struck from a flint, while the bystanders shivered with pleasurable apprehension. After this, Whiskers Wang went about in a daze for many days and dared not go near Ah Q, nor did the others.

Although we cannot say that in the eyes of the inhabitants of Weizhuang Ah Q's status at this time was superior to that of Mr Zhao, we can at least affirm without any danger of inaccuracy that it was approximately equivalent.

Before long, Ah Q's fame suddenly spread into the women's apartments of Weizhuang too. Although the only two families of any pretensions in Weizhuang were those of Qian and Zhao, and nine-tenths of the rest were poor, still women's apartments are women's apartments, and the way Ah Q's fame spread into them was quite miraculous. When the womenfolk met they would say to each other, "Mrs Zhou bought a blue silk skirt from Ah Q. Although it was old, it only cost ninety cents. And Zhao Baiyan's mother (this has yet to be verified, because some say it was Zhao Sichen's mother)

"你们可看见过杀头么?"阿Q说,"咳,好看。杀革命党。唉,好看好看,……"他摇摇头,将唾沫飞在正对面的赵司晨的脸上。这一节,听的人都凛然了。但阿Q又四面一看,忽然扬起右手,照着伸长脖子听得出神的王胡的后项窝上直劈下去道:

"嚓!"

王胡惊得一跳,同时电光石火似的赶快缩了头,而听的人又都悚然而且欣然了。从此王胡瘟头瘟脑的许多日,并且再不敢走近阿Q的身边;别的人也一样。

阿Q这时在未庄人眼睛里的地位,虽不敢说超过赵太爷,但谓之差不多,大约也就没有什么语病的了。

然而不多久,这阿Q的大名忽又传遍了未庄的闺中。虽然未庄只有钱赵两姓是大屋,此外十之九都是浅闺,但闺中究竟是闺中,所以也算得一件神异。女人们见面时一定说,邹七嫂在阿Q那里买了一条蓝绸裙,旧固然是旧的,但只化了九角钱。还有赵白眼的母亲,——说是赵司晨的母亲,待考,——也买了一件孩子

英汉对照
English-Chinese
中国文学宝库
Gems of Chinese Literature
现代文学系列
Modern Literature

bought a child's costume of crimson foreign calico which was nearly new for only three hundred cash."

Then those who had no silk skirt or needed foreign calico were most anxious to see Ah Q in order to buy from him. Far from avoiding him now, they sometimes followed him when he passed, calling to him to stop.

"Ah Q, have you any more silk skirts?" they would ask. "No? We want foreign calico too. Do you have any?"

This news later spread from the poor households to the rich ones, because Mrs Zhou was so pleased with her silk skirt that she took it to Mrs Zhao for her approval, and Mrs Zhao told Mr Zhao, speaking very highly of it.

Mr Zhao discussed the matter that evening at dinner with his son the successful county candidate, suggesting that there was certainly something strange about Ah Q and that they should be more careful about their doors and windows. They did not know, though, what if anything Ah Q had left — he might still have something good. Since Mrs Zhao happened to want a good cheap fur jacket, after a family council it was decided to ask Mrs Zou to find Ah Q for them at once. For this a third exception was made to the rule, special permission being given that evening for a lamp to be lit.

A considerable amount of oil had been burned, but still there was no sign of Ah Q. The whole Zhao household was yawning with impatience, some of them resenting Ah Q's casualness, others blaming Mrs Zou for not making a greater effort. Mrs Zhao was afraid that Ah Q dared not come because of the terms agreed upon that spring, but Mr Zhao did not think this anything to worry about

穿的大红洋纱衫,七成新,只用三百大钱九二串。于是伊们都眼巴巴的想见阿Q,缺绸裙的想问他买绸裙,要洋纱衫的想问他买洋纱衫,不但见了不逃避,有时阿Q已经走过了,也还要追上去叫住他,问道:

"阿Q,你还有绸裙么?没有?纱衫也要的,有罢?"

后来这终于从浅闺传进深闺里去了。因为邹七嫂得意之余,将伊的绸裙请赵太太去鉴赏,赵太太又告诉了赵太爷而且着实恭维了一番。赵太爷便在晚饭桌上,和秀才大爷讨论,以为阿Q实在有些古怪,我们门窗应该小心些;但他的东西,不知道可还有什么可买,也许有点好东西罢。加以赵太太也正想买一件价廉物美的皮背心。于是家族决议,便托邹七嫂即刻去寻阿Q,而且为此新辟了第三种的例外:这晚上也姑且特准点油灯。

油灯干了不少了,阿Q还不到。赵府的全眷都很焦急,打着呵欠,或恨阿Q太飘忽,或怨邹七嫂不上紧。赵太太还怕他因为春天的条件不敢来,而赵太爷以为不足虑:因为这是"我"去

英汉对照
English-Chinese
中国文学宝库
Gems of Chinese Literature
现代文学系列
Modern Literature

because, as he said, "This time I sent for him." Sure enough, Mr Zhao proved himself a man of insight, for Ah Q finally arrived with Mrs Zou.

"He keeps saying he has nothing left," panted Mrs Zou as she came in. "When I told him to come and tell you so himself he kept talking back. I told him..."

"Sir!" cried Ah Q with an attempt at a smile, coming to a halt under the eaves.

"I hear you did well for yourself in town, Ah Q," said Mr Zhao, going up to him and looking him over carefully. "Very good. Now... they say you have some old things... Bring them all here for us to look at. This is simply because I happen to want..."

"I told Mrs Zou — there's nothing left."

"Nothing left?" Mrs Zhao could not help sounding disappointed. "How could they go so quickly?"

"They belonged to a friend, and there wasn't much to begin with. People bought some..."

"There must be something left."

"Only a door curtain."

"Then bring the door curtain for us to see," said Mrs Zhao hurriedly.

"Well, tomorrow will do," said Mr Zhao without much enthusiasm. "When you have anything in future, Ah Q, you must bring it to us first..."

"We certainly won't pay less than other people!" said the successful county candidate. His wife shot a hasty glance at Ah Q to see his reaction.

叫他的。果然,到底赵太爷有见识,阿Q终于跟着邹七嫂进来了。

"他只说没有没有,我说你自己当面说去,他还要说,我说……"邹七嫂气喘吁吁的走着说。

"太爷!"阿Q似笑非笑的叫了一声,在檐下站住了。

"阿Q,听说你在外面发财,"赵太爷踱开去,眼睛打量着他的全身,一面说。"那很好,那很好的。这个,……听说你有些旧东西,……可以都拿来看一看,……这也并不是别的,因为我倒要……"

"我对邹七嫂说过了。都完了。"

"完了?"赵太爷不觉失声的说,"那里会完得这样快呢?"

"那是朋友的,本来不多。他们买了些,……"

"总该还有一点罢。"

"现在,只剩了一张门幕了。"

"就拿门幕来看看罢。"赵太太慌忙说。

"那么,明天拿来就是,"赵太爷却不甚热心了。"阿Q,你以后有什么东西的时候,你尽先送来给我们看,……"

"价钱决不会比别家出得少!"秀才说。秀才娘子忙一瞥阿Q的脸,看他感动了没有。

英汉对照
English-Chinese
中国文学宝库
Gems of Chinese Literature
现代文学系列
Modern Literature

"I need a fur jacket," said Mrs Zhao.

Although Ah Q agreed, he slouched out so carelessly that they did not know whether he had taken their instructions to heart or not. This so disappointed, annoyed and worried Mr Zhao that he even stopped yawning. The successful candidate was also far from satisfied with Ah Q's attitude. "People should be on their guard against such a turtle's egg," he said. "It might be best to order the bailiff to forbid him to live in Weizhuang."

Mr Zhao did not agree, saying that then Ah Q might bear a grudge, and that in a business like this it was probably a case of "the eagle does not prey on its own nest": his own village need not worry so long as they were a little more watchful at night. The successful candidate, much impressed by this parental instruction, immediately withdrew his proposal for banishing Ah Q but cautioned Mrs Zou on no account to repeat what had been said.

The next day, however, when Mrs Zou took her blue skirt to be dyed black she repeated these insinuations about Ah Q, although not actually mentioning what the successful candidate had said about driving him away. Even so, it was most damaging to Ah Q. In the first place, the bailiff appeared at his door and took away the door curtain. Although Ah Q protested that Mrs Zhao wanted to see it, the bailiff would not give it back and even demanded monthly hush money. In the second place, the villagers' respect for Ah Q suddenly changed. Although they still dared not take liberties, they avoided him as much as possible. While this differed from their previous fear of his "Off with his head!" it closely resembled the attitude of the ancients to spirits: they kept a respect-

"我要一件皮背心。"赵太太说。

阿Q虽然答应着,却懒洋洋的出去了,也不知道他是否放在心上。这使赵太爷很失望,气愤而且担心,至于停止了打呵欠。秀才对于阿Q的态度也很不平,于是说,这忘八蛋要提防,或者竟不如吩咐地保,不许他住在未庄。但赵太爷以为不然,说这也怕要结怨,况且做这路生意的大概是"老鹰不吃窝下食",本村倒不必担心的;只要自己夜里警醒点就是了。秀才听了这"庭训",非常之以为然,便即刻撤消了驱逐阿Q的提议,而且叮嘱邹七嫂,请伊万不要向人提起这一段话。

但第二日,邹七嫂便将那蓝裙去染了皂,又将阿Q可疑之点传扬出去了,可是确没有提起秀才要驱逐他这一节。然而这已经于阿Q很不利。最先,地保寻上门了,取了他的门幕去,阿Q说是赵太太要看的,而地保也不还,并且要议定每月的孝敬钱。其次,是村人对于他的敬畏忽而变相了,虽然还不敢来放肆,却很有远避的神情,而这神情和先前的防他来"嚓"的时

英汉对照
English-Chinese
中国文学宝库
Gems of Chinese Literature
现代文学系列
Modern Literature

ful distance.

Some idlers who wanted to get to the bottom of the business went to question Ah Q carefully. And with no attempt at concealment Ah Q told them proudly of his experiences. They learned that he had merely been a petty thief, not only unable to climb walls but even unable to go through openings: he simply stood outside an opening to receive the stolen goods.

One night he had just received a package and his chief had gone in again, when he heard a great uproar inside and took to his heels as fast as he could. He fled from the town that same night, back to Weizhuang; and after this he dared not return to do any more thieving. This story, however, was even more damaging to Ah Q, since the villagers had been keeping a respectful distance because they did not want to incur his enmity; for who could have guessed that he was only a thief who dared not steal again? Now they knew he was really too low to inspire fear.

CHAPTER 7

The Revolution

On the fourteenth day of the ninth month of the third year in the reign of Emperor Xuantong① — the day on which Ah Q sold his purse to Zhao Baiyan — at midnight, after the fourth stroke of the

---

① November 4, 1911, the day on which Shaoxing was freed in the 1911 Revolution.

候又不同,颇混着"敬而远之"的分子了。

只有一班闲人们却还要寻根究底的去探阿Q的底细。阿Q也并不讳饰,傲然的说出他的经验来。从此他们才知道,他不过是一个小脚色,不但不能上墙,并且不能进洞,只站在洞外接东西。有一夜,他刚才接到一个包,正手再进去,不一会,只听得里面大嚷起来,他便赶紧跑,连夜爬出城,逃回未庄来了,从此不敢再去做。然而这故事却于阿Q更不利,村人对于阿Q的"敬而远之"者,本因为怕结怨,谁料他不过是一个不敢再偷的偷儿呢?这实在是"斯亦不足畏也矣"。

第七章　革命

宣统三年九月十四日——即阿Q将搭连卖给赵白眼的这一天——三更四点,有一只大

third watch, a large boat with a big black awning arrived at the Zhao family's landing-place. This boat floated up in the darkness while the villagers were sound asleep, so that they knew nothing about it; but it left again about dawn, when quite a number of people saw it. Investigation revealed that this boat actually belonged to the successful provincial candidate!

This incident caused great uneasiness in Weizhuang, and before midday the hearts of all the villagers were beating faster. The Zhao family kept very quiet about the errand of the boat, but according to gossip in the tea-house and tavern, the revolutionaries were going to enter the town and the successful provincial candidate had come to the country to take refuge. Mrs Zou alone thought otherwise, maintaining that the successful candidate merely wanted to deposit a few battered cases in Weizhuang, but that Mr Zhao had sent them back. Actually the successful provincial candidate and the successful county candidate in the Zhao family were not on good terms, so that it was scarcely logical to expect them to prove friends in adversity; moreover, since Mrs Zou was a neighbour of the Zhao family and had a better idea of what was going on, she ought to have known.

Then a rumour spread that although the scholar had not come in person, he had sent a long letter tracing some distant relationship with the Zhao family; and since Mr Zhao after thinking it over had decided it could after all do him no harm to keep the cases, they were now stowed under his wife's bed. As for the revolutionaries, some people said they had entered the town that night in white

乌篷船到了赵府上的河埠头。这船从黑魆魆中荡来,乡下人睡得熟,都没有知道;出去时将近黎明,却很有几个看见的了。据探头探脑的调查来的结果,知道那竟是举人老爷的船!

那船便将大不安载给了未庄,不到正午,全村的人心就很摇动。船的使命,赵家本来是很秘密的,但茶坊酒肆里却都说,革命党要进城,举人老爷到我们乡下来逃难了。惟有邹七嫂不以为然,说那不过是几口破衣箱,举人老爷想来寄存,却已被赵太爷回复转去。其实举人老爷和赵秀才素不相能,在理本不能有"共患难"的情谊,况且邹七嫂又和赵家是邻居,见闻较为切近,所以大概该是伊对的。

然而谣言很旺盛,说举人老爷虽然似乎没有亲到,却有一封长信,和赵家排了"转折亲"。赵太爷肚里一轮,觉得于他总不会有坏处,便将箱子留下了,现就塞在太太的床底下。至于革命党,有的说是便在这一夜进了城,个个白盔白

英汉对照
English-Chinese
中国文学宝库
Gems of Chinese Literature
现代文学系列
Modern Literature

helmets and white armour — in mourning for Emperor Chong Zhen.①

Ah Q had long since known of revolutionaries and this year with his own eyes had seen revolutionaries decapitated. But since it had occurred to him that the revolutionaries were rebels and that a rebellion would make things difficult for him, he had always detested and kept away from them. Who could have guessed that they could strike such fear into a successful provincial candidate renowned for thirty miles around? In consequence, Ah Q could not help feeling rather fascinated, the terror of all the villagers only adding to his delight.

"Revolution is not a bad thing," thought Ah Q. "Finish off the whole lot of them... curse them!... I'd like to go over to the revolutionaries myself."

Ah Q had been hard up recently, which no doubt made him rather dissatisfied; moreover he had drunk two bowls of wine at noon on an empty stomach. Consequently he became drunk very quickly; and as he walked along thinking to himself, he seemed again to be treading on air. Suddenly, in some curious way, he felt as if he were a revolutionary and all the people in Weizhuang were his captives. Unable to contain himself for joy, he shouted at the top of his voice:

"Rebellion! Rebellion!"

---

① Chong Zhen, the last emperor of the Ming Dynasty, reigned from 1628 to 1644. He hanged himself before the insurgent peasant army under Li Zicheng entered Peking.

甲:穿着崇正皇帝的素。

阿Q的耳朵里,本来早听到过革命党这一句话,今年又亲眼见过杀掉革命党。但他有一种不知从那里来的意见,以为革命党便是造反,造反便是与他为难,所以一向是"深恶而痛绝之"的。殊不料这却使百里闻名的举人老爷有这样怕,于是他未免也有些"神往"了,况且未庄的一群鸟男女的慌张的神情,也使阿Q更快意。

"革命也好罢,"阿Q想,"革这伙妈妈的的命,太可恶!太可恨!……便是我,也要投降革命党了。"

阿Q近来用度窘,大约略略有些不平;加以午间喝了两碗空肚酒,愈加醉得快,一面想一面走,便又飘飘然起来。不知怎么一来,忽而似乎革命党便是自己,未庄人却都是他的俘虏了。他得意之余,禁不住大声的嚷道:

"造反了!造反了!"

英汉对照
English-Chinese
中国文学宝库
Gems of Chinese Literature
现代文学系列
Modern Literature

All the villagers stared at him in consternation. Ah Q had never seen such pitiful looks before; they refreshed him as much as a drink of iced water in summer. So he walked on even more happily, shouting:

"Fine!... I shall take what I want! I shall like whom I please!
"Tra la tra la!
Alas, in my cups I have slain my sworn brother Zheng.
Alas, ya-ya-ya...
Tra la, tra la, tum ti tum tum!
Steel mace in hand I shall trounce you."

Mr Zhao and his son were standing at their gate with two relatives discussing the revolution. Ah Q did not see them as he passed with his head thrown back, singing, *"Tra la la, tum ti tum!"*

"Q, old fellow!" called Mr Zhao timidly in a low voice.

"Tra la," sang Ah Q, unable to imagine that his name could be linked with those words "old fellow." Sure that he had heard wrongly and was in no way concerned, he simply went on singing, *"Tra la la, tum ti tum!"*

"Q, old fellow!"

"Alas, in my cups..."

"Ah Q!" The successful candidate had no choice but to name him outright.

Only then did Ah Q come to a stop. "Well?" he asked with his head on one side.

"Q, old fellow... now..." But Mr Zhao was at a loss for words again. "Are you well off now?"

"Well off? Of course. I get what I want..."

未庄人都用了惊惧的眼光对他看。这一种可怜的眼光,是阿Q从来没有见过的,一见之下,又使他舒服得如六月里喝了雪水。他更加高兴的走而且喊道:

"好,……我要什么就是什么,我欢喜谁就是谁。

得得,锵锵!

悔不该,酒醉错斩了郑贤弟,

悔不该,呀呀呀……

得得,锵锵,得,锵令锵!

我手执钢鞭将你打……"

赵府上的两位男人和两个真本家,也正站在大门口论革命,阿Q没有见,昂了头直唱过去。

"得得,……"

"老Q,"赵太爷怯怯的迎着低声的叫。

"锵锵,"阿Q料不到他的名字会和"老"字联结起来,以为是一句别的话,与己无干,只是唱。"得,锵,锵令锵,锵!"

"老Q。"

"悔不该……"

"阿Q!"秀才只得直呼其名了。

阿Q这才站住,歪着头问道,"什么?"

"老Q,……现在……"赵太爷却又没有话,"现在……发财么?"

"发财?自然。要什么就是什么…"

英汉对照
English-Chinese
中国文学宝库
Gems of Chinese Literature
现代文学系列
Modern Literature

"Ah Q, old man, poor friends of yours like us are of no consequence..." faltered Zhao Baiyan, as if sounding out the revolutionaries' attitude.

"Poor friends? You're richer anyway than I am." With this Ah Q walked away.

This left them in speechless dismay. Back home that evening Mr Zhao and his son discussed the question until it was time to light the lamps. And Zhao Baiyan once home took the purse from his waist and gave it to his wife to hide at the bottom of a chest.

For a while Ah Q walked upon air, but by the time he reached the Tutelary God's Temple he had come down to earth again. That evening the old man in charge of the temple was also unexpectedly friendly and offered him tea. Then Ah Q asked him for two pancakes, and after eating these demanded a four-ounce used candle and a candlestick. He lit the candle and lay down alone in his little room feeling inexpressibly refreshed and happy, while the candlelight leaped and flickered as if this were the Lantern Festival and his imagination soared with it.

"Revolt? It would be fine... A troop of revolutionaries would come, all in white helmets and white armour, with swords, steel maces, bombs, foreign guns, sharp-pointed double-edged knives, and spears with hooks. When they passed this temple they would call out, 'Ah Q! Come along with us!' And then I would go with them...

"Then the fun would start. All the villagers, the whole lousy lot, would kneel down and plead, 'Ah Q, spare us!' But who would listen to them! The first to die would be Young D and Mr

"阿……Q哥,像我们这样穷朋友是不要紧的……"赵白眼惴惴的说,似乎想探革命党的口风。

"穷朋友?你总比我有钱。"阿Q说着自去了。

大家都怃然,没有话。赵太爷父子回家,晚上商量到点灯。赵白眼回家,便从腰间扯下搭连来,交给他女人藏在箱底里。

阿Q飘飘然的飞了一通,回到土谷祠,酒已经醒透了。这晚上,管祠的老头子也意外的和气,请他喝茶;阿Q便向他要了两个饼,吃完之后,又要了一支点过的四两烛和一个树烛台,点起来,独自躺在自己的小屋里。他说不出的新鲜而且高兴,烛火像元夜似的闪闪的跳,他的思想也迸跳起来了:

"造反?有趣,……来了一阵白盔白甲的革命党,都拿着板刀,钢鞭,炸弹,洋炮,三尖两刃刀,钩镰枪,走过土谷祠,叫道,'阿Q!同去同去!'于是一同去。……

"这时未庄的一伙鸟男女才好笑哩,跪下叫道,'阿Q,饶命!'谁听他!第一个该死的是小

英汉对照
English-Chinese
中国文学宝库
Gems of Chinese Literature
现代文学系列
Modern Literature

Zhao, then the successful county candidate and the Bogus Foreign Devil... But perhaps I would spare a few. I would once have spared Whiskers Wang, but now I don't even want him...

"Things... I would go straight in and open the cases: silver ingots, foreign coins, foreign calico jackets... First I would move the Ningbo bed of the successful county candidate's wife to the temple, as well as the Qian family tables and chairs — or else just use the Zhaos'. I wouldn't lift a finger myself, but order Young D to move the things for me, and to look smart about it if he didn't want his face slapped...

"Zhao Sichen's younger sister is very ugly. In a few years Mrs Zou's daughter might be worth considering. The Bogus Foreign Devil's wife is willing to sleep with a man without a queue, hah! She can't be a good woman! The successful county candidate's wife has scars on her eyelids... I haven't seen Amah Wu for a long time and don't know where she is — what a pity her feet are so big."

Before Ah Q had reached a satisfactory conclusion, he started snoring. The four-ounce candle had burned down only half an inch, its flickering red light lighting up his open mouth.

"Ho, ho!" shouted Ah Q suddenly, raising his head and looking wildly around. But at sight of the four-ounce candle, he lay back and fell asleep again.

The next morning he got up very late, and when he went out into the street everything was the same as usual. He was still hungry, but though he racked his brains he did not seem able to think of anything. All of a sudden, however, an idea struck him and he

D和赵太爷,还有秀才,还有假洋鬼子,……留几条么?王胡本来还可留,但也不要了。……

"东西,……直走进去打开箱子来:元宝,洋钱,洋纱衫,……秀才娘子的一张宁式床先搬到土谷祠,此外便摆了钱家的桌椅,——或者也就用赵家的罢。自己是不动手的了,叫小D来搬,要搬得快,搬得不快打嘴巴。……

"赵司晨的妹子真丑。邹七嫂的女儿过几年再说。假洋鬼子的老婆会和没有辫子的男人睡觉,吓,不是好东西!秀才的老婆是眼胞上有疤的。……吴妈长久不见了,不知道在那里,——可惜脚太大。"

阿Q没有想得十分停当,已经发了鼾声,四两烛还只点去了小半寸,红焰焰的光照着他张开的嘴。

"荷荷!"阿Q忽而大叫起来,抬了头仓皇的四顾,待到看见四两烛,却又倒头睡去了。

第二天他起得很迟,走出街上看时,样样都照旧。他也仍然肚饿,他想着,想不起什么来;

英汉对照
English-Chinese
中国文学宝库
Gems of Chinese Literature
现代文学系列
Modern Literature

walked slowly off until, either by design or accident, he reached the Convent of Quiet Self-Improvement.

The convent was as peaceful as it had been that spring, with its white wall and shining black gate. After a moment's reflection he knocked at the gate, whereupon a dog on the other side started barking. He hastily picked up some broken bricks, then went back again to knock more heavily, until the black gate was pitted with pock-marks. At last he heard someone coming to open up.

Clutching a brick, Ah Q straddled there prepared to do battle with the black dog. The convent gate opened a crack, but no black dog rushed out. When he looked in all he could see was the old nun.

"What are you here for again?" She asked with a start.

"There's a revolution... didn't you know?" said Ah Q vaguely.

"Revolution, revolution... we've already had one." The old nun's eyes were red. "What more do you want to do to us?"

"What?" demanded Ah Q, dumbfounded.

"Didn't you know? The revolutionaries have already been here!"

"Who?" demanded Ah Q, still more dumbfounded.

"The successful county candidate and the Foreign Devil."

This completely took the wind out of Ah Q's sails. When the old nun saw there was no fight left in him she promptly shut the gate, so that when Ah Q pushed it again he could not budge it, and when he knocked again there was no answer.

It had happened that morning. The successful county candidate in the Zhao family was quick to learn the news. As soon as he heard that the revolutionaries had entered the town that night, he

但他忽而似乎有了主意了,慢慢的跨开步,有意无意的走到静修庵。

庵和春天时节一样静,白的墙壁和漆黑的门。他想了一想,前去打门,一只狗在里面叫。他急急拾了几块断砖,再上去较为用力的打,打到黑门上生出许多麻点的时候,才听得有人来开门。

阿Q连忙捏好砖头,摆开马步,准备和黑狗来开战。但庵门只开了一条缝,并无黑狗从中冲出,望进去只有一个老尼姑。

"你又来什么事?"伊大吃一惊的说。

"革命了……你知道?……"阿Q说得很含胡。

"革命革命,革过一革的,……你们要革得我们怎么样呢?"老尼姑两眼通红的说。

"什么?……"阿Q诧异了。

"你不知道,他们已经来革过了!"

"谁?……"阿Q更其诧异了。

"那秀才和洋鬼子!"

阿Q很出意外,不由的一错愕;老尼姑见他失了锐气,便飞速的关了门,阿Q再推时,牢不可开,再打时,没有回答了。

那还是上午的事。赵秀才消息灵,一知道革命党已在夜间进城,便将辫子盘在顶上,一早

英汉对照
English-Chinese
中国文学宝库
Gems of Chinese Literature
现代文学系列
Modern Literature

wound his queue up on his head and went out first thing to call on the Bogus Foreign Devil in the Qian family, with whom he had never been on very good terms. Because this was a time for all to work for reforms, they had a most satisfactory talk and on the spot became comrades who saw eye to eye and pledged themselves to make revolution.

After racking their brains for some time, they remembered that in the Convent of Quiet Self-Improvement there was an imperial tablet inscribed "Long live the Emperor" which ought to be done away with immediately. Thereupon they lost no time in going to the convent to carry out their revolutionary activities. Because the old nun tried to stop them and passed a few remarks, they considered her as the Qing government and gave her quite a few knocks on the head with a stick and with their knuckles. The nun, pulling herself together after they had gone, made an inspection. Naturally the imperial tablet had been smashed into fragments on the ground and the valuable Xuande censer[1] before the shrine of Guanyin, the goddess of mercy, had also disappeared.

Ah Q only learned this later. He deeply regretted having been asleep at the time, and resented the fact that they had not come to call him. Then he said to himself, "Maybe they still don't know I have joined the revolutionaries."

---

[1] Highly decorative bronze censers were made during the reign Xuande (1426-35) of the Ming Dynasty.

去拜访那历来也不相能的钱洋鬼子。这是"咸与维新"的时候了,所以他们便谈得很投机,立刻成了情投意合的同志,也相约去革命。他们想而又想,才想出静修庵里有一块"皇帝万岁万万岁"的龙牌,是应该赶紧革掉的,于是又立刻同到庵里去革命。因为老尼姑来阻挡,说了三句话,他们便将伊当作满政府,在头上很给了不少的棍子和栗凿。尼姑待他们走后,定了神来检点,龙牌固然已经碎在地上了,而且又不见了观音娘娘座前的一个宣德炉。

这事阿Q后来才知道。他颇悔自己睡着,但也深怪他们不来招呼他。他又退一步想道:

"难道他们还没有知道我已经投降了革命党么?"

英汉对照
English-Chinese
中国文学宝库
Gems of Chinese Literature
现代文学系列
Modern Literature

CHAPTER 8

Barred from the Revolution

The people of Weizhuang felt easier in their minds with each passing day. From the news brought they knew that although the revolutionaries had entered the town their coming had not made a great deal of difference. The magistrate was still the highest official, it was only his title that had changed; and the successful provincial candidate also had some post — the Weizhuang villagers could not remember these names clearly — some kind of official post; while the head of the military was still the same old captain. The only cause for alarm was that, the day after their arrival, some bad revolutionaries made trouble by cutting off people's queues. It was said that the boatman Seven Pounder from the next village had fallen into their clutches, and that he no longer looked presentable. Still, the danger of this was not great, because the Weizhuang villagers seldom went to town to begin with, and those who had been considering a trip there at once changed their minds in order to avoid this risk. Ah Q had been thinking of going to town to look up his old friends, but as soon as he heard the news he gave up the idea.

It would be wrong, however, to say that there were no reforms in Weizhuang. During the next few days the number of people who coiled their queues on their heads gradually increased and, as has already been said, the first to do so was naturally the successful

第八章 不准革命

未庄的人心日见其安静了。据传来的消息,知道革命党虽然进了城,倒还没有什么大异样。知县大老爷还是原官,不过改称了什么,而且举人老爷也做了什么——这些名目,未庄人都说不明白——官,带兵的也还是先前的老把总。只有一件可怕的事是另有几个不好的革命党夹在里面捣乱,第二天便动手剪辫子,听说那邻村的航船七斤便着了道儿,弄得不像人样子了。但这却还不算大恐怖,因为未庄人本来少上城,即使偶有想进城的,也就立刻变了计,碰不着这危险。阿Q本也想进城去寻他的老朋友,一得这消息,也只得作罢了。

但未庄也不能说是无改革。几天之后,将辫子盘在顶上的逐渐增加起来了,早经说过,最

county candidate; the next were Zhao Sichen and Zhao Baiyan, and after them Ah Q. If it had been summer it would not have been considered strange if everybody had coiled their queues on their heads or tied them in knots; but this was late, so that this autumn observance of a summer practice could be considered nothing short of a heroic decision, and as far as Weizhuang was concerned it could not be said to have had no connection with the reforms.

When Zhao Sichen approached with the nape of his neck bare, people who saw him remarked, "Ah! Here comes a revolutionary!"

When Ah Q heard this he was greatly impressed. Although he had long since heard how the successful county candidate had coiled his queue on his head, it had never occurred to him to do the same. Only now when he saw that Zhao Sichen had followed suit was he struck with the idea of doing the same himself. Making up his mind to copy them he used a bamboo chopstick to twist his queue up on his head, and after some hesitation eventually summoned up the courage to go out.

As he walked along the street people looked at him, but without any comment. Ah Q, disgruntled at first, soon waxed indignant. Recently he had been losing his temper very easily. As a matter of fact he was no worse off than before the revolution, people treated him politely, and the shops no longer demanded payment in cash. Yet Ah Q still felt dissatisfied. A revolution, he thought, should mean more than this. When he saw Young D, his anger boiled over.

Young D had also coiled his queue up on his head and, what

先自然是茂才公,其次便是赵司晨和赵白眼,后来是阿Q。倘在夏天,大家将辫子盘在头顶上或者打一个结,本不算什么稀奇事,但现在是暮秋,所以这"秋行夏令"的情形,在盘辫家不能不说是万分的英断,而在未庄也不能说无关于改革了。

赵司晨脑后空荡荡的走来,看见的人大嚷说,

"嚄,革命党来了!"

阿Q听到了很羡慕。他虽然早知道秀才盘辫的大新闻,但总没有想到自己可以照样做,现在看见赵司晨也如此,才有了学样的意思,定下实行的决心。他用一支竹筷将辫子盘在头顶上,迟疑多时,这才放胆的走去。

他在街上走,人也看他,然而不说什么话,阿Q当初很不快,后来便很不平。他近来很容易闹脾气了;其实他的生活,倒也并不比造反之前反艰难,人见他也客气,店铺也不说要现钱。而阿Q总觉得自己太失意:既然革了命,不应该只是这样的。况且有一回看见小D,愈使他气破肚皮了。

小D也将辫子盘在头顶上了,而且也居然

英汉对照
English-Chinese
中国文学宝库
Gems of Chinese Literature
现代文学系列
Modern Literature

was more, had actually used a bamboo chopstick too. Ah Q had never imagined that Young D would also have the courage to do this; he certainly could not tolerate such a thing! Who was Young D anyway? He was greatly tempted to seize him then and there, break his bamboo chopstick, let down his queue and slap his face several times into the bargain to punish him for forgetting his place and for his presumption in becoming a revolutionary. But in the end he let him off, simply fixing him with a furious glare, spitting, and exclaiming, "Pah!"

These last few days the only one to go to town was the Bogus Foreign Devil. The successful county candidate in the Zhao family had thought of using the deposited cases as a pretext to call on the successful provincial candidate, but the danger that he might have his queue cut off had made him defer his visit. He had written an extremely formal letter, and asked the Bogus Foreign Devil to take it to town; he had also asked the latter to introduce him to the Freedom Party. When the Bogus Foreign Devil came back he collected four dollars from the successful county candidate, after which the latter wore a silver peach on his chest. All the Weizhuang villagers were overawed, and said that this was the badge of the Persimmon Oil Party,[1] equivalent to the rank of a *hanlin*.[2] As a result, Mr Zhao's prestige suddenly increased, far more so in fact than when his son first passed the official examina-

---

[1] The Freedom Party was called Zi You Dang. The villagers, not understanding its meaning, turned Zi You into Shi You, which means persimmon oil.

[2] Member of the Imperial Academy in the Qing Dynasty.

用一支竹筷。阿Q万料不到他也敢这样做,自己也决不准他这样做!小D是什么东西呢?他很想即刻揪住他,拗断他的竹筷,放下他的辫子,并且批他几个嘴巴,聊且惩罚他忘了生辰八字,也敢来做革命党的罪。但他终于饶放了,单是怒目而视的吐一口唾沫道"呸!"

这几日里,进城去的只有一个假洋鬼子。赵秀才本也想靠着寄存箱子的渊源,亲身去拜访举人老爷的,但因为有剪辫的危险,所以也就中止了。他写了一封"黄伞格"的信,托假洋鬼子带上城,而且托他给自己绍介绍介,去进自由党。假洋鬼子回来时,向秀才讨还了四块洋钱,秀才便有一块银桃子挂在大襟上了;未庄人都惊服,说这是柿油党的顶子,抵得一个翰林,赵太爷因此也骤然大阔,远过于他儿子初隽秀才

英汉对照
English-Chinese
中国文学宝库
Gems of Chinese Literature
现代文学系列
Modern Literature

tion; consequently he started looking down on everyone else and when he saw Ah Q tended to ignore him a little.

Ah Q, disgruntled at finding himself cold-shouldered all the time, realized as soon as he heard of this silver peach why he was left out in the cold. Simply to say that you had gone over was not enough to make anyone a revolutionary; nor was it enough merely to wind your queue up on your head; the most important thing was to get into touch with the revolutionary party. In all his life he had known only two revolutionaries, one of whom had already lost his head in town, leaving only the Bogus Foreign Devil. His only course was to go at once to talk things over with the Bogus Foreign Devil.

The front gate of the Qian house happened to be open, and Ah Q crept timidly in. Once inside he gave a start, for there was the Bogus Foreign Devil standing in the middle of the courtyard dressed entirely in black, no doubt in foreign dress, and also wearing a silver peach. In his hand he held the stick with which Ah Q was already acquainted to his cost, while the foot-long queue which he had grown again had been combed out to hang loosely over his shoulders, giving him a resemblance to the immortal Liu Hai. ① Standing respectfully before him were Zhao Baiyan and three others, all of them listening with the utmost deference to what the Bogus Foreign Devil was saying.

Ah Q tiptoed inside and stood behind Zhao Baiyan, eager to pronounce some greeting, but not knowing what to say. Obviously he could not call the man "Bogus Foreign Devil," and neither

---

① A figure in Chinese folk legend, portrayed with flowing hair.

的时候,所以目空一切,见了阿Q,也就很有些不放在眼里了。

阿Q正在不平,又时时刻刻感着冷落,一听得这银桃子的传说,他立即悟出自己之所以冷落的原因了:要革命,单说投降,是不行的;盘上辫子,也不行的;第一着仍然要和革命党去结识。他生平所知道的革命党只有两个,城里的一个早已"嚓"的杀掉了,现在只剩了一个假洋鬼子。他除却赶紧去和假洋鬼子商量之外,再没有别的道路了。

钱府的大门正开着,阿Q便怯怯的蹩进去。他一到里面,很吃了惊,只见假洋鬼子正站在院子的中央,一身乌黑的大约是洋衣,身上也挂着一块银桃子,手里是阿Q曾经领教过的棍子,已经留到一尺多长的辫子都拆开了披在肩背上,蓬头散发的像一个刘海仙。对面挺直的站着赵白眼和三个闲人,正在必恭必敬的听说话。

阿Q轻轻的走近了,站在赵白眼的背后,心里想招呼,却不知道怎么说才好:叫他假洋鬼子固然是不行的了,洋人也不妥,革命党也不

英汉对照
English-Chinese
中国文学宝库
Gems of Chinese Literature
现代文学系列
Modern Literature

"Foreigner" nor "Revolutionary" seemed quite the thing. Perhaps the best form of address would be "Mr Foreigner."

But Mr Foreigner had not seen him, because with eyes upraised he was holding forth with great gusto:

"I am so impetuous that when we met I kept urging, 'Old Hong, let's get down to business!' But he always answered 'No!' — that's a foreign word which you wouldn't understand. Otherwise we should have succeeded long ago. This just goes to show how cautious he is. Time and again he asked me to go to Hubei, but I've not yet agreed. Who wants to work in this small Hubei town?..."

"Er — well — " Ah Q waited for him to pause, then screwed up his courage to speak. But for some reason or other he still did not call him Mr Foreigner.

The four men who had been listening gave a start and turned to stare at Ah Q. Mr Foreigner too caught sight of him for the first time.

"What is it?"

"I..."

"Clear out!"

"I want to join..."

"Get out!" Mr Foreigner raised the "mourner's stick."

Thereupon Zhao Baiyan and the others shouted, "Mr Qian tells you to get out, don't you hear!"

Ah Q put up his hands to protect his head, and without knowing what he was doing fled through the gate; but this time Mr Foreigner did not give chase. After running more than sixty steps Ah Q slowed down. Now his heart filled with dismay, because if Mr Foreigner would not allow him to be a revolutionary, there was no other way

妥，或者就应该叫洋先生了罢。

洋先生却没有见他，因为白着眼睛讲得正起劲：

"我是性急的，所以我们见面，我总是说：洪哥！我们动手罢！他却总说道 No！——这是洋话，你们不懂的。否则早已成功了。然而这正是他做事小心的地方。他再三再四的请我上湖北，我还没有肯。谁愿意在这小县城里做事情。……"

"唔，……这个……"阿 Q 候他略停，终于用十二分的勇气开口了，但不知道因为什么，又并不叫他洋先生。

听着说话的四个人都吃惊的回顾他。洋先生也才看见：

"什么？"

"我……"

"出去！"

"我要投……"

"滚出去！"洋先生扬起哭丧棒来了。

赵白眼和闲人们便都吆喝道："先生叫你滚出去，你还不听么！"

阿 Q 将手向头上一遮，不自觉的逃出门外；洋先生倒也没有追。他快跑了六十多步，这才慢慢的走，于是心里便涌起了忧愁：洋先生不准他革命，他再没有别的路；从此决不能望有白

英汉对照
English-Chinese
中国文学宝库
Gems of Chinese Literature
现代文学系列
Modern Literature

175

open to him. In future he could never hope to have men in white helmets and white armour come to call him. All his ambitions, aims, hope, and future had been blasted at one fell swoop. The fact that gossips might spread the news and make him a laughing-stock for the likes of Young D and Whiskers Wang was only a secondary consideration.

Never before had he felt so flat. Even coiling his queue on his head now struck him as pointless and ridiculous. As a form of revenge he was very tempted to let his queue down at once, but he did not do so. He wandered about till evening, when after drinking two bowls of wine on credit he began to feel in better spirits, and in his mind's eye saw fragmentary visions of white helmets and white armour once more.

One day he loafed about until late at night. Only when the tavern was about to close did he start to stroll back to the Tutelary God's Temple.

Crash-bang!

He suddenly heard an unusual sound, which could not have been firecrackers. Ah Q, always fond of excitement and of poking his nose into other people's business, headed straight for the noise in the darkness. He thought he heard footsteps ahead, and was listening carefully when a man fled past from the opposite direction. Ah Q instantly wheeled round to follow him. When that man turned, Ah Q turned too, and when having turned a corner that man stopped, Ah Q followed suit. He saw that there was no one after them and that the man was Young D.

"What's up?" demanded Ah Q resentfully.

"The Zhao... Zhao family has been robbed," panted Young D.

盔白甲的人来叫他,他所有的抱负,志向,希望,前程,全被一笔勾销了。至于闲人们传扬开去,给小D王胡等辈笑话,倒是还在其次的事。

他似乎从来没有经验过这样的无聊。他对于自己的盘辫子,仿佛也觉得无意味,要侮蔑;为报仇起见,很想立刻放下辫子来,但也没有竟放。他游到夜间,赊了两碗酒,喝下肚去,渐渐的高兴起来了,思想里才又出现白盔白甲的碎片。

有一天,他照例的混到夜深,待酒店要关门,才踱回土谷祠去。

拍,吧~~~!

他忽而听得一种异样的声音,又不是爆竹。阿Q本来是爱看热闹,爱管闲事的,便在暗中直寻过去。似乎前面有些脚步声;他正听,猛然间一个人从对面逃来了。阿Q一看见,便赶紧翻身跟着逃。那人转弯,阿Q也转弯,既转弯,那人站住了,阿Q也站住。他看后面并无什么,看那人便是小D。

"什么?"阿Q不平起来了。

"赵……赵家遭抢了!"小D气喘吁吁的说。

英汉对照
English-Chinese
中国文学宝库
Gems of Chinese Literature
现代文学系列
Modern Literature

Ah Q's heart went pit-a-pat. After saying this, Young D went off. But Ah Q kept on running by fits and starts. However, having been in the business himself made him unusually bold. Rounding the corner of a lane, he listened carefully and thought he heard shouting; while by straining his eyes he thought he could see a troop of men in white helmets and white armour carrying off cases, carrying off furniture, including the Ningbo bed of the successful county candidate's wife. He could not, however, see them very clearly. He wanted to go nearer, but his feet were rooted to the ground.

There was no moon that night, and Weizhuang was very still in the pitch darkness, as quiet as in the peaceful days of Emperor Fuxi.① Ah Q stood there until his patience ran out, yet there seemed no end to the business, distant figures kept moving to and fro, carrying off cases, carrying off furniture, carrying off the Ningbo bed of the successful county candidate's wife... carrying until he could hardly believe his own eyes. But he decided not to go any closer, and went back to the temple.

It was even darker in the Tutelary God's Temple. When he had closed the big gate he groped his way into his room, and only after he had been lying down for some time did he calm down sufficiently to begin thinking about how this affected him. The men in white helmets and white armour had evidently arrived, but they had not come to call him; they had taken away fine things, but there was no share for him — this was all the fault of the Bogus Foreign Devil, who had barred him from the rebellion. Otherwise how could he

---

① One of the earliest legendary monarchs in China.

阿Q的心怦怦的跳了。小D说了便走;阿Q却逃而又停的两三回。但他究竟是做过"这路生意"的人,格外胆大,于是蹩出路角,仔细的听,似乎有些嚷嚷,又仔细的看,似乎许多白盔白甲的人,络绎的将箱子抬出了,器具抬出了,秀才娘子的宁式床也抬出了,但是不分明,他还想上前,两只脚却没有动。

这一夜没有月,未庄在黑暗里很寂静,寂静到像羲皇时候一般太平。阿Q站着看到自己发烦,也似乎还是先前一样,在那里来来往往的搬,箱子抬出了,器具抬出了,秀才娘子的宁式床也抬出了,……抬得他自己有些不信他的眼睛了。但他决计不再上前,却回到自己的祠里去了。

土谷祠里更漆黑;他关好大门,摸进自己的屋子里。他躺了好一会,这才定了神,而且发出关于自己的思想来:白盔白甲的人明明到了,并不来打招呼,搬了许多好东西,又没有自己的份,——这全是假洋鬼子可恶,不准我造反,否

英汉对照
English-Chinese
中国文学宝库
Gems of Chinese Literature
现代文学系列
Modern Literature

have failed to have a share this time?

The more Ah Q thought of it the angrier he grew, until he was in a towering rage. "So no rebellion for me, only for you, eh?" he fumed, nodding maliciously. "Curse you, you Bogus Foreign Devil — all right, be a rebel! That's a crime for which you get your head chopped off. I'll inform on you, and see you dragged off to town to have your head cut off — your whole family executed...

To hell with you!"

CHAPTER 9

The Grand Finale

After the Zhao family was robbed most of the people in Weizhuang felt pleased yet fearful, and Ah Q was no exception. But four days later Ah Q was suddenly dragged into town in the middle of the night. It happened to be a dark night. A squad of soldiers, a squad of militia, a squad of police, and five detectives made their way quietly to Weizhuang and, after posting a machine-gun opposite the entrance, under cover of darkness surrounded the Tutelary God's Temple. But Ah Q did not bolt for it. For a long time nothing stirred till the captain, losing patience, offered a reward of twenty thousand cash. Only then did two militiamen summon up courage to jump over the wall and enter. With their co-operation, the others rushed in and dragged out Ah Q. But not until he had been carried out of the temple to somewhere near the machine-gun did he begin to wake up to what was happening.

则,这次何至于没有我的份呢?阿Q越想越气,终于禁不住满心痛恨起来,毒毒的点一点头:"不准我造反,只准你造反?妈妈的假洋鬼子,——好,你造反!造反是杀头的罪名呵,我总要告一状,看你抓进县里去杀头,——满门抄斩,——嚓!嚓!"

第九章 大团圆

赵家遭抢之后,未庄人大抵很快意而且恐慌,阿Q也很快意而且恐慌。但四天之后,阿Q在半夜里忽被抓进县城里去了。那时恰是暗夜,一队兵,一队团丁,一队警察,五个侦探,悄悄地到了未庄,乘昏暗围住土谷祠,正对门架好机关枪;然而阿Q不冲出。许多时没有动静,把总焦急起来了,悬了二十千的赏,才有两个团丁冒了险,逾垣进去,里应外合,一拥而入,将阿Q抓出来;直待擒出祠外面的机关枪左近,他才有些清醒了。

英汉对照
English-Chinese
中国文学宝库
Gems of Chinese Literature
现代文学系列
Modern Literature

It was already midday by the time they reached town, and Ah Q found himself carried to a dilapidated *yamen* where, after taking five or six turnings, he was pushed into a small room. No sooner had he stumbled inside than the door, in the form of a wooden grille, was slammed on his heels. The rest of the cell consisted of three blank walls, and when he looked carefully he saw two other men in a corner.

Although Ah Q was feeling rather uneasy, he was by no means depressed, because the room where he slept in the Tutelary God's Temple was in no way superior to this. The two other men also seemed to be villagers. They gradually fell into conversation with him, and one of them told him that the successful provincial candidate wanted to dun him for the rent owed by his grandfather; the other did not know why he was there. When they questioned Ah Q he answered quite frankly, "Because I wanted to revolt."

That afternoon he was dragged out through the grille and taken to a big hall, at the far end of which sat an old man with a cleanly shaven head. Ah Q took him for a monk at first, but when he saw soldiers standing guard and a dozen men in long coats on both sides, some with their heads clean-shaven like this old man and some with a foot or so of hair hanging over their shoulders like the Bogus Foreign Devil, all glaring furiously at him with grim faces, he knew that this man must be someone important. At once his knee-joints relaxed of their own accord, and he sank to his knees.

"Stand up to speak! Don't kneel!" shouted all the men in the long coats.

Although Ah Q understood, he felt quite incapable of standing

到进城,已经是正午,阿Q见自己被搡进一所破衙门,转了五六个弯,便推在一间小屋里。他刚刚一跄踉,那用整株的木料做成的栅栏门便跟着他的脚跟阖上了,其余的三面都是墙壁,仔细看时,屋角上还有两个人。

阿Q虽然有些忐忑,却并不很苦闷,因为他那土谷祠里的卧室,也并没有比这间屋子更高明。那两个也仿佛是乡下人,渐渐和他兜搭起来了,一个说是举人老爷要追他祖父欠下来的陈租,一个不知道为了什么事。他们问阿Q,阿Q爽利的答道,"因为我想造反。"

他下半天便又被抓出栅栏门去了,到得大堂,上面坐着一个满头剃得精光的老头子。阿Q疑心他是和尚,但看见下面站着一排兵,两旁又站着十几个长衫人物,也有满头剃得精光像这老头子的,也有将一尺来长的头发披在背后像那假洋鬼子的,都是一脸横肉,怒目而视的看他;他便知道这人一定有些来历,膝关节立刻自然而然的宽松,便跪了下去了。

"站着说!不要跪!"长衫人物都吆喝说。

阿Q虽然似乎懂得,但总觉得站不住,身

英汉对照
English-Chinese
中国文学宝库
Gems of Chinese Literature
现代文学系列
Modern Literature

up. He had involuntarily started squatting, improving on this finally to kneel down.

"What a slave!..." exclaimed the long-coated men contemptuously. They did not insist on his getting up, however.

"Tell the truth and you will receive a lighter sentence," said the old man with the shaven head in a low but clear voice, fixing his eyes on Ah Q. "We know everything already. When you have confessed, we will let you go."

"Confess!" repeated the long-coated men loudly.

"The fact is I wanted...to join..." muttered Ah Q disjointedly after a moment's confused thinking.

"In that case, why didn't you?" asked the old man gently.

"The Bogus Foreign Devil wouldn't let me."

"Nonsense. It's too late to talk now. Where are your accomplices?"

"What?..."

"The gang who robbed the Zhao family that night."

"They didn't come to call me. They moved the things away themselves." Mention of this made Ah Q indignant.

"Where are they now? When you tell me I will let you go," repeated the old man even more gently.

"I don't know... They didn't come to call me..."

Then, at a sign from the old man, Ah Q was dragged back through the grille. The following morning he was dragged out once more.

Everything was unchanged in the big hall. The old man with the clean-shaven head was still sitting there, and Ah Q knelt down

不由己的蹲了下去,而且终于趁势改为跪下了。

"奴隶性!……"长衫人物又鄙夷似的说,但也没有叫他起来。

"你从实招来罢,免得吃苦。我早都知道了。招了可以放你。"那光头的老头子看定了阿Q的脸,沉静的清楚的说。

"招罢!"长衫人物也大声说。

"我本来要……来投……"阿Q胡里胡涂的想了一通,这才断断续续的说。

"那么,为什么不来的呢?"老头子和气的问。

"假洋鬼子不准我!"

"胡说!此刻说,也迟了。现在你的同党在那里?"

"什么?……"

"那一晚打劫赵家的一伙人。"

"他们没有来叫我。他们自己搬走了。"阿Q提起来便愤愤。

"走到那里去了呢?说出来便放你了。"老头子更和气了。

"我不知道,……他们没有来叫我……"

然而老头子使了一个眼色,阿Q便又被抓进栅栏门里了。他第二次抓出栅栏门,是第二天的上午。

大堂的情形都照旧。上面仍然坐着光头的老头子,阿Q也仍然下了跪。

英汉对照
English-Chinese
中国文学宝库
Gems of Chinese Literature
现代文学系列
Modern Literature

again as before.

"Have you anything else to say?" asked the old man gently.

Ah Q thought, and decided there was nothing to say, so he answered, "Nothing."

Then a man in a long coat brought a sheet of paper and held a brush in front of Ah Q, which he wanted to thrust into his hand. Ah Q was now nearly frightened out of his wits, because this was the first time in his life that his hand had ever come into contact with a writing-brush. He was just wondering how to hold it when the man pointed out a place on the paper and told him to sign his name.

"I — I — can't write," said Ah Q, shamefaced, nervously holding the brush.

"In that case, to make it easy for you, draw a circle!"

Ah Q tried to draw a circle, but the hand with which he grasped the brush trembled, so the man spread the paper on the ground for him. Ah Q bent down and, painstakingly as if his life depended on it, drew a circle. Afraid people would laugh at him, he had determined to make the circle round; however, not only was that wretched brush very heavy, but it would not do his bidding. Instead it wobbled from side to side; and just as the circle was about to close the brush swerved out again, making a shape like a melon-seed.

While Ah Q was still feeling mortified by his failure to draw a circle, the man took away the paper and brush without any comment. A number of people then dragged him back for the third time through the grille.

老头子和气的问道,"你还有什么话说么?"

阿Q一想,没有话,便回答说,"没有。"

于是一个长衫人物拿了一张纸,并一支笔送到阿Q的面前,要将笔塞在他手里。阿Q这时很吃惊,几乎"魂飞魄散"了:因为他的手和笔相关,这回是初次。他正不知怎样拿;那人却又指着一处地方教他画花押。

"我……我……不认得字。"阿Q一把抓住了笔,惶恐而且惭愧的说。

"那么,便宜你,画一个圆圈!"

阿Q要画圆圈了,那手捏着笔却只是抖。于是那人替他将纸铺在地上,阿Q伏下去,使尽了平生的力画圆圈。他生怕被人笑话,立志要画得圆,但这可恶的笔不但很沉重,并且不听话,刚刚一抖一抖的几乎要合缝,却又向外一耸,画成瓜子模样了。

阿Q正羞愧自己画得不圆,那人却不计较,早已掣了纸笔去,许多人又将他第二次抓进栅栏门。

英汉对照
English-Chinese
中国文学宝库
Gems of Chinese Literature
现代文学系列
Modern Literature

By now he felt not too upset. He supposed that in this world it was the fate of everybody at some time to be dragged in and out of prison and to have to draw circles on paper; it was only his circle not being round that he felt a blot on his escutcheon. Presently, however, he regained composure by thinking, "Only idiots can make perfect circles." And with this thought he fell asleep.

That night, however, the successfoul provincial candidate was unable to sleep, because he had quarrelled with the captain. The successful provincial candidate had insisted that the main thing was to recover the stolen goods, while the captain said the main thing was to make a public example. Recently the captain had come to treat the successful provincial candidate quite disdainfully. So banging his fist on the table he said, "Punish one to awe one hundred! See now, I have been a member of the revolutionary party for less than twenty days, but there have been a dozen cases of robbery, none of them yet solved; think how badly that reflects on me. Now this one has been solved, you come and haggle. It won't do. This is my affair."

The successful provincial candidate, most put out, insisted that if the stolen goods were not recovered he would resign immediately as assistant civil administrator.

"As you please," said the captain.

In consequence the successful provincial candidate did not sleep that night; but he did not hand in his resignation the next day after all.

The third time that Ah Q was dragged out of the grille-door was the morning following the night on which the successful provincial

他第二次进了栅栏,倒也并不十分懊恼。他以为人生天地之间,大约本来有时要抓进抓出,有时要在纸上画圆圈的,惟有圈而不圆,却是他"行状"上的一个污点。但不多时也就释然了,他想:孙子才画得很圆的圆圈呢。于是他睡着了。

然而这一夜,举人老爷反而不能睡:他和把总呕了气。举人老爷主张第一要追赃,把总主张第一要示众。把总近来很不将举人老爷放在眼里了,拍案打凳的说道,"惩一儆百!你看,我做革命党还不上二十天,抢案就是十几件,全不破案,我的面子在那里?破了案,你又来迂。不成!这是我管的!"举人老爷窘急了,然而还坚持,说是倘若不追赃,他便立刻辞了帮办民政的职务。而把总却道,"请便罢!"于是举人老爷在这一夜竟没有睡,但幸而第二天倒也没有辞。

阿Q第三次抓出栅栏门的时候,便是举人

candidate had been unable to sleep. When he reached the hall, the old man with the clean-shaven head was sitting there as usual. And Ah Q knelt down as usual.

Very gently the old man questioned him: "Have you anything more to say?"

Ah Q thought for a moment, and decided there was nothing to say, so he answered, "Nothing."

A number of men in long coats and short jackets put on him a white vest of foreign cloth with some black characters on it. Ah Q felt most disconcerted, for this was very like a mourning dress and to wear mourning was unlucky. At the same time his hands were bound behind his back, and he was dragged out of the *yamen*.

Ah Q was lifted onto an uncovered cart, and several men in short jackets sat down beside him. The cart started off at once, following a number of soldiers and militiamen shouldering foreign rifles. On both sides were crowds of gaping spectators, while what was behind Ah Q could not see. Suddenly it occurred to him — "Can I be going to have my head cut off?" Panic seized him and everything turned dark before his eyes, while there was a humming in his ears as if he had fainted. But he did not really faint. Although he felt frightened some of the time, the rest of the time he was quite calm. It seemed to him that in this world probably it was the fate of everybody at some time to have his head cut off.

He still recognized the road and felt rather surprised: Why were they not going to the execution ground? He did not know that he was being paraded round the streets as a public example. But if he had known, it would have been the same: he would only have

老爷睡不着的那一夜的明天的上午了。他到了大堂,上面还坐着照例的光头老头子;阿Q也照例的下了跪。

老头子很和气的问道,"你还有什么话么?"

阿Q一想,没有话,便回答说,"没有。"

许多长衫和短衫人物,忽然给他穿上一件洋布的白背心,上面有些黑字。阿Q很气苦:因为这很像是带孝,而带孝是晦气的。然而同时他的两手反缚了,同时又被一直抓出衙门外去了。

阿Q被抬上了一辆没有篷的车,几个短衣人物也和他同坐在一处。这车立刻走动了,前面是一班背着洋炮的兵们和团丁,两旁是许多张着嘴的看客,后面怎样,阿Q没有见。但他突然觉到了:这岂不是去杀头么?他一急,两眼发黑,耳朵里嗥的一声,似乎发昏了。然而他又没有全发昏,有时虽然着急,有时却也泰然;他意思之间,似乎觉得人生天地间,大约本来有时也未免要杀头的。

他还认得路,于是有些诧异了:怎么不向着法场走呢?他不知道这是在游街,在示众。但即使知道也一样,他不过便以为人生天地间,大

英汉对照
English-Chinese
中国文学宝库
Gems of Chinese Literature
现代文学系列
Modern Literature

thought that in this world probably it was the fate of everybody at some time to be made a public example of.

Then he realized that they were making a detour to the execution ground, so after all he must be going to have his head cut off. He looked round him regretfully at the people swarming after him like ants, and unexpectedly in the crowd by the roadside he caught sight of Amah Wu. So that was why he had not seen her for so long: she was working in town.

Ah Q suddenly became ashamed of his lack of bravery, because he had not sung any lines from an opera. His thoughts revolved like a whirlwind: *The Young Widow at Her Husband's Grave* was not heroic enough. The passage "Alas, in my cups" in *The Battle of the Dragon and the Tiger* was too feeble. "Steel mace in hand I shall trounce you" was the best. But when he wanted to raise his hands, he remembered that they were bound together; so he did not sing "Steel mace in hand" either.

"In twenty years I shall be another..."[①] In his agitation Ah Q uttered half a saying which he had picked up for himself but never used before. "Good!!!" The roar of the crowd sounded like the growl of wolves.

The cart moved steadily forward. During the shouting Ah Q's eyes turned in search of Amah Wu, but she did not seem to have seen him for she was looking intently at the foreign rifles carried by

---

[①] "In twenty years I shall be another stout young fellow" was a phrase often used by criminals before execution to show their scorn of death. Believing in transmigration, they thought that after death their souls would enter other living bodies.

约本来有时也未免要游街要示众罢了。

　　他省悟了,这是绕到法场去的路,这一定是"嚓"的去杀头。他惘惘的向左右看,全跟着马蚁似的人,而在无意中,却在路旁的人丛中发见了一个吴妈。很久违,伊原来在城里做工了。阿Q忽然很羞愧自己没志气:竟没有唱几句戏。他的思想仿佛旋风似的在脑里一回旋:《小孤孀上坟》欠堂皇,《龙虎斗》里的"悔不该……"也太乏,还是"手执钢鞭将你打"罢。他同时想将手一扬,才记得这两手原来都捆着,于是"手执钢鞭"也不唱了。

　　"过了二十年又是一个……"阿Q在百忙中,"无师自通"的说出半句从来不说的话。

　　"好!!!"从人丛里,便发出豺狼的嗥叫一般的声音来。

　　车子不住的前行,阿Q在喝采声中,轮转眼睛去看吴妈,似乎伊一向并没有见他,却只是

英汉对照
English-Chinese
中国文学宝库
Gems of Chinese Literature
现代文学系列
Modern Literature

193

the soldiers.

So Ah Q took another look at the shouting crowd.

At that instant his thoughts revolved again like a whirlwind. Four years before, at the foot of the mountain, he had met a hungry wolf which had followed him at a set distance, wanting to eat him. He had nearly died of fright, but luckily he happened to have a knife in his hand which gave him the courage to get back to Weizhuang. He had never forgotten that wolf's eyes, fierce yet cowardly, gleaming like two will-o'-the-wisps, as if boring into him from a distance. Now he saw eyes more terrible even than the wolf's: dull yet penetrating eyes that having devoured his words still seemed eager to devour something beyond his flesh and blood. And these eyes kept following him at a set distance.

These eyes seemed to have merged into one, biting into his soul.

"Help, help!"

But Ah Q never uttered these words. All had turned black before his eyes, there was a buzzing in his ears, and he felt as if his whole body were being scattered like so much light dust.

As for the after-effects of the robbery, the most affected was the successful provincial candidate, because the stolen goods were never recovered. All his family lamented bitterly. Next came the Zhao household; for when the successful county candidate went into town to report the robbery, not only did he have his queue cut off by bad revolutionaries, but he had to pay a reward of twenty thousand cash into the bargain; so all the Zhao family lamented bitterly too. From that day forward they gradually assumed the air

出神的看着兵们背上的洋炮。

阿 Q 于是再看那些喝采的人们。

这刹那中,他的思想又仿佛旋风似的在脑里一回旋了。四年之前,他曾在山脚下遇见一只饿狼,永是不近不远的跟定他,要吃他的肉。他那时吓得几乎要死,幸而手里有一柄斫柴刀,才得仗这壮了胆,支持到未庄;可是永远记得那狼眼睛,又凶又怯,闪闪的像两颗鬼火,似乎远远的来穿透了他的皮肉。而这回他又看见从来没有见过的更可怕的眼睛了,又钝又锋利,不但已经咀嚼了他的话,并且还要咀嚼他皮肉以外的东西,永是不远不近的跟他走。

这些眼睛们似乎连成一气,已经在那里咬他的灵魂。

"救命,……"

然而阿 Q 没有说。他早就两眼发黑,耳朵里嗡的一声,觉得全身仿佛微尘似的迸散了。

至于当时的影响,最大的倒反在举人老爷,因为终于没有追赃,他全家都号咷了。其次是赵府,非特秀才因为上城去报官,被不好的革命党剪了辫子,而且又破费了二十千的赏钱,所以全家也号咷了。从这一天以来,他们便渐渐的

英汉对照
English-Chinese
中国文学宝库
Gems of Chinese Literature
现代文学系列
Modern Literature

of the survivors of a fallen dynasty.

As for any discussion of the event, no question was raised in Weizhuang. Naturally all agreed that Ah Q had been a bad man, the proof being that he had been shot; for if he had not been bad, how could he have been shot? But the consensus of opinion in town was unfavourable. Most people were dissatisfied, because a shooting was not such a fine spectacle as a decapitation; and what a ridiculous culprit he had been too, to pass through so many streets without singing a single line from an opera. They had followed him for nothing.

December 1921

都发生了遗老的气味。

至于舆论,在未庄是无异议,自然都说阿Q坏,被枪毙便是他的坏的证据;不坏又何至于被枪毙呢?而城里的舆论却不佳,他们多半不满足,以为枪毙并无杀头这般好看;而且那是怎样的一个可笑的死囚呵,游了那么久的街,竟没有唱一句戏:他们白跟一趟了。

一九二一年十二月。

英汉对照
English-Chinese
中国文学宝库
Gems of Chinese Literature
现代文学系列
Modern Literature

The New Year Sacrifice

The end of the year by the lunar calendar does seem a more natural end to the year for, to say nothing of the villages and towns, the very sky seems to proclaim the New Year's approach. Intermittent flashes from pallid, lowering evening clouds are followed by the rumble of crackers bidding farewell to the Hearth God[①] and, before the deafening reports of the bigger bangs close at hand have died away, the air is filled with faint whiffs of gunpowder. On one such night I returned to Luzhen, my hometown. I call it my hometown, but as I had not made my home there for some time I put up at the house of a certain Fourth Mr Lu, whom I was obliged to address as Fourth Uncle since he belonged to the generation before mine in our clan. A former Imperial College licentiate who believed in Neo-Confucianism,[②] he seemed very little changed, just slightly older, but without any beard as yet. Having exchanged some polite remarks upon meeting he observed that I was fatter, and having observed that I was fatter launched into a violent attack

---

[①] On the twenty-third of the twelfth lunar month the Hearth God was supposed to go up to Heaven to make a report.

[②] The Confucian school in the Song Dynasty (960 – 1279) which claimed that all things in the universe and the feudal order were ordained by "Reason" and could never change.

祝　福①

旧历的年底毕竟最像年底,村镇上不必说,就在天空中也显出将到新年的气象来。灰白色的沉重的晚云中间时时发出闪光,接着一声钝响,是送灶②的爆竹;近处燃放的可就更强烈了,震耳的大音还没有息,空气里已经散满了幽微的火药香。我是正在这一夜回到我的故乡鲁镇的。虽说故乡,然而已没有家,所以只得暂寓在鲁四老爷的宅子里。他是我的本家,比我长一辈,应该称之曰"四叔",是一个讲理学的老监生③。他比先前并没有什么大改变,单是老了些,但也还未留胡子,一见面是寒暄,寒暄之后

---

① 本篇最初发表于一九二四年三月二十五日上海《东方杂志》半月刊第二十一卷第六号。

② 送灶:旧俗以夏历十二月二十四日为灶神升天的日子,在这一天或前一天祭送灶神,称为送灶。

③ 理学:又称道学,是宋代周敦颐、程颢、程颐、朱熹等人阐释儒家学说而形成的唯心主义思想体系。它认为"理"是宇宙的本体,把"三纲五常"等封建伦理道德说成是"天理",提出"存天理,灭人欲"的主张。监生,国子监生员的简称。国子监原是封建时代中央最高学府,清代乾隆以后可以通过援例捐资取得监生名义,不一定在监读书。

英汉对照
English-Chinese
中国文学宝库
Gems of Chinese Literature
现代文学系列
Modern Literature

on the reformists.[1] I did not take this personally, however, as the object of his attack was Kang Youwei. Still, conversation proved so difficult that I shortly found myself alone in the study.

I rose late the next day and went out after lunch to visit relatives and friends, spending the following day in the same way. They were all very little changed, just slightly older; but every family was busy preparing for the New Year sacrifice. This is the great end-of-year ceremony in Luzhen, during which a reverent and splendid welcome is given to the God of Fortune so that he will send good luck for the coming year. Chickens and geese are killed, pork is bought, and everything is scrubbed and scoured until all the women's arms — some still in twisted silver bracelets — turn red in the water. After the meat is cooked chopsticks are thrust into it at random, and when this "offering" is set out at dawn, incense and candles are lit and the God of Fortune is respectfully invited to come and partake of it. The worshippers are confined to men and, of course, after worshipping they go on letting off firecrackers as before. This is done every year, in every household — so long as it can afford the offering and crackers — and naturally this year was no exception.

The sky became overcast and in the afternoon it was filled with a flurry of snowflakes, some as large as plum-blossom petals, which

---

[1] Referring to Kang Youwei, Liang Qichao and others who in 1898, supported by Emperor Guangxu, started a bourgeois reform movement. After this was crushed by the die-hards, Kang Youwei and others fled abroad and organized a royalist group advocating constitutional monarchy.

说我"胖了",说我"胖了"之后即大骂其新党①。但我知道,这并非借题在骂我:因为他所骂的还是康有为②。但是,谈话是总不投机的了,于是不多久,我便一个人剩在书房里。

第二天我起得很迟,午饭之后,出去看了几个本家和朋友;第三天也照样。他们也都没有什么大改变,单是老了些;家中却一律忙,都在准备着"祝福"③。这是鲁镇年终的大典,致敬尽礼,迎接福神,拜求来年一年中的好运气的。杀鸡,宰鹅,买猪肉,用心细细的洗,女人的臂膊都在水里浸得通红,有的还带着绞丝银镯子。煮熟之后,横七竖八的插些筷子在这类东西上,可就称为"福礼"了,五更天陈列起来,并且点上香烛,恭请福神们来享用;拜的却只限于男人,拜完自然仍然是放爆竹。年年如此,家家如此,——只要买得起福礼和爆竹之类的,——今年自然也如此。天色愈阴暗了,下午竟下起雪来,雪花大的有梅花那么大,满天飞舞,夹着烟霭和忙碌的气色,将鲁镇乱成一团糟。我回到四叔的书房里时,瓦楞上已经雪白,房里也映得

---

① 新党:清末对主张或倾向维新的人的称呼;辛亥革命前后,也用来称呼革命党人及拥护革命的人。

② 康有为(1858—1927),字广厦,号长素,广东南海人,清末维新运动领袖。他主张"变法维新",改君主专制为君主立宪。

③ "祝福":旧时江南一带每年年终的一种迷信习俗。清代范寅《越谚·风俗》载:"祝福,岁暮谢年,谢神祖,名此。"

英汉对照
English-Chinese
中国文学宝库
Gems of Chinese Literature
现代文学系列
Modern Literature

merged with the smoke and the bustling atmosphere to make the small town a welter of confusion. By the time I had returned to my uncle's study, the roof of the house was already white with snow which made the room brighter than usual, highlighting the red stone rubbing that hung on the wall of the big character "Longevity" as written by the Taoist saint Chen Tuan ①. One of the pair of scrolls flanking it had fallen down and was lying loosely rolled up on the long table. The other, still in its place, bore the inscription, "Understanding of principles brings peace of mind." Idly, I strolled over to the desk beneath the window to leaf through the pile of books on it, but only found an apparently incomplete set of *The Kangxi Dictionary*, *Selected Writings of Neo-Confucian Philosophers*, and *Commentaries on the Four Books*. ② At all events I must leave the next day, I decided.

Besides, the thought of my meeting with "Xianglin's Wife" the previous day was preying on my mind. It had happened in the afternoon. On my way back from calling on a friend in the eastern part of the town, I had met her by the river and knew from the fixed look in her eyes that she was going to accost me. Of all the people I had seen during this visit to Luzhen, none had changed so much as she had. Her hair, streaked with grey five years before, was now completely white, making her appear much older than one around forty. Her sallow, dark-tinged face that looked as if it had been carved out of wood was fearfully wasted and had lost the grief-

---

① A tenth-century hermit.
② Compiled by Luo Pei in the Qing Dynasty for use in the imperial examinations.

较光明,极分明的显出壁上挂着的朱拓① 的大"寿"字,陈抟② 老祖写的;一边的对联已经脱落,松松的卷了放在长桌上,一边的还在,道是"事理通达心气和平"③。我又无聊赖的到窗下的案头去一翻,只见一堆似乎未必完全的《康熙字典》,一部《近思录集注》和一部《四书衬》④。无论如何,我明天决计要走了。

况且,一想到昨天遇见祥林嫂的事,也就使我不能安住。那是下午,我到镇的东头访过一个朋友,走出来,就在河边遇见她;而且见她瞪着的眼睛的视线,就知道明明是向我走来的。我这回在鲁镇所见的人们中,改变之大,可以说无过于她的了:五年前的花白的头发,即今已经全白,全不像四十上下的人;脸上瘦削不堪,黄

---

① 朱拓:用银朱等红颜料从碑刻上拓下的文字或图形。

② 陈抟:据《宋史·隐逸列传》载:陈抟是五代时人,因科举不第,先后隐居武当山和华山修道。后人把他附会为"神仙"。

③ "事理通达心气和平":语出朱熹《论语集注》。朱熹在《季氏》篇中"不学诗无以言"和"不学礼无以立"语下分别注云:"事理通达而心气和平,故能言";"品节详明而德性坚定,故能立。"

④ 《康熙字典》:清代康熙年间张玉书、陈廷敬等奉旨编纂的一部大型字典,康熙五十五年(1716)刊行。《近思录》,是一部所谓理学入门书,宋代朱熹、吕祖谦选录周敦颐、程颢、程颐以及张载四人的文字编成,共十四卷。清初茅星来和江永分别为它作过集注。《四书衬》,清代骆培著,是一部解说"四书"(《论语》、《孟子》、《大学》、《中庸》)的书。

英汉对照
English-Chinese
中国文学宝库
Gems of Chinese Literature
现代文学系列
Modern Literature

stricken expression it had borne before. The only sign of life about her was the occasional flicker of her eyes. In one hand she had a bamboo basket containing a chipped, empty bowl; in the other, a bamboo pole, taller than herself, that was split at the bottom. She had clearly become a beggar pure and simple.

I stopped, waiting for her to come and ask for money.

"So you're back?" were her first words.

"Yes."

"That's good. You are a scholar who's travelled and seen the world. There's something I want to ask you." A sudden gleam lit up her lacklustre eyes.

This was so unexpected that surprise rooted me to the spot.

"It's this." She drew two paces nearer and lowered her voice, as if letting me into a secret. "Do dead people turn into ghosts or not?"

My flesh crept. The way she had fixed me with her eyes made a shiver run down my spine, and I felt far more nervous than when a surprise test is sprung on you at school and the teacher insists on standing over you. Personally, I had never bothered myself in the least about whether spirits existed or not, but what was the best answer to give her now? I hesitated for a moment, reflecting that the people here still believed in spirits, but she seemed to have her doubts, or rather hopes — she hoped for life after death and dreaded it at the same time. Why increase the sufferings of someone with a wretched life? For her sake, I thought, I'd better say there was.

"Quite possibly, I'd say," I told her falteringly.

中带黑,而且消尽了先前悲哀的神色,仿佛是木刻似的;只有那眼珠间或一轮,还可以表示她是一个活物。她一手提着竹篮,内中一个破碗,空的;一手拄着一支比她更长的竹竿,下端开了裂:她分明已经纯乎是一个乞丐了。

我就站住,豫备她来讨钱。

"你回来了?"她先这样问。

"是的。"

"这正好。你是识字的,又是出门人,见识得多。我正要问你一件事——"她那没有精采的眼睛忽然发光了。

我万料不到她却说出这样的话来,诧异的站着。

"就是——"她走近两步,放低了声音,极秘密似的切切的说,"一个人死了之后,究竟有没有魂灵的?"

我很悚然,一见她的眼钉着我的,背上也就遭了芒刺一般,比在学校里遇到不及豫防的临时考,教师又偏是站在身旁的时候,惶急得多了。对于魂灵的有无,我自己是向来毫不介意的;但在此刻,怎样回答她好呢?我在极短期的踌蹰中,想,这里的人照例相信鬼,然而她,却疑惑了,——或者不如说希望:希望其有,又希望其无……。人何必增添末路的人的苦恼,为她起见,不如说有罢。

"也许有罢,——我想。"我于是吞吞吐吐的说。

英汉对照
English-Chinese
中国文学宝库
Gems of Chinese Literature
现代文学系列
Modern Literature

"That means there must be a hell too?"

"What, hell?" I faltered, taken aback. "Hell? Logically speaking, there should be too — but not necessarily. Who cares anyway?"

"Then will all the members of a family meet again after death?"

"Well, as to whether they'll meet again or not ... " I realized now what an utter fool I was. All my hesitation and manoeuvring had been no match for her three questions. Promptly taking fright, I decided to recant. "In that case ... actually, I'm not sure ... In fact, I'm not sure whether there are ghosts or not either."

To avoid being pressed by any further questions I walked off, then beat a hasty retreat to my uncle's house, feeling thoroughly disconcerted. I might have given her a dangerous answer, I was thinking. Of course, she might just be feeling lonely because everybody else was celebrating now, but could she have had something else in mind? Some premonition? If she had had some other idea, and something happened as a result, then my answer should indeed be partly responsible... Then I laughed at myself for brooding so much over a chance meeting when it could have no serious significance. No wonder certain educationists called me neurotic. Besides, I had distinctly declared, "I'm not sure," contradicting the whole of my answer. This meant that even if something did happen, it would have nothing at all to do with me.

"I'm not sure" is a most useful phrase.

Bold inexperienced youngsters often take it upon themselves to solve problems or choose doctors for other people, and if by any chance things turn out badly they may well be held to blame; but

"那么,也就有地狱了?"

"阿!地狱?"我很吃惊,只得支梧着,"地狱?——论理,就该也有。——然而也未必,……谁来管这等事……。"

"那么,死掉的一家的人,都能见面的?"

"唉唉,见面不见面呢?……"这时我已知道自己也还是完全一个愚人,什么踌蹰,什么计画,都挡不住三句问。我即刻胆怯起来了,便想全翻过先前的话来,"那是,……实在,我说不清……。其实,究竟有没有魂灵,我也说不清。"

我乘她不再紧接的问,迈开步便走,匆匆的逃回四叔的家中,心里很觉得不安逸。自己想,我这答话怕于她有些危险。她大约因为在别人的祝福时候,感到自身的寂寞了,然而会不会含有别的什么意思的呢?——或者是有了什么豫感了?倘有别的意思,又因此发生别的事,则我的答话委实该负若干的责任……。但随后也就自笑,觉得偶尔的事,本没有什么深意义,而我偏要细细推敲,正无怪教育家要说是生着神经病;而况明明说过"说不清",已经推翻了答话的全局,即使发生什么事,于我也毫无关系了。

"说不清"是一句极有用的话。不更事的勇敢的少年,往往敢于给人解决疑问,选定医生,万一结果不佳,大抵反成了怨府,然而一用这说

英汉对照
English-Chinese
中国文学宝库
Gems of Chinese Literature
现代文学系列
Modern Literature

by concluding their advice with this evasive expression they achieve blissful immunity from reproach. The necessity for such a phrase was brought home to me still more forcibly now, since it was indispensable even in speaking with a beggar woman.

However, I remained uneasy, and even after a night's rest my mind dwelt on it with a certain sense of foreboding. The oppressive snowy weather and the gloomy study increased my uneasiness. I had better leave the next day and go back to the city. A large dish of plain shark's fin stew at the Fuxing Restaurant used to cost only a dollar. I wondered if this cheap delicacy had risen in price or not. Though my good companions of the old days had scattered, that shark's fin must still be sampled even if I were on my own. Whatever happened I would leave the next day, I decided.

Since, in my experience, things I hoped would not happen and felt should not happen invariably did occur all the same, I was much afraid this would prove another such case. And, sure enough, the situation soon took a strange turn. Towards evening I heard what sounded like a discussion in the inner room, but the conversation ended before long and my uncle walked away observing loudly: "What a moment to choose! Now of all times! Isn't that proof enough of a bad character?"

My initial astonishment gave way to a deep uneasiness; I felt that this had something to do with me. I looked out of the door, but no one was there. I waited impatiently till their servant came in before dinner to brew tea. Then at last I had a chance to make some inquiries.

"Who was Mr Lu so angry with just now?" I asked.

不清来作结束，便事事逍遥自在了。我在这时，更感到这一句话的必要，即使和讨饭的女人说话，也是万不可省的。

但是我总觉得不安，过了一夜，也仍然时时记忆起来，仿佛怀着什么不祥的豫感；在阴沉的雪天里，在无聊的书房里，这不安愈加强烈了。不如走罢，明天进城去。福兴楼的清燉鱼翅，一元一大盘，价廉物美，现在不知增价了否？往日同游的朋友，虽然已经云散，然而鱼翅是不可不吃的，即使只有我一个……。无论如何，我明天决计要走了。

我因为常见些但愿不如所料，以为未必竟如所料的事，却每每恰如所料的起来，所以很恐怕这事也一律。果然，特别的情形开始了。傍晚，我竟听到有些人聚在内室里谈话，仿佛议论什么事似的，但不一会，说话声也就止了，只有四叔且走而且高声的说：

"不早不迟，偏偏要在这时候，——这就可见是一个谬种！"

我先是诧异，接着是很不安，似乎这话于我有关系。试望门外，谁也没有。好容易待到晚饭前他们的短工来冲茶，我才得了打听消息的机会。

"刚才，四老爷和谁生气呢？"我问。

英汉对照
English-Chinese
中国文学宝库
Gems of Chinese Literature
现代文学系列
Modern Literature

"Why, Xianglin's Wife, of course," was the curt reply.

"Xianglin's Wife? Why?" I pressed.

"She's gone."

"Dead?" My heart missed a beat. I started and must have changed colour. But since the servant kept his head lowered, all this escaped him. I pulled myself together enough to ask:

"When did she die?"

"When? Last night or today — I'm not sure."

"How did she die?"

"How? Of poverty of course." After this stolid answer he withdrew, still without having raised his head to look at me.

My agitation was only short-lived, however. For now that my premonition had come to pass, I no longer had to seek comfort in my own "I'm not sure," or his "dying of poverty," and my heart was growing lighter. Only from time to time did I still feel a little guilty. Dinner was served, and my uncle impressively kept me company. Tempted as I was to ask about Xianglin's Wife, I knew that, although he had read that "ghosts and spirits are manifestations of the dual forces of Nature,"[1] he was still so superstitious that on the eve of the New Year sacrifice it would be unthinkable to mention anything like death or illness. In case of necessity one should use veiled allusions, but since this was unfortunately beyond me I had to bite the questions which kept rising to the tip of my tongue. And my uncle's solemn expression suddenly made me suspect that he looked on me too as a bad lot who had chosen this

---

[1] This was said by the Song-dynasty Neo-Confucian Zhang Zai.

"还不是和祥林嫂?"那短工简捷的说。

"祥林嫂?怎么了?"我又赶紧的问。

"老了。"

"死了?"我的心突然紧缩,几乎跳起来,脸上大约也变了色。但他始终没有抬头,所以全不觉。我也就镇定了自己,接着问:

"什么时候死的?"

"什么时候?——昨天夜里,或者就是今天罢。——我说不清。"

"怎么死的?"

"怎么死的?——还不是穷死的?"他淡然的回答,仍然没有抬头向我看,出去了。

然而我的惊惶却不过暂时的事,随着就觉得要来的事,已经过去,并不必仰仗我自己的"说不清"和他之所谓"穷死的"的宽慰,心地已经渐渐轻松;不过偶然之间,还似乎有些负疚。晚饭摆出来了,四叔俨然的陪着。我也还想打听些关于祥林嫂的消息,但知道他虽然读过"鬼神者二气之良能也"①,而忌讳仍然极多,当临近祝福时候,是万不可提起死亡疾病之类的话的;倘不得已,就该用一种替代的隐语,可惜我又不知道,因此屡次想问,而终于中止了。我从他俨然的脸色上,又忽而疑他正以为我不早不

---

① 语见宋代张载的《张子全书·正蒙》,也见《近思录》。意思是:鬼神是阴阳二气自然变化而成的。

moment, now of all times, to come and trouble him. To set his mind at rest as quickly as I could, I told him at once of my plan to leave Luzhen the next day and go back to the city. He did not press me to stay, and at last the uncomfortably quiet meal came to an end.

Winter days are short, and because it was snowing, darkness had already enveloped the whole town. All was stir and commotion in the lighted houses, but outside was remarkably quiet. And the snowflakes hissing down on the thick snowdrifts intensified one's sense of loneliness. Seated alone in the amber light of the vegetable-oil lamp I reflected that this wretched and forlorn woman, abandoned in the dust like a worn-out toy its owners had tired of, had once left her own imprint in the dust, and those who enjoyed life must have wondered at her for wishing to live on, but now at last she had been swept away by death. Whether spirits existed or not I did not know; but in this world of ours the end of a futile existence, the removal of someone whom others are tired of seeing, was just as well, both for them and for the individual concerned. Occupied with these reflections, I listened quietly to the hissing of the snow outside, until little by little I felt more relaxed.

But the fragments of her life that I had seen or heard about before combined now to form a whole.

She was not from Luzhen. Early one winter, when my uncle's family wanted a new maid, Old Mrs Wei the go-between had brought her along. She had a white mourning band round her hair and was wearing a black skirt, blue jacket, and pale green

迟,偏要在这时候来打搅他,也是一个谬种,便立刻告诉他明天要离开鲁镇,进城去,趁早放宽了他的心。他也不很留。这样闷闷的吃完了一餐饭。

冬季日短,又是雪天,夜色早已笼罩了全市镇。人们都在灯下匆忙,但窗外很寂静。雪花落在积得厚厚的雪褥上面,听去似乎瑟瑟有声,使人更加感得沉寂。我独坐在发出黄光的菜油灯下,想,这百无聊赖的祥林嫂,被人们弃在尘芥堆中的,看得厌倦了的陈旧的玩物,先前还将形骸露在尘芥里,从活得有趣的人们看来,恐怕要怪讶她何以还要存在,现在总算被无常①打扫得干干净净了。魂灵的有无,我不知道;然而在现世,则无聊生者不生,即使厌见者不见,为人为己,也还都不错。我静听着窗外似乎瑟瑟作响的雪花声,一面想,反而渐渐的舒畅起来。

然而先前所见所闻的她的半生事迹的断片,至此也联成一片了。

她不是鲁镇人。有一年的冬初,四叔家里要换女工,做中人的卫老婆子带她进来了,头上扎着白头绳,乌裙,蓝夹袄,月白背心,年纪大约

---

① 无常:佛家语,原指世间一切事物都在变异灭坏的过程中;后引申为死的意思,也用作迷信传说中"勾魂使者"的名称。

bodice. She was about twenty-six, and though her face was sallow her cheeks were red. Old Mrs Wei had introduced her as "Xianglin's Wife," a neighbour of her mother's family, who wanted to go out to work now that her husband had died. My uncle frowned at this, and my aunt knew that he disapproved of taking on a widow. She looked just the person for them, though, with her big strong hands and feet; and, judging by her downcast eyes and silence, she was a good worker who would know her place. So my aunt ignored my uncle's frown and kept her. During her trial period she worked from morning till night as if she found resting irksome, and proved strong enough to do the work of a man; so on the third day she was taken on for five hundred cash a month.

Everybody called her Xianglin's Wife and no one asked her own name, but since she had been introduced by someone from Wei Village as a neighbour, her surname was presumably also Wei. She was taciturn, only answering briefly when asked a question. Thus it took them a dozen days or so to find out bit by bit that she had a strict mother-in-law at home and a brother-in-law of ten or so, old enough to cut wood. Her husband, who had died that spring, had been a woodcutter too, and had been ten years younger than she was. This little was all they could learn.

Time passed quickly. She went on working as hard as ever, not caring what she ate, never sparing herself. It was generally agreed that the Lu family's maid actually got through more work than a hard-working man. At the end of the year, she swept and mopped the floors, killed the fowl, and sat up to boil the sacrificial meat, all single-handedly, so that they did not need to hire extra help.

二十六七,脸色青黄,便两颊却还是红的。卫老婆子叫她祥林嫂,说是自己母家的邻居,死了当家人,所以出来做工了。四叔皱了皱眉,四婶已经知道了他的意思,是在讨厌她是一个寡妇。但看她模样还周正,手脚都壮大,又只是顺着眼,不开一句口,很像一个安分耐劳的人,便不管四叔的皱眉,将她留下了。试工期内,她整天的做,似乎闲着就无聊,又有力,简直抵得过一个男子,所以第三天就定局,每月工钱五百文。

大家都叫她祥林嫂;没问她姓什么,但中人是卫家山人,既说是邻居,那大概也就姓卫了。她不很爱说话,别人问了才回答,答的也不多。直到十几天之后,这才陆续的知道她家里还有严厉的婆婆;一个小叔子,十多岁,能打柴了;她是春天没了丈夫的;他本来也打柴为生,比她小十岁:大家所知道的就只是这一点。

日子很快的过去了,她的做工却毫没有懈,食物不论,力气是不惜的。人们都说鲁四老爷家里雇着了女工,实在比勤快的男人还勤快。到年底,扫尘,洗地,杀鸡,宰鹅,彻夜的煮福礼,全是一人担当,竟没有添短工。然而她反满足,

And she for her part was quite contented. Little by little the trace of a smile appeared at the corners of her mouth, while her face became whiter and plumper.

Just after the New Year she came back from washing rice by the river most upset because in the distance she had seen a man, pacing up and down on the opposite bank, who looked like her husband's elder cousin — very likely he had come in search of her. When my aunt in alarm pressed her for more information, she said nothing. As soon as my uncle knew of this he frowned.

"That's bad," he observed. "She must have run away."

Before very long this inference was confirmed.

About a fortnight later, just as this incident was beginning to be forgotten, Old Mrs Wei suddenly brought along a woman in her thirties whom she introduced as Xianglin's mother. Although this woman looked like the hill-dweller she was, she behaved with great self-possession and had a ready tongue in her head. After the usual civilities she apologized for coming to take her daughter-in-law back, explaining that early spring was a busy time and they were short-handed at home with only old people and children around.

"If her mother-in-law wants her back, there's nothing more to be said," was my uncle's comment.

Thereupon her wages were reckoned up. They came to 1,750 cash, all of which she had left in the keeping of her mistress without spending any of it. My aunt gave the entire sum to Xianglin's mother, who took her daughter-in-law's clothes as well, expressed her thanks, and left. By this time it was noon.

"Oh, the rice! Didn't Xianglin's Wife go to wash the rice?"

口角边渐渐的有了笑影,脸上也白胖了。

新年才过,她从河边淘米回来时,忽而失了色,说刚才远远地看见一个男人在对岸徘徊,很像夫家的堂伯,恐怕是正为寻她而来的。四婶很惊疑,打听底细,她又不说。四叔一知道,就皱一皱眉,道:

"这不好。恐怕她是逃出来的。"

她诚然是逃出来的,不多久,这推想就证实了。

此后大约十几天,大家正已渐渐忘却了先前的事,卫老婆子忽而带了一个三十多岁的女人进来了,说那是祥林嫂的婆婆。那女人虽是山里人模样,然而应酬很从容,说话也能干,寒暄之后,就赔罪,说她特来叫她的儿媳回家去,因为开春事务忙,而家中只有老的和小的,人手不够了。

"既是她的婆婆要她回去,那有什么话可说呢。"四叔说。

于是算清了工钱,一共一千七百五十文,她全存在主人家,一文也还没有用,便都交给她的婆婆。那女人又取了衣服,道过谢,出去了。其时已经是正午。

"阿呀,米呢?祥林嫂不是去淘米的么?

英汉对照
English-Chinese
中国文学宝库
Gems of Chinese Literature
现代文学系列
Modern Literature

exclaimed my aunt some time later. It was probably hunger that reminded her of lunch.

A general search started then for the rice-washing basket. My aunt searched the kitchen, then the hall, then the bedroom, but not a sign of the basket was to be seen. My uncle could not find it outside either, until he went right down to the riverside. Then he saw it set squarely on the bank, with some vegetables beside it.

Some people on the bank told him that a boat with a white awning had moored there that morning but, since the awning covered the boat completely, they had no idea who was inside and had paid no special attention to begin with. But when Xianglin's Wife had arrived and was kneeling down to wash rice, two men who looked like hill-dwellers had jumped off the boat and seized her. Between them they had dragged her on board. She had wept and shouted at first but soon fell silent, probably because she was gagged. Then along came two women, a stranger and Old Mrs Wei. It was difficult to see clearly into the boat, but the victim seemed to be lying, tied up, on the planking.

"Disgraceful! Still ..." said my uncle.

That day my aunt cooked the midday meal herself, and their son Ah Niu lit the fire.

After lunch Old Mrs Wei came back.

"Disgraceful!" said my uncle.

"What's the meaning of this? How dare you show your face here again?" My aunt, who was washing up, started fuming as soon as she saw her. "First you recommended her, then helped them carry her off, causing such a shocking commotion. What will people

……"好一会,四婶这才惊叫起来。她大约有些饿,记得午饭了。

于是大家分头寻淘箩。她先到厨下,次到堂前,后到卧房,全不见淘箩的影子。四叔踱出门外,也不见,直到河边,才见平平正正的放在岸上,旁边还有一株菜。

看见的人报告说,河里面上午就泊了一只白篷船,篷是全盖起来的,不知道什么人在里面,但事前也没有人去理会他。待到祥林嫂出来淘米,刚刚要跪下去,那船里便突然跳出两个男人来,像是山里人,一个抱住她,一个帮着,拖进船去了。祥林嫂还哭喊了几声,此后便再没有什么声息,大约给用什么堵住了罢。接着就走上两个女人来,一个不认识,一个就是卫婆子。窥探舱里,不很分明,她像是捆了躺在船板上。

"可恶!然而……。"四叔说。

这一天是四婶自己煮午饭;他们的儿子阿牛烧火。

午饭之后,卫老婆子又来了。

"可恶!"四叔说。

"你是什么意思?亏你还会再来见我们。"四婶洗着碗,一见面就愤愤的说,"你自己荐她来,又合伙劫她去,闹得沸反盈天的,大家看了

英汉对照
English-Chinese
中国文学宝库
Gems of Chinese Literature
现代文学系列
Modern Literature

think? Are you trying to make fools of our family?"

"*Aiya*, I was completely taken in! I've come specially to clear this up. How was I to know she'd left home without permission from her mother-in-law when she asked me to find her work? I'm sorry, Mr Lu, I'm sorry, Mrs Lu. I'm growing so stupid and careless in my old age, I've let my patrons down. It's lucky for me you're such kind, generous people, never hard on those below you. I promise to make it up to you by finding someone good this time."

"Still..." said my uncle.

That had concluded the affair of Xianglin's Wife, and before long it was forgotten.

My aunt was the only one who still spoke of Xianglin's Wife. This was because most of the maids taken on afterwards turned out to be lazy or greedy, or both, none of them satisfactory. At such times she would invariably say to herself, I wonder what's become of her now? — implying that she would like to have her back. But by the next New Year she too had given up hope.

The first month was nearing its end when Old Mrs Wei called on my aunt to wish her a happy New Year. Already tipsy, she explained that the reason for her coming so late was that she had been visiting her family in Wei Village in the hills for a few days. The conversation, naturally, soon touched on Xianglin's Wife.

"Xianglin's Wife?" cried Old Mrs Wei cheerfully. "She's in luck now. When her mother-in-law dragged her home, she'd promised her to the sixth son of the He family in He Glen. So a

成个什么样子?你拿我们家里开玩笑么?"

"阿呀阿呀,我真上当。我这回,就是为此特地来说说清楚的。她来求我荐地方,我那里料得到是瞒着她的婆婆的呢。对不起,四老爷,四太太。总是我老发昏不小心,对不起主顾。幸而府上是向来宽洪大量,不肯和小人计较的。这回我一定荐一个好的来折罪……。"

"然而……。"四叔说。

于是祥林嫂事件便告终结,不久也就忘却了。

只有四婶,因为后来雇用的女工,大抵非懒即馋,或者馋而且懒,左右不如意,所以也还提起祥林嫂。每当这些时候,她往往自言自语的说,"她现在不知道怎么样了?"意思是希望她再来。但到第二年的新正,她也就绝了望。

新正将尽,卫老婆子来拜年了,已经喝得醉醺醺的,自说因为回了一趟卫家山的娘家,住下几天,所以来得迟了。她们问答之间,自然就谈到祥林嫂。

"她么?"卫老婆子高兴的说,"现在是交了好运了。她婆婆来抓她回去的时候,是早已许给了贺家墺的贺老六的,所以回家之后不几天,

英汉对照
English-Chinese
中国文学宝库
Gems of Chinese Literature
现代文学系列
Modern Literature

few days after her return they put her in the bridal chair and sent her off."

"Gracious! What a mother-in-law!" exclaimed my aunt.

"Ah, madam, you really talk like a great lady! This is nothing to poor folk like us who live up in the hills. That young brother-in-law of hers still had no wife. If they didn't marry her off, where would the money have come from to get him one? Her mother-in-law is a clever, capable woman, a fine manager, who married her off into the mountains. If she'd betrothed her to a family in the same village, she wouldn't have made so much; but as very few girls are willing to take a husband deep in the mountains at the back of beyond, she got eighty thousand cash. Now the second son has a wife, who cost only fifty thousand; and after paying the wedding expenses she's still over ten thousand in hand. Wouldn't you call her a fine manager?"

"But was Xianglin's Wife willing?"

"It wasn't a question of willing or not. Of course any woman would make a row about it. All they had to do was tie up, shove her into the chair, carry her to the man's house, force on her the bridal headdress, make her bow in the ceremonial hall, lock the two of them into their room — and that was that. But Xianglin's Wife is quite a character. I heard that she made a terrible scene. It was working for a scholar's family, everyone said, that made her different from other people. We go-betweens see life, madam. Some widows sob and shout when they remarry; some threaten to kill themselves; some refuse to go through the ceremony of bowing to heaven and earth after they've been carried to the man's house;

也就装在花轿里抬去了。"

"阿呀,这样的婆婆!……"四婶惊奇的说。

"阿呀,我的太太!你真是大户人家的太太的话。我们山里人,小户人家,这算得什么?她有小叔子,也得娶老婆。不嫁了她,那有这一注钱来做聘礼?她的婆婆倒是精明强干的女人呵,很有打算,所以就将她嫁到里山去。倘许给本村人,财礼就不多;惟独肯嫁进深山野墺里去的女人少,所以她就到手了八十千①。现在第二个儿子的媳妇也娶进了,财礼只花了五十,除去办喜事的费用,还剩十多千。吓,你看,这多么好打算?……"

"祥林嫂竟肯依?……"

"这有什么依不依。——闹是谁也总要闹一闹的;只要用绳子一捆,塞在花轿里,抬到男家,捺上花冠,拜堂,关上房门,就完事了。可是祥林嫂真出格,听说那时实在闹得利害,大家还都说大约因为在念书人家做过事,所以与众不同呢。太太,我们见得多了:回头人出嫁,哭喊的也有,说要寻死觅活的也有,抬到男家闹得拜

---

① 八十千:旧时以一千文钱为一贯或一吊,所以几千文钱也称为几贯或几吊,但也有些地方直称为多少千。八十千即八十吊。

英汉对照
English-Chinese
中国文学宝库
Gems of Chinese Literature
现代文学系列
Modern Literature

some even smash the wedding candlesticks. But Xianglin's Wife was really extraordinary. They said she screamed and cursed all the way to He Glen, so that she was completely hoarse by the time they got there. When they dragged her out of the chair, no matter how the two chair-bearers and her brother-in-law held her, they couldn't make her go through the ceremony. The moment they were off guard and had loosened their grip — gracious Buddha! — she bashed her head on a corner of the altar, gashing it so badly that the blood spurted out. Even though they smeared on two handfuls of incense ashes and tied it up with two pieces of red cloth, they couldn't stop the bleeding. It took quite a few of them to shut her up finally with the man in the bridal chamber, but even then she went on cursing. Oh, it was really..." Shaking her head, she lowered her eyes and fell silent.

"And what then?" asked my aunt.

"They said that the next day she didn't get up." Old Mrs Wei raised her eyes.

"And after?"

"After? She got up. At the end of the year she had a baby, a boy, who must be two this New Year. These few days when I was at home, some people back from a visit to He Glen said they'd seen her and her son, and both mother and child are plump. There's no mother-in-law over her, her man is a strong fellow who can earn a living, and the house belongs to them. Oh, yes, she's in luck all right."

After this event my aunt gave up talking of Xianglin's Wife.

But one autumn, after two New Years had passed since this good

不成天地的也有,连花烛都砸了的也有。祥林嫂可是异乎寻常,他们说她一路只是嚎,骂,抬到贺家墺,喉咙已经全哑了。拉出轿来,两个男人和她的小叔子使劲的擒住她也还拜不成天地。他们一不小心,一松手,阿呀,阿弥陀佛,她就一头撞在香案角上,头上碰了一个大窟窿,鲜血直流,用了两把香灰,包上两块红布还止不住血呢。直到七手八脚的将她和男人反关在新房里,还是骂,阿呀呀,这真是……"。她摇一摇头,顺下眼睛,不说了。

"后来怎么样呢?"四婶还问。

"听说第二天也没有起来。"她抬起眼来说。

"后来呢?"

"后来?——起来了。她到年底就生了一个孩子,男的,新年就两岁了。我在娘家这几天,就有人到贺家墺去,回来说看见他们娘儿俩,母亲也胖,儿子也胖;上头又没有婆婆;男人所有的是力气,会做活;房子是自家的。——唉唉,她真是交了好运了。"

从此之后,四婶也就不再提起祥林嫂。

但有一年的秋季,大约是得到祥林嫂好运

news of Xianglin's Wife, she once more crossed the threshold of my uncle's house, placing her round bulb-shaped basket on the table and her small bedding-roll under the eaves. As before, she had a white mourning band round her hair and was wearing a black skirt, blue jacket, and pale green bodice. Her face was sallow, her cheeks no longer red; and her downcast eyes, stained with tears, had lost their brightness. Just as before, it was Old Mrs Wei who brought her to my aunt.

"It was really a bolt from the blue," she explained compassionately. "Her husband was a strong young fellow — who'd have thought that typhoid fever would carry him off? He'd taken a turn for the better, but then he ate some cold rice and got worse again. Luckily she had the boy and she can work — she's able to gather firewood, pick tea, or raise silkworms — so she could have managed on her own. But who'd have thought that the child would be carried off by a wolf? It was nearly the end of spring, yet a wolf came to the glen — who could have guessed that? Now she's all on her own. Her husband's elder brother has taken over the house and turned her out. So she's no way to turn for help except to her former mistress. Luckily this time there's nobody to stop her and you happen to be needing someone, madam. That's why I've brought her here. I think someone used to your ways is much better than a new hand..."

"I was really too stupid, really..." put in Xianglin's Wife, raising her lacklustre eyes. "All I knew was that when it snowed and the wild beasts up in the hills had nothing to eat, they might come to the villages. I didn't know that in spring they might come

的消息之后的又过了两个新年,她竟又站在四叔家的堂前了。桌上放着一个荸荠式的圆篮,檐下一个小铺盖。她仍然头上扎着白头绳,乌裙,蓝夹袄,月白背心,脸色青黄,只是两颊上已经消失了血色,顺着眼,眼角上带些泪痕,眼光也没有先前那样精神了。而且仍然是卫老婆子领着,显出慈悲模样,絮絮的对四婶说:

"……这实在是叫作'天有不测风云',她的男人是坚实人,谁知道年纪青青,就会断送在伤寒上?本来已经好了的,吃了一碗冷饭,复发了。幸亏有儿子;她又能做,打柴摘茶养蚕都来得,本来还可以守着,谁知道那孩子又会给狼衔去的呢?春天快完了,村上倒反来了狼,谁料到?现在她只剩了一个光身了。大伯来收屋,又赶她。她真是走投无路了,只好来求老主人。好在她现在已经再没有什么牵挂,太太家里又凑巧要换人,所以我就领她来。——我想,熟门熟路,比生手实在好得多……。"

"我真傻,真的,"祥林嫂抬起她没有神采的眼睛来,接着说。"我单知道下雪的时候野兽在山墺里没有食吃,会到村里来;我不知道春天也

英汉对照
English-Chinese
中国文学宝库
Gems of Chinese Literature
现代文学系列
Modern Literature

too. I got up at dawn and opened the door, filled a small basket with beans and told our Ah Mao to sit on the doorstep and shell them. He was such a good boy, he always did as he was told, and out he went. Then I went to the back to chop wood and wash the rice, and when the rice was in the pot I wanted to steam the beans. I called Ah Mao, but there was no answer. When I went out to look there were beans all over the ground but no Ah Mao. He never went to the neighbours' houses to play; and, sure enough, though I asked everywhere he wasn't there. I got so worried, I begged people to help me find him. Not until that afternoon, after searching high and low, did they try the gully. There they saw one of his little shoes caught on a bramble. 'That's bad,' they said. 'A wolf must have got him.' And sure enough, further on, there he was lying in the wolf's den, all his innards eaten away, still clutching that little basket tight in his hand..." At this point she broke down and could not go on.

My aunt had been undecided at first, but the rims of her eyes were rather red the time Xianglin's Wife broke off. After a moment's thought she told her to take her things to the servants' quarters. Old Mrs Wei heaved a sigh, as if a great weight had been lifted from her mind; and Xianglin's Wife, looking more relaxed than when she first came, went off quietly to put away her bedding without having to be told the way. So she started work again as a maid in Luzhen.

She was still known as Xianglin's Wife.

But now she was a very different woman. She had not worked there more than two or three days before her mistress realized that

会有。我一清早起来就开了门,拿小篮盛了一篮豆,叫我们的阿毛坐在门槛上剥豆去。他是很听话的,我的话句句听;他出去了。我就在屋后劈柴,淘米,米下了锅,要蒸豆。我叫阿毛,没有应,出去一看,只见豆撒得一地,没有我们的阿毛了。他是不到别家去玩的;各处去一问,果然没有。我急了,央人出去寻。直到下半天,寻来寻去寻到山墺里,看见刺柴上挂着一只他的小鞋。大家都说,糟了,怕是遭了狼了。再进去;他果然躺在草窠里,肚里的五脏已经都给吃空了,手上还紧紧的捏着那只小篮呢。……"她接着但是呜咽,说不出成句的话来。

四婶起初还踌蹰,待到听完她自己的话,眼圈就有些红了。她想了一想,便教拿圆篮和铺盖到下房去。卫老婆子仿佛卸了一肩重担似的嘘一口气;祥林嫂比初来时候神气舒畅些,不待指引,自己驯熟的安放了铺盖。她从此又在鲁镇做女工了。

大家仍然叫她祥林嫂。

然而这一回,她的境遇却改变得非常大。上工之后的两三天,主人们就觉得她手脚已没

英汉对照
English-Chinese
中国文学宝库
Gems of Chinese Literature
现代文学系列
Modern Literature

she was not as quick as before. Her memory was much worse too, while her face, like a death-mask, never showed the least trace of a smile. Already my aunt was expressing herself as not too satisfied. Though my uncle had frowned as before when she first arrived, they always had such trouble finding servants that he raised no serious objections, simply warning his wife on the quiet that while such people might seem very pathetic they exerted a bad moral influence. She could work for them but must have nothing to do with ancestral sacrifices. They would have to prepare all the dishes themselves. Otherwise they would be unclean and the ancestors would not accept them.

The most important events in my uncle's household were ancestral sacrifices, and formerly these had kept Xianglin's Wife especially busy, but now she had virtually nothing to do. As soon as the table had been placed in the centre of the hall and a front curtain fastened round its legs, she started setting out the winecups and chopsticks in the way she still remembered.

"Put those down, Xianglin's Wife," cried my aunt hastily. "Leave that to me."

She drew back sheepishly then and went for the candlesticks.

"Put those down, Xianglin's Wife," cried my aunt again in haste. "I'll fetch them."

After walking round in the hall several times without finding anything to do, she moved doubtfully away. All she could do that day was to sit by the stove and feed the fire.

The townspeople still called her Xianglin's Wife, but in quite a different tone from before; and although they still talked to her,

有先前一样灵活,记性也坏得多,死尸似的脸上又整日没有笑影,四婶的口气上,已颇有些不满了。当她初到的时候,四叔虽然照例皱过眉,但鉴于向来雇用女工之难,也就并不大反对,只是暗暗地告诫四婶说,这种人虽然似乎很可怜,但是败坏风俗的,用她帮忙还可以,祭祀时候可用不着她沾手,一切饭菜,只好自己做,否则,不干不净,祖宗是不吃的。

四叔家里最重大的事件是祭祀,祥林嫂先前最忙的时候也就是祭祀,这回她却清闲了。桌子放在堂中央,系上桌帏,她还记得照旧的去分配酒杯和筷子。

"祥林嫂,你放着罢!我来摆。"四婶慌忙的说。

她讪讪的缩了手,又去取烛台。

"祥林嫂,你放着罢!我来拿。"四婶又慌忙的说。

她转了几个圆圈,终于没有事情做,只得疑惑的走开。她在这一天可做的事是不过坐在灶下烧火。

镇上的人们也仍然叫她祥林嫂,但音调和先前很不同;也还和她讲话,但笑容却冷冷的

their manner was colder. Quite impervious to this, staring straight in front of her, she would tell everybody the story which night or day was never out of her mind.

"I was really too stupid, really," she would say. "All I knew was that when it snowed and the wild beasts up in the hills had nothing to eat, they might come to the villages. I didn't know that in spring they might come too. I got up at dawn and opened the door, filled a small basket with beans and told our Ah Mao to sit on the doorstep and shell them. He was such a good boy, he always did as he was told, and out he went. Then I went to the back to chop wood and wash the rice, and when the rice was in the pot I wanted to steam the beans. I called Ah Mao, but there was no answer. When I went out to look, there were beans all over the ground but no Ah Mao. He never went to the neighbours' houses to play; and, sure enough, though I asked everywhere he wasn't there. I got so worried, I begged people to help me find him. Not until that afternoon, after searching high and low, did they try the gully. There they saw one of his little shoes caught on a bramble. 'That's bad,' they said. 'A wolf must have got him.' And sure enough, further on, there he was lying in the wolf's den, all his innards eaten away, still clutching that little basket tight in his hand..." At this point her voice would be choked with tears.

This story was so effective that men hearing it often stopped smiling and walked blankly away, while the women not only seemed to forgive her but wiped the contemptuous expression off their faces and added their tears to hers. Indeed, some old women who had not heard her in the street sought her out specially to hear

了。她全不理会那些事,只是直着眼睛,和大家讲她自己日夜不忘的故事:

"我真傻,真的,"她说。"我单知道下雪的时候野兽在深山里没有食吃,会到村里来;我不知道春天也会有。我一大早起来就开了门,拿小篮盛了一篮豆,叫我们的阿毛坐在门槛上剥豆去。他是很听话的孩子,我的话句句听;他就出去了。我就在屋后劈柴,淘米,米下了锅,打算蒸豆。我叫,'阿毛!'没有应。出去一看,只见豆撒得满地,没有我们的阿毛了。各处去一问,都没有。我急了,央人去寻去。直到下半天,几个人寻到山墺里,看见刺柴上挂着一只他的小鞋。大家都说,完了,怕是遭了狼了。再进去;果然他躺在草窠里,肚里的五脏已经都给吃空了,可怜他手上还紧紧的捏着那只小篮呢。……"她于是淌下眼泪来,声音也呜咽了。

这故事倒颇有效,男人听到这里,往往敛起笑容,没趣的走了开去;女人们却不独宽恕了她似的,脸上立刻改换了鄙薄的神气,还要陪出许多眼泪来。有些老女人没有在街头听到她的话,便特意寻来,要听她这一段悲惨的故事。直

英汉对照
English-Chinese
中国文学宝库
Gems of Chinese Literature
现代文学系列
Modern Literature

her sad tale. And when she broke down, they too shed the tears which had gathered in their eyes, after which they sighed and went away satisfied, exchanging eager comments.

As for her, she asked nothing better than to tell her sad story over and over again, often gathering three or four listeners around her. But before long everybody knew it so well that no trace of a tear could be seen even in the eyes of the most kindly, Buddha-invoking old ladies. In the end, practically the whole town could recite it by heart and became bored and exasperated to hear it repeated.

"I was really too stupid, really," she would begin.

"Yes. All you knew was that in snowy weather, when the wild beasts in the mountains had nothing to eat, they might come down to the villages." Cutting short her recital abruptly, they walked away.

She would stand there open-mouthed, staring after them stupidly, and then wander off as if she too were bored by the story. But she still tried hopefully to lead up from other topics such as small baskets, and other people's children to the story of her Ah Mao. At the sight of a child of two or three she would say, "Ah, if my Ah Mao were alive he'd be just that size..."

Children would take fright at the look in her eyes and clutch the hem of their mother's clothes to tug them away. Left by herself again, she would eventually walk blankly away. In the end everybody knew what she was like. If a child were present they would ask with a spurious smile: "If your Ah Mao were alive, Xianglin's Wife, wouldn't he be just that size?"

到她说到呜咽,她们也就一齐流下那停在眼角上的眼泪,叹息一番,满足的去了,一面还纷纷的评论着。

她就只是反复的向人说她悲惨的故事,常常引住了三五个人来听她。但不久,大家也都听得纯熟了,便是最慈悲的念佛的老太太们,眼里也再不见有一点泪的痕迹。后来全镇的人们几乎都能背诵她的话,一听到就烦厌得头痛。

"我真傻,真的,"她开首说。

"是的,你是单知道雪天野兽在深山没有食吃,才会到村里来的。"他们立即打断她的话,走开去了。

她张着口怔怔的站着,直着眼睛看他们,接着也就走了,似乎自己也觉得没趣。但她还妄想,希图从别的事,如小篮,豆,别人的孩子上,引出她的阿毛的故事来。倘一看见两三岁的小孩子,她就说:

"唉唉,我们的阿毛如果还在,也就有这么大了。……"

孩子看见她的眼光就吃惊,牵着母亲的衣襟催她走。于是又只剩下她一个,终于没趣的也走了。后来大家又都知道了她的脾气,只要有孩子在眼前,便似笑非笑的先问她,道:

"祥林嫂,你们的阿毛如果还在,不是也就有这么大了么?"

英汉对照
English-Chinese
中国文学宝库
Gems of Chinese Literature
现代文学系列
Modern Literature

She may not have realized that her tragedy, after being generally savoured for so many days, had long since grown so stale that it now aroused only revulsion and disgust. But she seemed to sense the cold mockery in their smiles, and the fact that there was no need for her to say any more. So she would simply look at them in silence.

New Year preparations always start in Luzhen on the twentieth day of the twelfth lunar month. That year my uncle's household had to take on a temporary man-servant. And since there was more than he could do they asked Amah Liu to help by killing the fowl; but being a devout vegetarian who would not kill living creatures, she would only wash the sacrificial vessels. Xianglin's Wife, with nothing to do but feed the fire, sat there at loose ends watching Amah Liu as she worked. A light snow began to fall.

"Ah, I was really too stupid," said Xianglin's Wife as if to herself, looking at the sky and sighing.

"There you go again, Xianglin's Wife." Amah Liu glanced with irritation at her face. "Tell me, wasn't that when you got that scar on your forehead?"

All the reply she received was a vague murmur.

"Tell me this: what made you willing after all?"

"Willing?"

"Yes. Seems to me you must have been willing. Otherwise..."

"Oh, you don't know how strong he was."

"I don't believe it. I don't believe he was so strong that you with your strength couldn't have kept him off. You must have ended up willing. That talk of his being so strong is just an excuse."

她未必知道她的悲哀经大家咀嚼赏鉴了许多天,早已成为渣滓,只值得烦厌和唾弃;但从人们的笑影上,也仿佛觉得这又冷又尖,自己再没有开口的必要了。她单是一瞥他们,并不回答一句话。

鲁镇永远是过新年,腊月二十以后就忙起来了。四叔家里这回须雇男短工,还是忙不过来,另叫柳妈做帮手,杀鸡,宰鹅;然而柳妈是善女人①,吃素,不杀生的,只肯洗器皿。祥林嫂除烧火之外,没有别的事,却闲着了,坐着只看柳妈洗器皿。微雪点点的下来了。

"唉唉,我真傻,"祥林嫂看了天空,叹息着,独语似的说。

"祥林嫂,你又来了。"柳妈不耐烦的看着她的脸,说。"我问你:你额角上的伤疤,不就是那时撞坏的么?"

"唔唔。"她含胡的回答。

"我问你:你那时怎么后来竟依了呢?"

"我么?……"

"你呀。我想:这总是你自己愿意了,不然……。"

"阿阿,你不知道他力气多么大呀。"

"我不信。我不信你这么大的力气,真会拗他不过。你后来一定是自己肯了,倒推说他力气大。"

英汉对照
English-Chinese
中国文学宝库
Gems of Chinese Literature
现代文学系列
Modern Literature

---

① 善女人:佛家语,指信佛的女人。

237

"Why ... just try for yourself and see." She smiled.

Amah Liu's lined face broke into a smile too, wrinkling up like a walnut-shell. Her small beady eyes swept the other woman's forehead, then fastened on her eyes. At once Xianglin's Wife stopped smiling, as if embarrassed, and turned her eyes away to watch the snow.

"That was really a bad bargain you struck, Xianglin's Wife," said Amah Liu mysteriously. "If you'd held out longer or knocked yourself to death outright, that would have been better. As it is, you're guilty of a great sin though you lived less than two years with your second husband. Just think: when you go down to the lower world, the ghosts of both men will start fighting over you. Which ought to have you? The King of Hell will have to saw you into two and divide you between them. I feel it really is..."

Xianglin's Wife's face registered terror then. This was something no one had told her up in the mountains.

"Better guard against that in good time, I say. Go to the Temple of the Tutelary God and buy a threshold to be trampled in your place by thousands of people. If you atone for your sins in this life you'll escape torment after death."

Xianglin's Wife said nothing at the time, but she must have taken this advice to heart for when she got up the next morning there were dark rims round her eyes. After breakfast she went to the Temple of the Tutelary God at the west end of the town and asked to buy a threshold as an offering. At first the priest refused, only giving a grudging consent after she was reduced to tears of desperation. The price charged was twelve thousand cash.

"阿阿,你……你倒自己试试看。"她笑了。

柳妈的打皱的脸也笑起来,使她蹙缩得像一个核桃;干枯的小眼睛一看祥林嫂的额角,又钉住她的眼。祥林嫂似乎很局促了,立刻敛了笑容,旋转眼光,自去看雪花。

"祥林嫂,你实在不合算。"柳妈诡秘的说。"再一强,或者索性撞一个死,就好了。现在呢,你和你的第二个男人过活不到两年,倒落了一件大罪名。你想,你将来到阴司去,那两个死鬼的男人还要争,你给了谁好呢?阎罗大王只好把你锯开来,分给他们。我想,这真是……。"

她脸上就显出恐怖的神色来,这是在山村里所未曾知道的。

"我想,你不如及早抵当。你到土地庙里去捐一条门槛,当作你的替身,给千人踏,万人跨,赎了这一世的罪名,免得死了去受苦。"

她当时并不回答什么话,但大约非常苦闷了,第二天早上起来的时候,两眼上便都围着大黑圈。早饭之后,她便到镇的西头的土地庙里去求捐门槛。庙祝① 起初执意不允许,直到她急得流泪,才勉强答应了。价目是大钱十二千。

---

① 庙祝:旧时庙宇中管理香火的人。

英汉对照
English-Chinese
中国文学宝库
Gems of Chinese Literature
现代文学系列
Modern Literature

She had long since given up talking to people after their contemptuous reception of Ah Mao's story; but as word of her conversation with Amah Liu spread, many of the townsfolk took a fresh interest in her and came once more to provoke her into talking. The topic, of course, had changed to the scar on her forehead.

"Tell me, Xianglin's Wife, what made you willing in the end?" one would ask.

"What a waste, to have bashed yourself like that for nothing," another would chime in, looking at her scar.

She must have known from their smiles and tone of voice that they were mocking her, for she simply stared at them without a word and finally did not even turn her head. All day long she kept her lips tightly closed, bearing on her head the scar considered by everyone as a badge of shame, while she shopped, swept the floor, washed the vegetables and prepared the rice in silence. Nearly a year went by before she took her accumulated wages from my aunt, changed them for twelve silver dollars, and asked for leave to go to the west end of town. In less time than it takes for a meal she was back again, looking much comforted. With an unaccustomed light in her eyes, she told my aunt contentedly that she had now offered up a threshold in the Temple of the Tutelary God.

When the time came for the ancestral sacrifice at the winter solstice she worked harder than ever, and as soon as my aunt took out the sacrificial vessels and helped Ah Niu to carry the table into the middle of the hall, she went confidently to fetch the winecups and chopsticks.

"Put those down, Xianglin's Wife!" my aunt called hastily.

她久已不和人们交口,因为阿毛的故事是早被大家厌弃了的;但自从和柳妈谈了天,似乎又即传扬开去,许多人都发生了新趣味,又来逗她说话了。至于题目,那自然是换了一个新样,专在她额上的伤疤。

"祥林嫂,我问你:你那时怎么竟肯了?"一个说。

"唉,可惜,白撞了这一下。"一个看着她的疤,应和道。

她大约从他们的笑容和声调上,也知道是在嘲笑她,所以总是瞪着眼睛,不说一句话,后来连头也不回了。她整日紧闭了嘴唇,头上带着大家以为耻辱的记号的那伤痕,默默的跑街,扫地,洗菜,淘米。快够一年,她才从四婶手里支取了历来积存的工钱,换算了十二元鹰洋①,请假到镇的西头去。但不到一顿饭时候,她便回来,神气很舒畅,眼光也分外有神,高兴似的对四婶说,自己已经在土地庙捐了门槛了。

冬至的祭祖时节,她做得更出力,看四婶装好祭品,和阿牛将桌子抬到堂屋中央,她便坦然的去拿酒杯和筷子。

"你放着罢,祥林嫂!"四婶慌忙大声说。

---

① 鹰洋:指墨西哥银元,币面铸有鹰的图案。鸦片战争后曾大量流入我国。

She withdrew her hand as if scorched, her face turned ashen grey, and instead of fetching the candlesticks she just stood there in a daze until my uncle came in to burn some incense and told her to go away. This time the change in her was phenomenal: the next day her eyes were sunken, her spirit seemed broken. She took fright very easily too, afraid not only of the dark and shadows, but of meeting anyone. Even the sight of her own master or mistress set her trembling like a mouse that had strayed out of its hole in broad daylight. The rest of the time she would sit stupidly as if carved out of wood. In less than half a year her hair had turned grey, and her memory had deteriorated so much that she often forgot to go and wash the rice.

"What's come over Xianglin's Wife? We should never have taken her on again," my aunt would sometimes say in front of her, as if to warn her.

But there was no change in her, no sign that she would ever recover her wits. So they decided to get rid of her and told her to go back to Old Mrs Wei. That was what they were saying, at least, when I had been there; and, judging by subsequent developments, this was evidently what they must have done. But whether she started begging as soon as she left my uncle's house, or whether she went first to Old Mrs Wei and later became a beggar, I do not know.

I was woken up by the noisy explosion of crackers close at hand and, from the faint glow shed by the yellow oil lamp and the bangs of fireworks as my uncle's household celebrated the sacrifice, I knew that it must be nearly dawn. Listening drowsily I vaguely

她像是受了炮烙①似的缩手,脸色同时变作灰黑,也不再去取烛台,只是失神的站着。直到四叔上香的时候,教她走开,她才走开。这一回她的变化非常大,第二天,不但眼睛窈陷下去,连精神也更不济了。而且很胆怯,不独怕暗夜,怕黑影,即使见人,虽是自己的主人,也总惴惴的,有如白天出穴游行的小鼠;否则呆坐着,直是一个木偶人。不半年,头发也花白起来了,记性尤其坏,甚而至于常常忘却了去淘米。

"祥林嫂怎么这样了?倒不如那时不留她。"四婶有时当面就这样说,似乎是警告她。

然而她总如此,全不见有怜悧起来的希望。他们于是想打发她走了,教她回到卫老婆子那里去。但当我还在鲁镇的时候,不过单是这样说;看现在的情状,可见后来终于实行了。然而她是从四叔家出去就成了乞丐的呢,还是先到卫老婆子家然后再成乞丐的呢?那我可不知道。

我给那些因为在近旁而极响的爆竹声惊醒,看见豆一般大的黄色的灯火光,接着又听得毕毕剥剥的鞭炮,是四叔家正在"祝福"了;知道已是五更将近时候。我在蒙胧中,又隐约听到

---

① 炮烙:亦作炮格,相传为殷纣王时的一种酷刑。据《史记·殷本纪》裴骃集解引《列女传》:"膏铜柱,下加之炭,令有罪者行焉,辄堕炭中,妲己笑,名曰炮格之刑。"

heard the ceaseless explosion of crackers in the distance. It seemed to me that the whole town was enveloped by the dense cloud of noise in the sky, mingling with the whirling snowflakes. Blanketed in this medley of sound I relaxed; the doubt which had preyed on my mind from dawn till night was swept away by the festive atmosphere, and I felt only that the saints of heaven and earth had accepted the sacrifice and incense and were reeling with intoxication in the sky, preparing to give Luzhen's people boundless good fortune.

February 7, 1924

远处的爆竹声联绵不断,似乎合成一天音响的浓云,夹着团团飞舞的雪花,拥抱了全市镇。我在这繁响的拥抱中,也懒散而且舒适,从白天以至初夜的疑虑,全给祝福的空气一扫而空了,只觉得天地圣众歆享了牲醴和香烟,都醉醺醺的在空中蹒跚,豫备给鲁镇的人们以无限的幸福。

一九二四年二月七日。

英汉对照
English-Chinese
中国文学宝库
Gems of Chinese Literature
现代文学系列
Modern Literature

In the Tavern

During my travels from the north to the southeast I made a detour to my home and then went on to S —. This town, only thirty *li* from my native place, can be reached in less than half a day by a small boat. I had taught for a year in a school here. In the depth of winter after snow the landscape was bleak; but a combination of indolence and nostalgia made me put up briefly in the Luo Si Hotel, a new hotel since my time. The town was small. I looked for several old colleagues I thought I might find, but not one of them was there. They had long since gone their different ways. And when I passed the gate of the school that too had changed its name and appearance, making me feel quite a stranger. In less than two hours my enthusiasm had waned and I rather reproached myself for coming.

The hotel I was in let rooms but did not serve meals, which had to be ordered from outside, but these were about as unpalatable as mud. Outside the window was only a stained and spotted wall, covered with withered moss. Above was the leaden sky, a colourless dead white; moreover a flurry of snow had begun to fall. Since my lunch had been poor and I had nothing to do to while away the time, my thoughts turned quite naturally to a small tavern I had known well in the past called One Barrel House, which I reckoned could not be far from the hotel. I immediately locked my door and

在酒楼上①

　　我从北地向东南旅行,绕道访了我的家乡,就到S城。这城离我的故乡不过三十里,坐了小船,小半天可到,我曾在这里的学校里当过一年的教员。深冬雪后,风景凄清,懒散和怀旧的心绪联结起来,我竟暂寓在S城的洛思旅馆里了;这旅馆是先前所没有的。城圈本不大,寻访了几个以为可以会见的旧同事,一个也不在,早不知散到那里去了;经过学校的门口,也改换了名称和模样,于我很生疏。不到两个时辰,我的意兴早已索然,颇悔此来为多事了。

　　我所住的旅馆是租房不卖饭的,饭菜必须另外叫来,但又无味,入口如嚼泥土。窗外只有渍痕斑驳的墙壁,帖着枯死的莓苔;上面是铅色的天,白皑皑的绝无精采,而且微雪又飞舞起来了。我午餐本没有饱,又没有可以消遣的事情,便很自然的想到先前有一家很熟识的小酒楼,叫一石居的,算来离旅馆并不远。我于是立即

---

①　本篇最初发表于一九二四年五月十日上海《小说月报》第十五卷第五号。

英汉对照
English-Chinese
中国文学宝库
Gems of Chinese Literature
现代文学系列
Modern Literature

In the Tavern

set out to find it. Actually, all I wanted was to escape the boredom of my stay, not to do any serious drinking. One Barrel House was still there, its narrow mouldering front and dilapidated signboard unchanged. But from the landlord down to the waiters there was not a soul I knew — in One Barrel House too I had become a complete stranger. Still I climbed the familiar stairway in the corner to the little upper storey. The five small wooden tables up here were unchanged; only the window at the back, originally latticed, had been fitted with glass panes.

"A catty of yellow wine. To go with it? Ten pieces of fried beancurd with plenty of paprika sauce."

As I gave this order to the waiter who had come up with me I went and sat down at the table by the back window. The fact that the place was empty enabled me to pick the best seat, one with a view of the deserted garden below. Most likely this did not belong to the tavern. I had looked out at it many times in the past, sometimes too in snowy weather. But now, to eyes accustomed to the north, the sight was sufficiently striking. Several old plum trees in full bloom were braving the snow as if oblivious of the depth of winter; while among the thick dark green foliage of a camellia beside the crumbling pavilion a dozen crimson blossoms blazed bright as flame in the snow, indignant and arrogant, as if despising the wanderer's wanderlust. At this I suddenly remembered the moistness of the heaped snow here, clinging, glistening and shining, quite unlike the dry northern snow which when a high wind blows will fly up to fill the sky like mist...

"Your wine, sir..." said the waiter carelessly, putting down my

锁了房门,出街向那酒楼去。其实也无非想姑且逃避客中的无聊,并不专为买醉。一石居是在的,狭小阴湿的店面和破旧的招牌都依旧;但从掌柜以至堂倌却已没有一个熟人,我在这一石居中也完全成了生客。然而我终于跨上那走熟的屋角的扶梯去了,由此径到小楼上。上面也依然是五张小板桌;独有原是木棂的后窗却换嵌了玻璃。

"一斤绍酒。——菜?十个油豆腐,辣酱要多!"

我一面说给跟我上来的堂倌听,一面向后窗走,就在靠窗的一张桌旁坐下了。楼上"空空如也",任我拣得最好的坐位:可以眺望楼下的废园。这园大概是不属于酒家的,我先前也曾眺望过许多回,有时也在雪天里。但现在从惯于北方的眼睛看来,却很值得惊异了:几株老梅竟斗雪开着满树的繁花,仿佛毫不以深冬为意;倒塌的亭子边还有一株山茶树,从暗绿的密叶里显出十几朵红花来,赫赫的在雪中明得如火,愤怒而且傲慢,如蔑视游人的甘心于远行。我这时又忽地想到这里积雪的滋润,著物不去,晶莹有光,不比朔雪的粉一般干,大风一吹,便飞得满空如烟雾。……

"客人,酒。……"

堂倌懒懒的说着,放下杯,筷,酒壶和碗碟,

cup, chopsticks, wine-pot and dish. The wine had come. I turned to the table, set everything straight and filled my cup. I felt that the north was certainly not my home, yet when I came south I could only count as a stranger. The powdery dry snow which whirled through the air up there and the clinging soft snow here were equally alien to me. In a slightly melancholy mood I took a leisurely sip of wine. The wine tasted pure and the fried beancurd was excellently cooked, only the paprika sauce was not hot enough; but then the people of S — had never understood pungent flavours.

Probably because it was the afternoon, the place had none of the atmosphere of a tavern. By the time I had drunk three cups, the four other tables were still unoccupied. A sense of loneliness stole over me as I stared at the deserted garden, yet I did not want other customers to come up. Thus I could not help being irritated by the occasional footsteps on the stairs, and was relieved to find it was only the waiter. And so I drank another two cups of wine.

"This time it must be a customer," I thought, at the sound of footsteps much slower than those of the waiter. When I judged that he must be at the top of the stairs, I raised my head rather apprehensively to look at this extraneous company and stood up with a start. It had never occurred to me that I might run into a friend here — if such he would still let me call him. The newcomer was an old classmate who had been my colleague when I was a teacher, and although he had changed a great deal I knew him at a glance. Only he had become very slow in his movements, quite unlike the spry dynamic Lü Weifu of the old days.

酒到了。我转脸向了板桌,排好器具,斟出酒来。觉得北方固不是我的旧乡,但南来又只能算一个客子,无论那边的干雪怎样纷飞,这里的柔雪又怎样的依恋,于我都没有什么关系了。我略带些哀愁,然而很服帖的呷一口酒。酒味很纯正;油豆腐也煮得十分好;可惜辣酱太淡薄,本来S城人是不懂得吃辣的。

大概因为正在下午的缘故罢,这虽说是酒楼,却毫无酒楼气,我已经喝下三杯酒去了,而我以外还是四张空板桌。我看着废园,渐渐的感到孤独,但又不愿有别的酒客上来。偶然听得楼梯上脚步响,便不由的有些懊恼,待到看见是堂倌,才又安心了,这样的又喝了两杯酒。

我想,这回定是酒客了,因为听得那脚步声比堂倌的要缓得多。约略料他走完了楼梯的时候,我便害怕似的抬头去看这无干的同伴,同时也就吃惊的站起来。我竟不料在这里意外的遇见朋友了,——假如他现在还许我称他为朋友。那上来的分明是我的旧同窗,也是做教员时代的旧同事,面貌虽然颇有些改变,但一见也就认识,独有行动却变得格外迂缓,很不像当年敏捷精悍的吕纬甫了。

英汉对照
English-Chinese
中国文学宝库
Gems of Chinese Literature
现代文学系列
Modern Literature

In the Tavern

"Well, Weifu, is it you? Fancy meeting you here!"

"Well, well, is it you? Just fancy..."

I invited him to join me, but he seemed to hesitate before doing so. This struck me as strange, then I felt rather hurt and annoyed. A closer look revealed that Lü had still the same unkempt hair and beard, but his pale lantern-jawed face was thin and wasted. He appeared very quiet if not dispirited, and his eyes beneath their thick black brows had lost their alertness; but while looking slowly around, at sight of the deserted garden they suddenly flashed with the same piercing light I had seen so often at school.

"Well," I said cheerfully but very awkwardly, "it must be ten years since last we saw each other. I heard long ago that you were at Jinan, but I was so wretchedly lazy I never wrote..."

"It was the same with me. I've been at Taiyuan for more than two years now with my mother. When I came back to fetch her I learned that you had already left, left for good and all."

"What are you doing at Taiyuan?" I asked.

"Teaching in the family of a fellow-provincial."

"And before that?"

"Before that?" He took a cigarette from his pocket, lit it and put it to his lips, then watching the smoke he puffed out said reflectively, "Just futile work, amounting to nothing at all."

He in turn asked what I had been doing all these years. I gave him a rough idea, at the same time calling the waiter to bring a cup and chopsticks in order that Lü could share my wine while we had another two catties heated. We also ordered dishes. In the past we had never stood on ceremony, but now we began deferring

"阿,——纬甫,是你么?我万想不到会在这里遇见你。"

"阿阿,是你?我也万想不到……"

我就邀他同坐,但他似乎略略踌躇之后,方才坐下来。我起先很以为奇,接着便有些悲伤,而且不快了。细看他相貌,也还是乱蓬蓬的须发;苍白的长方脸,然而衰瘦了。精神很沉静,或者却是颓唐;又浓又黑的眉毛底下的眼睛也失了精采,但当他缓缓的四顾的时候,却对废园忽地闪出我在学校时代常常看见的射人的光来。

"我们,"我高兴的,然而颇不自然的说,"我们这一别,怕有十年了罢。我早知道你在济南,可是实在懒得太难,终于没有写一封信。……"

"彼此都一样。可是现在我在太原了,已经两年多,和我的母亲。我回来接她的时候,知道你早搬走了,搬得很干净。"

"你在太原做什么呢?"我问。

"教书,在一个同乡的家里。"

"这以前呢?"

"这以前么?"他从衣袋里掏出一支烟卷来,点了火衔在嘴里,看着喷出的烟雾,沉思似的说,"无非做了些无聊的事情,等于什么也没有做。"

他也问我别后的景况;我一面告诉他一个大概,一面叫堂倌先取杯筷来,使他先喝着我的酒,然后再去添二斤。其间还点菜,我们先前原是毫不客气的,但此刻却推让起来了,终于说不

英汉对照
English-Chinese
中国文学宝库
Gems of Chinese Literature
现代文学系列
Modern Literature

to each other so that finally we fixed on four dishes suggested by the waiter: peas spiced with aniseed, jellied pork, fried beancurd and salted mackerel.

"As soon as I came back I knew I was a fool." Holding his cigarette in one hand and the winecup in the other, he spoke with a bitter smile. "When I was young, I saw the way bees or flies stuck to one spot. If something frightened them they would buzz off, but after flying in a small circle they would come back to stop in the same place; and I thought this really ridiculous as well as pathetic. Little did I think I'd be flying back myself too after only describing a small circle. And I didn't think you'd come back either. Couldn't you have flown a little further?"

"That's difficult to say. Probably I too have simply described a small circle." I also spoke with a rather bitter smile. "But why did you fly back?"

"For something quite futile." In one gulp he emptied his cup, then took several pulls at his cigarette and his eyes widened a little. "Futile — but you may as well hear about it."

The waiter brought up the freshly heated wine and dishes and set them on the table. The smoke and the fragrance of fried beancurd seemed to make the upstairs room more cheerful, while outside the snow fell still more thickly.

"Perhaps you knew," he went on, "that I had a little brother who died when he was three and was buried in the country here. I can't even remember clearly what he looked like, but I've heard my mother say he was a very lovable child and very fond of me. Even now it brings tears to her eyes to speak of him. This spring

清那一样是谁点的,就从堂倌的口头报告上指定了四样菜:茴香豆,冻肉,油豆腐,青鱼干。

"我一回来,就想到我可笑。"他一手擎着烟卷,一只手扶着酒杯,似笑非笑的向我说。"我在少年时,看见蜂子或蝇子停在一个地方,给什么来一吓,即刻飞去了,但是飞了一个小圈子,便又回来停在原地点,便以为这实在很可笑,也可怜。可不料现在我自己也飞回来了,不过绕了一点小圈子。又不料你也回来了。你不能飞得更远些么?"

"这难说,大约也不外乎绕点小圈子罢。"我也似笑非笑的说。"但是你为什么飞回来的呢?"

"也还是为了无聊的事。"他一口喝干了一杯酒,吸几口烟,眼睛略为张大了。"无聊的。——但是我们就谈谈罢。"

堂倌搬上新添的酒菜来,排满了一桌,楼上又添了烟气和油豆腐的热气,仿佛热闹起来了;楼外的雪也越加纷纷的下。

"你也许本来知道,"他接着说,"我曾经有一个小兄弟,是三岁上死掉的,就葬在这乡下。我连他的模样都记不清楚了,但听母亲说,是一个很可爱念的孩子,和我也很相投,至今她提起来还似乎要下泪。今年春天,一个堂兄就来了

英汉对照
English-Chinese
中国文学宝库
Gems of Chinese Literature
现代文学系列
Modern Literature

an elder cousin wrote to tell us that the ground beside his grave was gradually being swamped, and he was afraid before long it would slip into the river: we should go at once and do something about it. This upset my mother so much that she couldn't sleep for several nights — she can read letters herself, you know. But what could I do? I had no money, no time: there was nothing that could be done.

"Now at last, because I'm on holiday over New Year, I've been able to come south to move his grave." He tossed off another cup of wine and looking out of the window exclaimed: "Could you find anything like this up north? Blossom in thick snow, and the soil beneath the snow not frozen. So the day before yesterday I bought a small coffin in town — because I reckoned that the one under the ground must have rotted long ago — took cotton and bedding, hired four workmen, and went into the country to move his grave. I suddenly felt most elated, eager to dig up the grave, eager to see the bones of the little brother who had been so fond of me: this was a new experience for me. When we reached the grave, sure enough, the river was encroaching on it and the water was less than two feet away. The poor grave not having had any earth added to it for two years was subsiding. Standing there in the snow, I pointed to it firmly and ordered the workmen: 'Dig it up.'

"I really am a commonplace fellow. I felt that my voice at this juncture was rather unnatural, and that this order was the greatest I had given in all my life. But the workmen didn't find it strange in the least, and set to dig. When they reached the enclosure I had a look, and sure enough the coffin had rotted almost completely

一封信,说他的坟边已经渐渐的浸了水,不久怕要陷入河里去了,须得赶紧去设法。母亲一知道就很着急,几乎几夜睡不着,——她又自己能看信的。然而我能有什么法子呢?没有钱,没有工夫:当时什么法也没有。

"一直挨到现在,趁着年假的闲空,我才得回南给他来迁葬。"他又喝干一杯酒,看着窗外,说,"这在那边那里能如此呢?积雪里会有花,雪地下会不冻。就在前天,我在城里买了一口小棺材,——因为我豫料那地下的应该早已朽烂了,——带着棉絮和被褥,雇了四个土工,下乡迁葬去。我当时忽而很高兴,愿意掘一回坟,愿意一见我那曾经和我很亲睦的小兄弟的骨殖:这些事我生平都没有经历过。到得坟地,果然,河水只是咬进来,离坟已不到二尺远。可怜的坟,两年没有培土,也平下去了。我站在雪中,决然的指着他对土工说,'掘开来!'我实在是一个庸人,我这时觉得我的声音有些希奇,这命令也是一个在我一生中最为伟大的命令。但土工们却毫不骇怪,就动手掘下去了。待到掘着圹穴,我便过去看,果然,棺木已经快要烂尽

英汉对照
English-Chinese
中国文学宝库
Gems of Chinese Literature
现代文学系列
Modern Literature

away: there was nothing left but a heap of splinters and chips of wood. My heart beat faster as I set these aside myself, very carefully, wanting to see my little brother. However, I was in for a surprise. Bedding, clothes, skeleton, all had gone!

"I thought: 'These have all disappeared, but hair, I have always heard, is the last thing to rot. There may still be some hair.' So I bent down and searched carefully in the mud where the pillow should have been, but there was none. Not a trace remained."

I suddenly noticed that the rims of his eyes were rather red, but immediately attributed this to the effect of the wine. He had scarcely touched the dishes but had been drinking incessantly and must have drunk more than a catty; his looks and gestures had become more animated, more like the Lü Weifu whom I had known. I called the waiter to heat two more catties of wine, then turned back to face my companion, my cup in my hand, as I listened to him in silence.

"Actually there was really no need to move it: I had only to level the ground, sell the coffin and make an end of the business. Although it might have seemed odd my going to sell the coffin, if the price were low enough the shop from which I bought it would have taken it, and I could at least have recouped a few cents for wine. But I didn't. I still spread out the bedding, wrapped up in cotton some of the clay where his body had been, covered it up, put it in the new coffin, moved it to my father's grave and buried it beside him. And having a brick vault built kept me busy most of yesterday too, supervising the work. But in this way I can count the affair ended, at least enough to deceive my mother and set her mind at

了,只剩下一堆木丝和小木片。我的心颤动着,自去拨开这些,很小心的,要看一看我的小兄弟。然而出乎意外!被褥,衣服,骨骼,什么也没有。我想,这些都消尽了,向来听说最难烂的是头发,也许还有罢。我便伏下去,在该是枕头所在的泥土里仔仔细细的看,也没有。踪影全无!"

我忽而看见他眼圈微红了,但立即知道是有了酒意。他总不很吃菜,单是把酒不停的喝,早喝了一斤多,神情和举动都活泼起来,渐近于先前所见的吕纬甫了。我叫堂倌再添二斤酒,然后回转身,也拿着酒杯,正对面默默的听着。

"其实,这本已可以不必再迁,只要平了土,卖掉棺材,就此完事了的。我去卖棺材虽然有些离奇,但只要价钱极便宜,原铺子就许要,至少总可以捞回几文酒钱来。但我不这样,我仍然铺好被褥,用棉花裹了些他先前身体所在的地方的泥土,包起来,装在新棺材里,运到我父亲埋着的坟地上,在他坟旁埋掉了。因为外面用砖砌,昨天又忙了我大半天:监工。但这样总算完了一件事,足够去骗骗我的母亲,使她安

rest. Well, well, the look you're giving me shows you are wondering why I've changed so much. Yes, I still remember the time when we went together to the tutelary god's temple to pull off the idols' beards, and how for days on end we used to discuss methods of reforming China until we even came to blows. But this is how I am now, willing to let things slide and to compromise. Sometimes I think: 'If my old friends were to see me now, probably they would no longer acknowledge me as a friend.' But this is what I am like now."

He took out another cigarette, put it to his lips and lit it.

"Judging by your expression, you still expect something of me. Naturally I am much more obtuse than before, but I'm not completely blind yet. This makes me grateful to you, at the same time rather uneasy. I'm afraid I've let down the old friends who even now still wish me well..." He stopped and took several puffs at his cigarette before going on slowly: "Only today, just before coming to this One Barrel House, I did something futile yet something I was glad to do. My former neighbour on the east side was called Chang Fu. He was a boatman and had a daughter named A Shun. When you came to my house in those days you may have seen her but you certainly wouldn't have paid any attention to her, because she was still small then. She didn't grow up to be pretty either, having just an ordinary thin oval face and pale skin. Only her eyes were unusually large with very long lashes and whites as clear as a cloudless night sky — I mean the cloudless sky of the north on a windless day; here it is not so clear. She was very capable. She lost her mother while in her teens, and had to look after a small

心些。——阿阿,你这样的看我,你怪我何以和先前太不相同了么?是的,我也还记得我们同到城隍①庙里去拔掉神像的胡子的时候,连日议论些改革中国的方法以至于打起来的时候。但我现在就是这样了,敷敷衍衍,模模胡胡。我有时自己也想到,倘若先前的朋友看见我,怕会不认我做朋友了。——然而我现在就是这样。"

他又掏出一支烟卷来,衔在嘴里,点了火。

"看你的神情,你似乎还有些期望我,——我现在自然麻木得多了,但是有些事也还看得出。这使我很感激,然而也使我很不安:怕我终于辜负了至今还对我怀着好意的老朋友。……"他忽而停住了,吸几口烟,才又慢慢的说,"正在今天,刚在我到这一石居来之前,也就做了一件无聊事,然而也是我自己愿意做的。我先前的东边的邻居叫长富,是一个船户。他有一个女儿叫阿顺,你那时到我家里来,也许见过的,但你一定没有留心,因为那时她还小。后来她也长得并不好看,不过是平常的瘦瘦的瓜子脸,黄脸皮;独有眼睛非常大,睫毛也很长,眼白又青得如夜的晴天,而且是北方的无风的晴天,这里的就没有那么明净了。她很能干,十多岁没了母亲,招呼两个小弟妹都靠她;又得服侍父

① 城隍:迷信中主管城池的神。

英汉对照
English-Chinese
中国文学宝库
Gems of Chinese Literature
现代文学系列
Modern Literature

brother and sister besides waiting on her father; and all this she did very competently. She was so economical too that the family gradually grew better off. There was scarcely a neighbour who didn't praise her, and even Chang Fu often expressed his appreciation. When I was setting off on my journey this time, my mother remembered her — old folk's memories are so long. She recalled that once A Shun saw someone wearing red velvet flowers in her hair, and wanted a spray for herself. When she couldn't get one she cried nearly all night, so that her father beat her and her eyes remained red and swollen for two or three days. These red flowers came from another province and couldn't be bought even in S — , so how could she ever hope to have any? Since I was coming south this time, my mother told me to buy two sprays for her.

"Far from feeling vexed at this commission, I was actually delighted, really glad of the chance to do something for A Shun. The year before last I came back to fetch my mother, and one day when Chang Fu was at home I dropped in for some reason to chat with him. By way of refreshment he offered me some buckwheat mush, remarking that they added white sugar to it. As you can see, a boatman who could afford white sugar was obviously not poor and must eat pretty well. I let myself be persuaded but begged them to give me only a small bowl. He quite understood and instructed A Shun: 'These scholars have no appetite. Give him a small bowl, but add more sugar,' However when she had prepared the concoction and brought it in, it gave me quite a turn, because it was a large bowl, as much as I could eat in a whole day. Though compared with Chang Fu's bowl, admittedly, it was small. This was

亲,事事都周到;也经济,家计倒渐渐的稳当起来了。邻居几乎没有一个不夸奖她,连长富也时常说些感激的话。这一次我动身回来的时候,我的母亲又记得她了,老年人记性真长久。她说她曾经知道顺姑因为看见谁的头上戴着红的剪绒花,自己也想有一朵,弄不到,哭了,哭了小半夜,就挨了她父亲的一顿打,后来眼眶还红肿了两三天。这种剪绒花是外省的东西,S城里尚且买不出,她那里想得到手呢?趁我这一次回南的便,便叫我买两朵去送她。

"我对于这差使倒并不以为烦厌,反而很喜欢;为阿顺,我实在还有些愿意出力的意思的。前年,我回来接我母亲的时候,有一天,长富正在家,不知怎的我和他闲谈起来了。他便要请我吃点心,荞麦粉,并且告诉我所加的是白糖。你想,家里能有白糖的船户,可见决不是一个穷船户了,所以他也吃得很阔绰。我被劝不过,答应了,但要求只要用小碗。他也很识世故,便嘱咐阿顺说,'他们文人,是不会吃东西的。你就用小碗,多加糖!'然而等到调好端来的时候,仍然使我吃一吓,是一大碗,足够我吃一天。但是和长富吃的一碗比起来,我的也确乎算小碗。

英汉对照
English-Chinese
中国文学宝库
Gems of Chinese Literature
现代文学系列
Modern Literature

the first time I had eaten buckwheat mush, and I just could not stomach it though it was so sweet. I gulped down a few mouthfuls and decided to leave the rest when I happened to notice A Shun standing some distance away in one corner of the room, and I simply hadn't the heart to put down my chopsticks. In her face I saw both hope and fear — fear presumably that she had prepared it badly, and hope that we would find it to our liking. I knew that if I left most of my bowl she would feel very disappointed and sorry. I made up my mind to finish it and shovelled the stuff down, eating almost as fast as Chang Fu. That taught me how painful it is forcing oneself to eat; and I remembered experiencing the same difficulty as a child when I had to finish a bowl of worm-medicine mixed with brown sugar. I didn't hold it against her though, because her half-suppressed smile of satisfaction when she came to take away our empty bowls more than repaid me for all my discomfort. So that night, although indigestion kept me from sleeping well and I had a series of nightmares, I still wished her a lifetime of happiness and hoped that for her sake the world would change for the better. But such thoughts were only the residue of my old dreams. The next instant I laughed at myself, and promptly forgot them.

"I hadn't known before that she had been beaten on accout of a spray of velvet flowers, but when my mother spoke of it I remembered the buckwheat mush incident and became unaccountably diligent. First I made a search in Taiyuan, but none of the shops had them. It was only when I went to Jinan..."

There was a rustle outside the window as a pile of snow slithered

我生平没有吃过荞麦粉,这回一尝,实在不可口,却是非常甜。我漫然的吃了几口,就想不吃了,然而无意中,忽然间看见阿顺远远的站在屋角里,就使我立刻消失了放下碗筷的勇气。我看她的神情,是害怕而且希望,大约怕自己调得不好,愿我们吃得有味。我知道如果剩下大半碗来,一定要使她很失望,而且很抱歉。我于是同时决心,放开喉咙灌下去了,几乎吃得和长富一样快。我由此才知道硬吃的苦痛,我只记得还做孩子时候的吃尽一碗拌着驱除蛔虫药粉的沙糖才有这样难。然而我毫不抱怨,因为她过来收拾空碗时候的忍着的得意的笑容,已尽够赔偿我的苦痛而有余了。所以我这一夜虽然饱胀得睡不稳,又做了一大串恶梦,也还是祝赞她一生幸福,愿世界为她变好。然而这些意思也不过是我的那些旧日的梦的痕迹,即刻就自笑,接着也就忘却了。

"我先前并不知道她曾经为了一朵剪绒花挨打,但因为母亲一说起,便也记得了荞麦粉的事,意外的勤快起来了。我先在太原城里搜求了一遍,都没有;一直到济南……"

窗外沙沙的一阵声响,许多积雪从被他压

英汉对照
English-Chinese
中国文学宝库
Gems of Chinese Literature
现代文学系列
Modern Literature

off the camellia which had been bending beneath its weight; then the branches of the tree straightened themselves, flaunting their thick dark foliage and blood-red flowers even more clearly. The sky had grown even more leaden. Sparrows were twittering, no doubt because dusk was falling and finding nothing to eat on the snow-covered ground they were going back early to their nests to sleep.

"It was only when I went to Jinan..." He glanced out of the window then turned back, drained a cup of wine, took several puffs at his cigarette and went on, "Only then did I buy the artificial flowers. I didn't know whether they were the same as those she had been beaten for, but at least they were made of velvet. And not knowing whether she liked deep or light colours, I bought one spray of red, one spray of pink, and brought them both here.

"This afternoon straight after lunch I went to see Chang Fu, having stayed on an extra day just for this. Though his house was still there it seemed to me rather gloomy, but perhaps that was simply my imagination. His son and second daughter A Qiao were standing at the gate. Both of them had grown. A Qiao is quite unlike her sister, she looks simply ghastly; but at my approach she rushed into the house. I learned from the boy that Chang Fu was not at home. 'And your elder sister?' I asked. At that he glared at me and demanded what my business with her was. He looked fierce enough to fling himself at me and bite me. I dithered, then walked away. Nowadays I just let things slide...

"You can have no idea how I dread calling on people, much more so than in the old days. Because I know what a nuisance I

弯了的一枝山茶树上滑下去了,树枝笔挺的伸直,更显出乌油油的肥叶和血红的花来。天空的铅色来得更浓;小鸟雀啾唧的叫着,大概黄昏将近,地面又全罩了雪,寻不出什么食粮,都赶早回巢来休息了。

"一直到了济南,"他向窗外看了一回,转身喝干一杯酒,又吸几口烟,接着说。"我才买到剪绒花。我也不知道使她挨打的是不是这一种,总之是绒做的罢了。我也不知道她喜欢深色还是浅色,就买了一朵大红的,一朵粉红的,都带到这里来。

"就是今天午后,我一吃完饭,便去看长富,我为此特地耽搁了一天。他的家倒还在,只是看去很有些晦气色了,但这恐怕不过是我自己的感觉。他的儿子和第二个女儿——阿昭,都站在门口,大了。阿昭长得全不像她姊姊,简直像一个鬼,但是看见我走向她家,便飞奔的逃进屋里去。我就问那小子,知道长富不在家。'你的大姊呢?'他立刻瞪起眼睛,连声问我寻她什么事,而且恶狠狠的似乎就要扑过来,咬我。我支吾着退走了,我现在是敷敷衍衍……

"你不知道,我可是比先前更怕去访人了。

英汉对照
English-Chinese
中国文学宝库
Gems of Chinese Literature
现代文学系列
Modern Literature

am, I am even sick of myself; so, knowing this, why inflict myself on others? But since this commission had to be carried out, after some reflection I went back to the firewood shop almost opposite their house. The proprietor's mother old Mrs Fa was still there and, what's more, still recognized me. She actually asked me into the shop to sit down. After the usual polite preliminaries I told her why I had come back to S — and was looking for Chang Fu. I was taken aback when she sighed:

"'What a pity A Shun hadn't the luck to wear these velvet flowers.'

"Then she told me the whole story. 'It was probably last spring that A Shun began to look pale and thin. Later she had fits of crying, but if asked why she wouldn't say. Sometimes she even cried all night until Chang Fu couldn't help losing his temper and swearing at her for carrying on like a crazy old maid. But when autumn came she caught a chill, then she took to her bed and never got up again. Only a few days before she died she confessed to Chang Fu that she had long ago started spitting blood and perspiring at night like her mother. But she hadn't told him for fear of worrying him. One evening her uncle Chang Keng came to demand a loan — he was always sponging on them — and when she wouldn't give him any money he sneered: "Don't give yourself airs; your man isn't even up to me!" That upset her, but she was too shy to ask any questions and could only cry. As soon as Chang Fu knew this, he told her what a decent fellow the man chosen for her was; but it was too late. Besides, she didn't believe him. "It's a good thing I'm already this way," she said. "Now nothing matters any more."

因为我已经深知道自己之讨厌,连自己也讨厌,又何必明知故犯的去使人暗暗地不快呢?然而这回的差使是不能不办妥的,所以想了一想,终于回到就在斜对门的柴店里。店主的母亲,老发奶奶,倒也还在,而且也还认识我,居然将我邀进店里坐去了。我们寒暄几句之后,我就说明了回到 S 城和寻长富的缘故。不料她叹息说:

"'可惜顺姑没有福气戴这剪绒花了。'

"她于是详细的的告诉我,说是'大约从去年春天以来,她就见得黄瘦,后来忽而常常下泪了,问她缘故又不说;有时还整夜的哭,哭得长富也忍不住生气,骂她年纪大了,发了疯。可是一到秋初,起先不过小伤风,终于躺倒了,从此就起不来。直到咽气的前几天,才肯对长富说,她早就像她母亲一样,不时的吐红和流夜汗。但是瞒着,怕他因此要担心。有一夜,她的伯伯长庚又来硬借钱,——这是常有的事,——她不给,长庚就冷笑着说:你不要骄气,你的男人比我还不如!她从此就发了愁,又怕羞,不好问,只好哭。长富赶紧将她的男人怎样的挣气的话说给她听,那里还来得及?况且她也不信,反而说:好在我已经这样,什么也不要紧了。'

英汉对照
English-Chinese
中国文学宝库
Gems of Chinese Literature
现代文学系列
Modern Literature

"Old Mrs Fa also said, 'If her man really hadn't been up to Chang Keng, that would have been truly frightful. Not up to a chicken thief — what man of creature would that be? But I saw him with my own eyes at the funeral: dressed in clean clothes and quite presentable. And he said with tears in his eyes that he'd worked hard all those years on the boat to save up money to marry, but now the girl was dead. Obviously he was really a good sort, and Chang Keng had been lying. It was too bad that A Shun believed such a rascally liar and died for nothing. Still, we can't blame anyone else: this was A Shun's fate.'

"Since that was the case, my business was finished too. But what about the two sprays of artificial flowers I had brought with me? Well, I asked her to give them to A Qiao. This A Qiao had fled at the sight of me as if I were a wolf or monster; I really didn't want to give them to her. However, give them I did, and I have only to tell my mother that A Shun was delighted with them and that will be that. Who cares about such futile affairs anyway? One only wants to muddle through them somehow. When I have muddled through New Year I shall go back to teaching the Confucian classics."

"Is that what you're teaching?" I asked in astonishment.

"Of course. Did you think I was teaching English? First I had two pupils, one studying the *Book of Songs*, the other *Mencius*. Recently I have got another, a girl, who is studying the *Canon for*

"她还说,'如果她的男人真比长庚不如,那就真可怕呵!比不上一个偷鸡贼,那是什么东西呢?然而他来送殓的时候,我是亲眼看见他的,衣服很干净,人也体面;还眼泪汪汪的说,自己撑了半世小船,苦熬苦省的积起钱来聘了一个女人,偏偏又死掉了。可见他实在是一个好人,长庚说的全是谎。只可惜顺姑竟会相信那样的贼骨头的谎话,白送了性命。——但这也不能去怪谁,只能怪顺姑自己没有这一份好福气。'

"那倒也罢,我的事情又完了。但是带在身边的两朵剪绒花怎么办呢?好,我就托她送了阿昭。这阿昭一见我就飞跑,大约将我当作一只狼或是什么,我实在不愿意去送她。——但是我也就送她了,对母亲只要说阿顺见了喜欢的了不得就是。这些无聊的事算什么?只要模模胡胡。模模胡胡的过了新年,仍旧教我的'子曰诗云'去。"

"你教的是'子曰诗云'么?"我觉得奇异,便问。

"自然。你还以为教的是 ABCD 么?我先是两个学生,一个读《诗经》①,一个读《孟子》②。

---

① 《诗经》:我国最早的诗歌总集,共三百零五篇。编成于春秋时代,大抵是周初到春秋中期的作品,相传曾经孔丘删定。

② 《孟子》:记载战国中期儒家学派代表人物孟轲(约前372—前289)的言行的书,由他的弟子纂辑而成。

英汉对照
English-Chinese
中国文学宝库
Gems of Chinese Literature
现代文学系列
Modern Literature

Girls.① I don't even teach mathematics; not that I wouldn't teach it, but they don't want it taught."

"I could really never have guessed that you would be teaching such books."

"Their father wants them to study these. I'm an outsider, it's all the same to me. Who cares about such futile affairs anyway? There's no need to take them seriously..."

His whole face was scarlet as if he were quite drunk, but the gleam in his eyes had died down. I gave a slight sigh, not knowing what to say. There was a clatter on the stairs as several customers came up. The first was short, with a round bloated face; the second was tall, with a conspicuous red nose. Behind them followed others, and as they walked up the small upper floor shook. I turned to Lü Weifu who was trying to catch my eye, then called for the bill.

"Is your salary enough to live on?" I asked as we prepared to leave.

"I have twenty dollars a month, not quite enough to manage on."

"What are your future plans then?"

"Future plans? I don't know. Just think: has any single thing turned out as we hoped of all we planned in the past? I'm not sure of anything now, not even of what tomorrow will bring, not even of the next minute..."

---

① A book describing the feudal standard of behaviour for girls and the virtues they should cultivate.

新近又添了一个,女的,读《女儿经》①。连算学也不教,不是我不教,他们不要教。"

"我实在料不到你倒去教这类的书,……"

"他们的老子要他们读这些;我是别人,无乎不可的。这些无聊的事算什么?只要随随便便,……"

他满脸已经通红,似乎很有些醉,但眼光却又消沉下去了。我微微的叹息,一时没有话可说。楼梯上一阵乱响,拥上几个酒客来:当头的是矮子,拥肿的圆脸;第二个是长的,在脸上很惹眼的显出一个红鼻子;此后还有人,一叠连的走得小楼都发抖。我转眼去看吕纬甫,他也正转眼来看我,我就叫堂倌算酒账。

"你借此还可以支持生活么?"我一面准备走,一面问。

"是的。——我每月有二十元,也不大能够敷衍。"

"那么,你以后豫备怎么办呢?"

"以后?——我不知道。你看我们那时豫想的事可有一件如意?我现在什么也不知道,连明天怎样也不知道,连后一分……"

---

① 《女儿经》:一种向妇女宣传封建礼教的通俗读物。版本较多,作者不一,较流行的有明代赵南星注刻本。

英汉对照
English-Chinese
中国文学宝库
Gems of Chinese Literature
现代文学系列
Modern Literature

In the Tavern

The waiter brought up the bill and handed it to me. Lü Weifu had abandoned his earlier formality. He just glanced at me, went on smoking, and allowed me to pay.

We left the tavern together, parting at the door because our hotels lay in opposite directions. As I walked back alone to my hotel, the cold wind buffeted my face with snowflakes, but I found this thoroughly refreshing. I saw that the sky, already dark, had interwoven with the houses and streets in the white, shifting web of thick snow.

February 16, 1924

堂倌送上账来,交给我;他也不像初到时候的谦虚了,只向我看了一眼,便吸烟,听凭我付了账。

我们一同走出店门,他所住的旅馆和我的方向正相反,就在门口分别了。我独自向着自己的旅馆走,寒风和雪片扑在脸上,倒觉得很爽快。见天色已是黄昏,和屋宇和街道都织在密雪的纯白而不定的罗网里。

一九二四年二月一六日。

英汉对照
English-Chinese
中国文学宝库
Gems of Chinese Literature
现代文学系列
Modern Literature

Regret for the Past
Juansheng's Notes

I want, if I can, to describe my remorse and grief for Zijun's sake as well as for my own. This shabby room, tucked away in a forgotten corner of the hostel, is so quiet and empty. Time really flies. A whole year has passed since I fell in love with Zijun, and, thanks to her, escaped from this dead quiet and emptiness. On my return, as ill luck would have it, this was the only room vacant. The broken window with the half dead locust tree and old wistaria outside and square table inside are the same as before. The same too are the mouldering wall and wooden bed beside it. At night I lie in bed alone just as I did before I started living with Zijun. The past year has been blotted out as if it had never been — as if I never moved out of this shabby room to set up a small home so hopefully in Jizhao Street.

Nor is that all. A year ago this silence and emptiness were different — there was often an expectancy about them. I was expecting Zijun's arrival. As I waited long and impatiently, the tapping of high heels on the brick pavement would galvanize me into life. Then I would see her pale round face dimpling in a smile, her thin white arms, striped cotton blouse and black skirt. And she would bring in a new leaf from the half withered locust tree outside the window for me to look at, or clusters of the mauve flowers that hung from the old wistaria tree, the trunk of which looked as if

伤 逝①
——涓生的手记

如果我能够,我要写下我的悔恨和悲哀,为子君,为自己。

会馆②里的被遗忘在偏僻里的破屋是这样地寂静和空虚。时光过得真快,我爱子君,仗着她逃出这寂静和空虚,已经满一年了。事情又这么不凑巧,我重来时,偏偏空着的又只有这一间屋。依然是这样的破窗,这样的窗外的半枯的槐树和老紫藤,这样的窗前的方桌,这样的败壁,这样的靠壁的板床。深夜中独自躺在床上,就如我未曾和子君同居以前一般,过去一年中的时光全被消灭,全未有过,我并没有曾经从这破屋子搬出,在吉兆胡同创立了满怀希望的小小的家庭。

不但如此。在一年之前,这寂静和空虚是并不这样的,常常含着期待;期待子君的到来。在久待的焦躁中,一听到皮鞋的高底尖触着砖路的清响,是怎样地使我骤然生动起来呵!于是就看见带着笑涡的苍白的圆脸,苍白的瘦的臂膊,布的有条纹的衫子,玄色的裙。她又带了窗外的半枯的槐树的新叶来,使我看见,还有挂

---

① 本篇在收入《彷徨》前未在报刊上发表过。
② 会馆:旧时都市同乡会或同业公会设立的馆舍,供同乡或同业旅居、聚会之用。

英汉对照
English-Chinese
中国文学宝库
Gems of Chinese Literature
现代文学系列
Modern Literature

made of iron.

But now there is only the old silence and emptiness. Zijun will not be coming again — never, never again.

In Zijun's absence, I could see nothing in this shabby room. Out of sheer boredom I would pick up a book — science or literature, it was all the same to me — and read on and on, till I realized I had turned a dozen pages without taking in a word I had read. Only my ears were so sensitive, I seemed able to hear all the footsteps outside the gate, those of among the rest. Her steps often sounded as if they were drawing nearer and nearer — only to grow fainter again, until they were lost in the tramping of other feet. I hated the servant's son who wore cloth-soled shoes which sounded quite different from Zijun's. I hated the young pansy next door who used face cream, who often wore new leather shoes, and whose steps sounded all too like Zijun's.

Could her rickshaw have been upset? Could she have been knocked over by a tram?...

I would be on the point of putting on my hat to go and see her, but her uncle had cursed me to my face.

Suddenly I would hear her coming nearer step by step, and by the time I was out to meet her she would already have passed the wistaria trellis, her face dimpling in a smile. Probably she wasn't badly treated after all in her uncle's home. I would calm down and, after we had gazed at each other in silence for a moment, the shabby room would be filled with the sound of my voice as I held forth on the tyranny of the home, the need to break with tradition, the equality of men and women, Ibsen, Tagore and Shelley... She

在铁似的老干上的一房一房的紫白的藤花。

然而现在呢,只有寂静和空虚依旧,子君却决不再来了,而且永远,永远地!……

子君不在我这破屋里时,我什么也看不见。在百无聊赖中,随手抓过一本书来,科学也好,文学也好,横竖什么都一样;看下去,看下去,忽而自己觉得,已经翻了十多页了,但是毫不记得书上所说的事。只是耳朵却分外地灵,仿佛听到大门外一切往来的履声,从中便有子君的,而且橐橐地逐渐临近,——但是,往往又逐渐渺茫,终于消失在别的步声的杂沓中了。我憎恶那不像子君鞋声的穿布底鞋的长班①的儿子,我憎恶那太像子君鞋声的常常穿着新皮鞋的邻院的搽雪花膏的小东西!

莫非她翻了车么?莫非她被电车撞伤了么?……

我便要取了帽子去看她,然而她的胞叔就曾经当面骂过我。

蓦然,她的鞋声近来了,一步响于一步,迎出去时,却已经走过紫藤棚下,脸上带着微笑的酒窝。她在她叔子的家里大约并未受气;我的心宁帖了,默默地相视片时之后,破屋里便渐渐充满了我的语声,谈家庭专制,谈打破旧习惯,

---

① 长班:旧时官员的随身仆人,也用来称呼一般的"听差"。

would nod her head, smiling, her eyes filled with a childlike look of wonder. On the wall was nailed a copperplate bust of Shelley, cut out from a magazine. It was one of the best likenesses of him, but when I pointed it out to her she only gave it a hasty glance, then hung her head as if in embarrassment. In matters like this, Zijun probably hadn't yet freed herself entirely from old ideas. It occurred to me later it might be better to substitute a picture of Shelley being drowned in the sea, or a portrait of Ibsen. But I never got round to it. And now even this picture has vanished.

"I'm my own mistress. None of them has any right to interfere with me."

She came out with this statement clearly, firmly and gravely, after a thoughtful silence — we had been talking about her uncle who was here and her father who was at home. We had then known each other for half a year. By that time I had told her all my views, all that had happened to me, and what my failings were. I had hidden very little, and she understood me completely. These few words of hers stirred me to the bottom of my heart, and rang in my ears for many days after. I was unspeakably happy to know that Chinese women were not as hopeless as the pessimists made out, and that we should see them in the not too distant future in all their glory.

Each time I saw her out, I always kept several paces behind her. And always the old man's face with its whiskers like fishy tentacles would be pressed so hard against the dirty windowpane, even the tip of his nose was flattened. While when we reached the outer

谈男女平等,谈伊孛生,谈泰戈尔,谈雪莱①……。她总是微笑点头,两眼里弥漫着稚气的好奇的光泽。壁上就钉着一张铜板的雪莱半身像,是从杂志上裁下来的,是他的最美的一张像。当我指给她看时,她却只草草一看,便低了头,似乎不好意思了。这些地方,子君就大概还未脱尽旧思想的束缚,——我后来也想,倒不如换一张雪莱淹死在海里的记念像或是伊孛生的罢;但也终于没有换,现在是连这一张也不知那里去了。

"我是我自己的,他们谁也没有干涉我的权利!"

这是我们交际了半年,又谈起她在这里的胞叔和在家的父亲时,她默想了一会之后,分明地,坚决地,沉静地说了出来的话。其时是我已经说尽了我的意见,我的身世,我的缺点,很少隐瞒;她也完全了解的了。这几句话很震动了我的灵魂,此后许多天还在耳中发响,而且说不出的狂喜,知道中国女性,并不如厌世家所说那样的无法可施,在不远的将来,便要看见辉煌的

---

① 伊孛生(H.Ibsen,1828—1906):通译易卜生,挪威剧作家。泰戈尔(R.Tagore,1861—1941),印度诗人。一九二四年曾来过我国。当时他的诗作译成中文的有《新月集》、《飞鸟集》等。雪莱(P.B.Shelley, 1792—1822),英国诗人。曾参加爱尔兰民族独立运动,因传播革命思想和争取婚姻自由屡遭迫害。后在海里覆舟淹死。他的《西风颂》、《云雀颂》等著名短诗,"五四"后被介绍到我国。

courtyard, against the bright glass window there was that little fellow's face, plastered with face cream. But walking out proudly, without looking right or left, Zijun did not see them. And I walked proudly back.

"I'm my own mistress. None of them has any right to interfere with me." Her mind was completely made up on this point. She was by far the more thoroughgoing and resolute of the two of us. What did she care about the half pot of face cream or the flattened nose tip?

I can't remember clearly now how I expressed my true, passionate love for her. Not only now — even just after it happened, my impression was very blurred. When I thought back at night, I could only remember snatches of what I had said; while during the month or two after we started living together, even these fragments vanished like a dream without a trace. I only remember how for about a fortnight beforehand I had reflected very carefully what attitude to adopt, prepared what to say, and decided what to do if I were refused. But when the time came it was all no use. In my nervousness, I unconsciously used the method I had seen in the movies. The memory of this makes me thoroughly ashamed, yet this is the one thing I remember clearly. Even today it is like a solitary lamp in a dark room, lighting me up as I clasped her hand with tears in my eyes, and went down on one knee...

I did not even see clearly how Zijun reacted at the time. All I know was that she accepted me. However, I seem to remember her face first turned pale then gradually flushed red — redder than I

曙色的。

　　送她出门,照例是相离十多步远;照例是那鲇鱼须的老东西的脸又紧贴在脏的窗玻璃上了,连鼻尖都挤成一个小平面;到外院,照例又是明晃晃的玻璃窗里的那小东西的脸,加厚的雪花膏。她目不邪视地骄傲地走了,没有看见;我骄傲地回来。

　　"我是我自己的,他们谁也没有干涉我的权利!"这彻底的思想就在她的脑里,比我还透澈,坚强得多。半瓶雪花膏和鼻尖的小平面,于她能算什么东西呢?

　　我已经记不清那时怎样地将我的纯真热烈的爱表示给她。岂但现在,那时的事后便已模胡,夜间回想,早只剩了一些断片了;同居以后一两月,便连这些断片也化作无可追踪的梦影。我只记得那时以前的十几天,曾经很仔细地研究过表示的态度,排列过措辞的先后,以及倘或遭了拒绝以后的情形。可是临时似乎都无用,在慌张中,身不由己地竟用了在电影上见过的方法了。后来一想到,就使我很愧恧,但在记忆上却偏只有这一点永远留遗,至今还如暗室的孤灯一般,照见我含泪握着她的手,一条腿跪了下去……。

　　不但我自己的,便是子君的言语举动,我那时就没有看得分明;仅知道她已经允许我了。但也还仿佛记得她脸色变成青白,后来又渐渐

英汉对照
English-Chinese
中国文学宝库
Gems of Chinese Literature
现代文学系列
Modern Literature

have ever seen it before or since. Sadness and joy flashed from her childlike eyes, mingled with apprehension, although she struggled to avoid my gaze, looking as if she would like to fly out of the window in her confusion. Then I knew she consented, although I didn't know what she said, or whether she said anything at all.

She, however, remembered everything. She could recite all that I said non-stop, as if she had learned it by heart; and describe all my actions in detail, to the life, like a film unfolding itself before my eyes, which included, naturally, that shallow scene from the movies which I was anxious to forget. At night, when all was still, it was our time for review. I was often questioned and examined, or ordered to retell all that had been said on that occasion; but she often had to fill up gaps and correct my mistakes, as if I were a Grade D student.

Gradually these reviews became few and far between. But whenever I saw her gazing raptly into space, a tender look coming over her and dimpling, I knew she was going over that old lesson again, and would be afraid she was seeing my ridiculous act from the movies. I knew, though, that she must have seen it, and that she insisted on seeing it.

But she didn't find it ridiculous. Though I thought it laughable, even contemptible, she didn't find it so at all. And I knew this was because she loved me so truly and passionately.

Late spring last year was our happiest and busiest time. I was calmer then, although one part of my mind became as active as my body. This was when we started going out together. We went

转作绯红,——没有见过,也没有再见的绯红;孩子似的眼里射出悲喜,但是夹着惊疑的光,虽然力避我的视线,张皇地似乎要破窗飞去。然而我知道她已经允许我了,没有知道她怎样说或是没有说。

她却是什么都记得:我的言辞,竟至于读熟了的一般,能够滔滔背诵;我的举动,就如有一张我所看不见的影片挂在眼下,叙述得如生,很细微,自然连那使我不愿再想的浅薄的电影的一闪。夜阑人静,是相对温习的时候了,我常是被质问,被考验,并且被命复述当时的言语,然而常须由她补足,由她纠正,像一个丁等的学生。

这温习后来也渐渐稀疏起来。但我只要看见她两眼注视空中,出神似的凝想着,于是神色越加柔和,笑窝也深下去,便知道她又在自修旧课了,只是我很怕她看到我那可笑的电影的一闪。但我又知道,她一定要看见,而且也非看不可的。

然而她并不觉得可笑。即使我自己以为可笑,甚而至于可鄙的,她也毫不以为可笑。这事我知道得很清楚,因为她爱我,是这样地热烈,这样地纯真。

去年的暮春是最为幸福,也是最为忙碌的时光。我的心平静下去了,但又有别一部分和身体一同忙碌起来。我们这时才在路上同行,

英汉对照
English-Chinese
中国文学宝库
Gems of Chinese Literature
现代文学系列
Modern Literature

several times to the park, but more often to look for lodgings. On the road I was conscious of searching looks, sarcastic smiles or lewd and contemptuous glances which tended, if I was not careful, to make me shiver. At every instant I had to summon all my pride and defiance to my support. She was quite fearless, however, and completely impervious to all this. She proceeded slowly forward, as calmly as if there were nobody in sight.

It was no easy matter finding lodgings. In most cases we were refused on some pretext, while some places we turned down as unsuitable. In the beginning we were very particular — and yet not too particular either, because we saw most of these lodgings did not look like places where we could live. Later on, all we asked was to be tolerated. We had looked at over twenty places, before we found one we could make do — two rooms facing north in a small house in Jizhao Street. The owner of the house was a small official, but an intelligent man, who only occupied the central and side rooms. His household consisted simply of a wife, a baby a few months old, and a maid from the country. As long as the child didn't cry, it would be very quiet.

Our furniture, simple as it was, had already taken the greater part of the money I had raised; and Zijun had sold her only gold ring and ear-rings too. I tried to stop her, but she insisted, so I didn't press the point. I knew, if she hadn't a share in our home, she would feel uncomfortable.

She had already quarrelled with her uncle — in fact he was so angry that he had disowned her. And I had broken with several friends who thought they were giving me good advice but were

也到过几回公园,最多的是寻住所。我觉得在路上时时遇到探索,讥笑,猥亵和轻蔑的眼光,一不小心,便使我的全身有些瑟缩,只得即刻提起我的骄傲和反抗来支持。她却是大无畏的,对于这些全不关心,只是镇静地缓缓前行,坦然如入无人之境。

寻住所实在不是容易事,大半是被托辞拒绝,小半是我们以为不相宜。起先我们选择得很苛酷,——也非苛酷,因为看去大抵不像是我们的安身之所;后来,便只要他们能相容了。看了二十多处,这才得到可以暂且敷衍的处所,是吉兆胡同一所小屋里的两间南屋;主人是一个小官,然而倒是明白人,自住着正屋和厢房。他只有夫人和一个不到周岁的女孩子,雇一个乡下的女工,只要孩子不啼哭,是极其安闲幽静的。

我们的家具很简单,但已经用去了我的筹来的款子的大半;子君还卖掉了她唯一的金戒指和耳环。我拦阻她,还是定要卖,我也就不再坚持下去了;我知道不给她加入一点股分去,她是住不舒服的。

和她的叔子,她早经闹开,至于使他气愤到不再认她做侄女;我也陆续和几个自以为忠告,

英汉对照
English-Chinese
中国文学宝库
Gems of Chinese Literature
现代文学系列
Modern Literature

actually either afraid for me, or jealous. Still, this meant we were very quiet. Although it was nearly dark when I left the office, and the rickshaw man went so slowly, the time always came when we were together again. First we would look at each other in silence, then relax and talk intimately, and finally fall silent again, bowing our heads without thinking of anything in particular. Gradually I was able to read her soberly like a book, body and soul. In a mere three weeks I learned much more about her, and broke down barriers which I had not known to exist, but now discovered had been real barriers.

As the days passed, Zijun became more lively. However, she didn't like flowers. I bought two pots of flowers at the fair, but after four days without watering they died neglected in a corner. I hadn't the time to see to everything. She had a liking for animals, though, which she may have picked up from the official's wife; and in less than a month our household was greatly increased. Four chicks of ours started picking their way across the courtyard with the landlady's dozen. But the two mistresses could tell them apart, each able to spot her own. Then there was a spotted dog, bought at the fair. I believe he had a name to begin with, but Zijun gave him a new one — Ahsui. And I called him Ahsui too, though I didn't like the name.

It is true that love must be constantly renewed, must grow and create. When I spoke of this to Zijun, she nodded understandingly.

Ah, what peaceful, happy evenings those were!

其实是替我胆怯,或者竟是嫉妒的朋友绝了交。然而这倒很清静。每日办公散后,虽然已近黄昏,车夫又一定走得这样慢,但究竟还有二人相对的时候。我们先是沉默的相视,接着是放怀而亲密的交谈,后来又是沉默。大家低头沉思着,却并未想着什么事。我也渐渐清醒地读遍了她的身体,她的灵魂,不过三星期,我似乎于她已经更加了解,揭去许多先前以为了解而现在看来却是隔膜,即所谓真的隔膜了。

子君也逐日活泼起来。但她并不爱花,我在庙会①时买来的两盆小草花,四天不浇,枯死在壁角了,我又没有照顾一切的闲暇。然而她爱动物,也许是从官太太那里传染的罢,不一月,我们的眷属便骤然加得很多,四只小油鸡,在小院子里和房主人的十多只在一同走。但她们却认识鸡的相貌,各知道那一只是自家的。还有一只花白的叭儿狗,从庙会买来,记得似乎原有名字,子君却给它另起了一个,叫作阿随。我就叫它阿随,但我不喜欢这名字。

这是真的,爱情必须时时更新,生长,创造。我和子君说起这,她也领会地点点头。

唉唉,那是怎样的宁静而幸福的夜呵!

---

① 庙会:又称"庙市",旧时在节日或规定的日子,设在寺庙或其附近的集市。

英汉对照
English-Chinese
中国文学宝库
Gems of Chinese Literature
现代文学系列
Modern Literature

Tranquillity and happiness must be consolidated, so that they may last for ever. When we were in the hostel, we had occasional differences of opinion or misunderstandings; but after we moved into Jizhao Street even these slight differences vanished. We just sat opposite each other in the lamplight, reminiscing, savouring again the joy of the new harmony which had followed our disputes.

Zijun grew plumper and her cheeks became rosier; the only pity was she was too busy. Her housekeeping left her no time even to chat, much less to read or go out for walks. We often said we would have to get a maid.

Another thing that upset me when I got back in the evening, was to see her try to hide a look of unhappiness or — and this depressed me even more — force a smile onto her face. Luckily I discovered this was owing to her secret feud with the petty official's wife, and the bone of contention was the chicks. But why wouldn't she tell me? People ought to have a home of their own. This was no place to live in.

I had my routine too. Six days of the week I went from home to the office and from the office home. In the office I sat at my desk endlessly copying official documents and letters. At home I kept her company or helped her light the stove, cook rice or steam bread. This was when I learned to cook.

Still, I ate much better than when I was in the hostel. Although cooking was not Zijun's strongest point, she threw herself into it heart and soul. Her ceaseless anxieties on this score made me anxious too, and in this way we shared the sweet and the bitter together. She kept at it so hard all day, perspiration made her short hair

安宁和幸福是要凝固的,永久是这样的安宁和幸福。我们在会馆里时,还偶有议论的冲突和意思的误会,自从到吉兆胡同以来,连这一点也没有了;我们只在灯下对坐的怀旧谭中,回味那时冲突以后的和解的重生一般的乐趣。

子君竟胖了起来,脸色也红活了;可惜的是忙。管了家务便连谈天的工夫也没有,何况读书和散步。我们常说,我们总还得雇一个女工。

这就使我也一样地不快活,傍晚回来,常见她包藏着不快活的颜色,尤其使我不乐的是她要装作勉强的笑容。幸而探听出来了,也还是和那小官太太的暗斗,导火线便是两家的小油鸡。但又何必硬不告诉我呢?人总该有一个独立的家庭。这样的处所,是不能居住的。

我的路也铸定了,每星期中的六天,是由家到局,又由局到家。在局里便坐在办公桌前钞,钞,钞些公文和信件;在家里是和她相对或帮她生白炉子,煮饭,蒸馒头。我的学会了煮饭,就在这时候。

但我的食品却比在会馆里时好得多了。做菜虽不是子君的特长,然而她于此却倾注着全力;对于她的日夜的操心,使我也不能不一同操心,来算作分甘共苦。况且她又这样地终日汗流满面,短发都粘在脑额上;两只手又只是这样

英汉对照
English-Chinese
中国文学宝库
Gems of Chinese Literature
现代文学系列
Modern Literature

stick to her head, and her hands grew rough.

And then she had to feed Ahsui and the chicks ... nobody else could do this.

I told her, I would rather not eat than see her work herself to the bone like this. She just gazed at me without a word, rather wistfully; and I couldn't very well say any more. But she went on working as hard as ever.

Finally the blow I had been expecting fell. The evening before the Double Tenth Festival, I was sitting idle while she was washing the dishes, when we heard a knock on the door. When I went to open it I found the messenger from our office who handed me a mimeographed slip of paper. I guessed what it was, and when I took it to the lamp, sure enough, it read:

> By order of the commissioner, Shi Juansheng is discharged.
> The Secretariat.
> October 9th.

I had foreseen this while we were still in the hostel. That Face Cream was one of the gambling friends of the commissioner's son. He was bound to spread rumours and try to make trouble. I was only surprised this hadn't happened sooner. In fact this was really no blow, because I had already decided I could work as a clerk somewhere else or teach, or, although it was a little more difficult, do some translation work. I knew the editor of *Freedom's Friend*,

地粗糙起来。

况且还要饲阿随,饲油鸡,……都是非她不可的工作。

我曾经忠告她:我不吃,倒也罢了;却万不可这样地操劳。她只看了我一眼,不开口,神色却似乎有点凄然;我也只好不开口。然而她还是这样地操劳。

我所豫期的打击果然到来。双十节的前一晚,我呆坐着,她在洗碗。听到打门声,我去开门时,是局里的信差,交给我一张油印的纸条。我就有些料到了,到灯下去一看,果然,印着的就是:

奉
局长谕史涓生着毋庸到局办事
秘书处启　十月九号

这在会馆里时,我就早已料到了;那雪花膏便是局长的儿子的赌友,一定要去添些谣言,设法报告的。到现在才发生效验,已经要算是很晚了。其实这在我不能算是一个打击,因为我早就决定,可以给别人去钞写,或者教读,或者虽然费力,也还可以译点书,况且《自由之友》

英汉对照
English-Chinese
中国文学宝库
Gems of Chinese Literature
现代文学系列
Modern Literature

and had corresponded with him a couple of months previously. But all the same, my heart was thumping. What distressed me most was that even Zijun, fearless as she was, had turned pale. Recently she seemed to have grown weaker.

"What does it matter?" she said. "We'll make a new start, won't we? We'll...."

She didn't finish, and her voice sounded flat. The lamplight seemed unusually dim. Humans are really laughable creatures, so easily upset by trifles. First we gazed at each other in silence, then started discussing what to do. Finally we decided to live as economically as possible on the money we had, to advertise in the paper for a post as clerk or teacher, and to write at the same time to the editor of *Freedom's Friend*, explaining my present situation and asking him to accept a translation to help me out of this difficulty.

"As good said as done! Let's make a fresh start."

I went straight to the table and pushed aside the bottle of vegetable oil and dish of vinegar, while Zijun brought over the dim lamp. First I drew up the advertisement; then I made a selection of books to translate. I hadn't looked at my books since we moved house, and each volume was thick with dust. Finally I wrote the letter.

I hesitated for a long time over the wording of the letter, and when I stopped writing to think, and glanced at her in the dusky lamplight, she was looking very wistful again. I had never imagined a trifle like this could cause such a striking change in someone so firm and fearless as Zijun. She really had grown much

的总编辑便是见过几次的熟人,两月前还通过信。但我的心却跳跃着。那么一个无畏的子君也变了色,尤其使我痛心;她近来似乎也较为怯弱了。

"那算什么。哼,我们干新的。我们……。"她说。

她的话没有说完;不知怎地,那声音在我听去却只是浮浮的;灯光也觉得格外黯淡。人们真是可笑的动物,一点极微末的小事情,便会受着很深的影响。我们先是默默地相视,逐渐商量起来,终于决定将现有的钱竭力节省,一面登"小广告"去寻求钞写和教读,一面写信给《自由之友》的总编辑,说明我目下的遭遇,请他收用我的译本,给我帮一点艰辛时候的忙。

"说做,就做罢!来开一条新的路!"

我立刻转身向了书案,推开盛香油的瓶子和醋碟,子君便送过那黯淡的灯来。我先拟广告;其次是选定可译的书,迁移以来未曾翻阅过,每本的头上都满漫着灰尘了;最后才写信。

我很费踌蹰,不知道怎样措辞好,当停笔凝思的时候,转眼去一瞥她的脸,在昏暗的灯光下,又很见得凄然。我真不料这样微细的小事情,竟会给坚决的,无畏的子君以这么显著的变

英汉对照
English-Chinese
中国文学宝库
Gems of Chinese Literature
现代文学系列
Modern Literature

weaker lately — it wasn't something that had just started that evening. This made me feel more put out. I had a sudden vision of a peaceful life — the quiet of my shabby room in the hostel flashed before my eyes, and I was just going to take a good look at it when I found myself back in the dusky lamplight again.

After a long time the letter was finished. It was very lengthy, and I was so tired after writing it, I realized I must have grown weaker myself lately too. We decided to send in the advertisement and post the letter the next day. Then with one accord we straightened up, silently, as if conscious of each other's fortitude and strength, and able to see new hope growing from this fresh beginning.

Actually, this blow from outside infused a new spirit into us. In the office I had lived like a wild bird in a cage, given just enough canary-seed by its captor to keep alive, but not to grow fat. And as time passed it would lose the use of its wings, so that if ever it were let out of the cage it could no longer fly. Now, at any rate, I had got out of the cage, and must soar anew in the wide sky before it was too late, while I could still flap my wings.

Of course we could not expect results from a small advertisement right away. However, translating is not so simple either. You read something and think you understand it, but when you come to translate it difficulties crop up everywhere, and it's very slow going. Still, I determined to do my best. In less than a fortnight, the edge of a fairly new dictionary was black with my finger-prints, which

化。她近来实在变得很怯弱了,但也并不是今夜才开始的。我的心因此更缭乱,忽然有安宁的生活的影像——会馆里的破屋的寂静,在眼前一闪,刚刚想定睛凝视,却又看见了昏暗的灯光。

许久之后,信也写成了,是一封颇长的信;很觉得疲劳,仿佛近来自己也较为怯弱了。于是我们决定,广告和发信,就在明日一同实行。大家不约而同地伸直了腰肢,在无言中,似乎又都感到彼此的坚忍崛强的精神,还看见从新萌芽起来的将来的希望。

外来的打击其实倒是振作了我们的新精神。局里的生活,原如鸟贩子手里的禽鸟一般,仅有一点小米维系残生,决不会肥胖;日子一久,只落得麻痹了翅子,即使放出笼外,早已不能奋飞。现在总算脱出这牢笼了,我从此要在新的开阔的天空中翱翔,趁我还未忘却了我的翅子的扇动。

小广告是一时自然不会发生效力的;但译书也不是容易事,先前看过,以为已经懂得的,一动手,却疑难百出了,进行得很慢。然而我决计努力地做,一本半新的字典,不到半月,边上便有了一大片乌黑的指痕,这就证明着我的工

英汉对照
English-Chinese
中国文学宝库
Gems of Chinese Literature
现代文学系列
Modern Literature

shows how seriously I took my work. The editor of *Freedom's Friend* had said that his magazine would never ignore a good manuscript.

Unfortunately, there was no room where I could be undisturbed, and Zijun was not as quiet or considerate as she had been. Our room was so cluttered up with dishes and bowls and filled with smoke it was impossible to work steadily there. But of course I had only myself to blame for this — it was my fault for not being able to afford a study. On top of this there was Ahsui and the chicks. And the chicks had grown into hens now, and were more of a bone of contention than ever between the two families.

Then there was the never-ending business of eating every day. All Zijun's efforts seemed to be devoted to our meals. One ate to earn, and earned to eat; while Ahsui and the hens had to be fed too. Apparently she had forgotten all she had ever learned, and did not realize that she was interrupting my train of thought when she called me to meals. And although I sometimes showed a little displeasure as I sat down, she paid no attention at all, just went on munching away quite unconcerned.

It took her five weeks to learn that my work could not be restricted by regular eating hours. When she did realize it she was probably annoyed, but she said nothing. After that my work did go forward faster, and soon I had translated 50,000 words. I had only to polish the manuscript, and it could be sent in with two short essays of my own to *Freedom's Friend*. Those meals were still a headache though. It didn't matter if the dishes were cold, but there wasn't enough of them. My appetite was much smaller than before, now that I was sitting at home all day using my brain, but even so there

作的切实。《自由之友》的总编辑曾经说过,他的刊物是决不会埋没好稿子的。

可惜的是我没有一间静室,子君又没有先前那么幽静,善于体帖了,屋子里总是散乱着碗碟,弥漫着煤烟,使人不能安心做事,但是这自然还只能怨我自己无力置一间书斋。然而又加以阿随,加以油鸡们。加以油鸡们又大起来了,更容易成为两家争吵的引线。

加以每日的"川流不息"的吃饭;子君的功业,仿佛就完全建立在这吃饭中。吃了筹钱,筹来吃饭,还要喂阿随,饲油鸡;她似乎将先前所知道的全都忘掉了,也不想到我的构思就常常为了这催促吃饭而打断。即使在坐中给看一点怒色,她总是不改变,仍然毫无感触似的大嚼起来。

使她明白了我的作工不能受规定的吃饭的束缚,就费去五星期。她明白之后,大约很不高兴罢,可是没有说。我的工作果然从此较为迅速地进行,不久就共译了五万言,只要润色一回,便可以和做好的两篇小品,一同寄给《自由之友》去。只是吃饭却依然给我苦恼。菜冷,是无妨的,然而竟不够;有时连饭也不够,虽然我因为终日坐在家里用脑,饭量已经比先前要减

英汉对照
English-Chinese
中国文学宝库
Gems of Chinese Literature
现代文学系列
Modern Literature

wasn't always even enough rice. It had been given to Ahsui, sometimes along with the mutton which I myself rarely had a chance of eating recently. She said Ahsui was so thin, it was really pathetic, and it made the landlady sneer at us. She couldn't stand being laughed at.

So there were only the hens to eat my left-overs. It was a long time before I realized this. I was very conscious, however, that my "place in the universe," as Huxley describes it, was only somewhere between the dog and the hens.

Later on, after much argument and insistence, the hens started appearing on our table, and we and Ahsui were able to enjoy them for over the days. They were very thin, though, because for a long time they had only been fed a few grains of *gaoliang* a day. After that life became much more peaceful. Only Zijun was very dispirited, and seemed so sad and bored without them, she grew rather sulky. How easily people change!

However, Ahsui too would have to be given up. We had stopped hoping for a letter from anywhere, and for a long time Zijun had had no food left to get the dog to beg or stand on his hind legs. Besides, winter was coming on very fast, and we didn't know what to do about a stove. His appetite had long been a heavy liability, of which we were all too conscious. So even the dog had to go.

If we had tied a tag to him and taken him to the market to sell, we might have made a few coppers. But neither of us could bring ourselves to do this.

Finally I muffled his head in a cloth and took him outside the West Gate where I let him loose. When he ran after me, I pushed

少得多。这是先去喂了阿随了,有时还并那近来连自己也轻易不吃的羊肉。她说,阿随实在瘦得太可怜,房东太太还因此嗤笑我们了,她受不住这样的奚落。

于是吃我残饭的便只有油鸡们。这是我积久才看出来的,但同时也如赫胥黎① 的论定"人类在宇宙间的位置"一般,自觉了我在这里的位置:不过是叭儿狗和油鸡之间。

后来,经多次的抗争和催逼,油鸡们也逐渐成为肴馔,我们和阿随都享用了十多日的鲜肥;可是其实都很瘦,因为它们早已每日只能得到几粒高粱了。从此便清静得多。只有子君很颓唐,似乎常觉得凄苦和无聊,至于不大愿意开口。我想,人是多么容易改变呵!

但是阿随也将留不住了。我们已经不能再希望从什么地方会有来信,子君也早没有一点食物可以引它打拱或直立起来。冬季又逼近得这么快,火炉就要成为很大的问题;它的食量,在我们其实早是一个极易觉得的很重的负担。于是连它也留不住了。

倘使插了草标② 到庙市去出卖,也许能得几文钱罢,然而我们都不能,也不愿这样做。终于是用包袱蒙着头,由我带到西郊去放掉了,还

---

① 赫胥黎 (T. Huxley, 1825—1895):英国生物学家。他的《人类在宇庙间的位置》(今译《人类在自然界的位置》),是宣传达尔文的进化论的重要著作。

② 草标:旧时在被卖的人身或物品上插置的草标,作为出卖的标志。

英汉对照
English-Chinese
中国文学宝库
Gems of Chinese Literature
现代文学系列
Modern Literature

him into a pit that wasn't too deep.

When I got home, I found it more peaceful; but I was quite taken aback by Zijun's tragic expression. I had never seen her so woebegone. Of course, it was because of Ahsui, but why take it so to heart? And I hadn't told her about pushing him into the pit.

That night, something icy crept into her expression too.

"Really!" I couldn't help saying. "What's got into you today, Zijun?"

"What?" She didn't even look at me.

"You look so..."

"It's nothing — nothing at all."

Eventually I realized she must consider me callous. Actually, when I was on my own I had got along very well, although I was too proud to mix much with family acquaintances. But since my move I had become estranged from all my old friends. Still, if I could only get away from all this, there were plenty of ways open to me. Now I had to put up with all these hardships mainly because of her sake — getting rid of Ahsui was a case in point. But Zijun seemed too obtuse now even to understand that.

When I took an opportunity to hint this to her, she nodded as if she understood. But judging by her later behaviour, she either didn't take it in or else didn't believe me.

The cold weather and her cold looks made it impossible for me to be comfortable at home. But where could I go? I could get away from her icy looks in the street and parks, but the cold wind outside just whistled through you. Finally I found a haven in the

要追上来,便推在一个并不很深的土坑里。

我一回寓,觉得又清静得多多了;但子君的凄惨的神色,却使我很吃惊。那是没有见过的神色,自然是为阿随。但又何至于此呢?我还没有说起推在土坑里的事。

到夜间,在她的凄惨的神色中,加上冰冷的分子了。

"奇怪。——子君,你怎么今天这样儿了?"我忍不住问。

"什么?"她连看也不看我。

"你的脸色……。"

"没有什么,——什么也没有。"

我终于从她言动上看出,她大概已经认定我是一个忍心的人。其实,我一个人,是容易生活的,虽然因为骄傲,向来不与世交来往,迁居以后,也疏远了所有旧识的人,然而只要能远走高飞,生路还宽广得很。现在忍受着这生活压迫的苦痛,大半倒是为她,便是放掉阿随,也何尝不如此。但子君的识见却似乎只是浅薄起来,竟至于连这一点也想不到了。

我拣了一个机会,将这些道理暗示她;她领会似的点头。然而看她后来的情形,她是没有懂,或者是并不相信的。

天气的冷和神情的冷,逼迫我不能在家庭中安身。但是往那里去呢?大道上,公园里,虽然没有冰冷的神情,冷风究竟也刺得人皮肤欲裂。我终于在通俗图书馆里觅得了我的天堂。

英汉对照
English-Chinese
中国文学宝库
Gems of Chinese Literature
现代文学系列
Modern Literature

303

public library.

Admission was free, and there were two stoves in the reading room. Although the fire was very low, the mere sight of the stoves made one warm. There were no books worth reading: the old ones were out of date, and there were practically no new ones.

But I didn't go there to read. There were usually a few other people there, sometimes as many as a dozen, all thinly clad like me. We kept up a pretence of reading, in order to keep out of the cold. This suited me down to the ground. You were liable to meet people you knew on the road who would glance at you contemptuously, but here there was no trouble of that kind, because my acquaintances were all gathered round other stoves or warming themselves at the stoves in their own homes.

Although there were no books for me to read there, I found quiet in which to think. As I sat there alone thinking over the past, I felt that during the last half year for love — blind love — I had neglected all the important things in life. First and foremost, livelihood. A man must make a living before there can be any place for love. There must be a way out for those who struggle, and I hadn't yet forgotten how to flap my wings, though I was much weaker than before...

The room and the readers gradually faded. I saw fishermen in the angry sea, soldiers in the trenches, dignitaries in their cars, speculators at the stock exchange, heroes in mountain forests, teachers on their platforms, night prowlers, thieves in the dark... Zijun was far away. She had lost all her courage in her resentment over Ahsui and absorption in her cooking. The strange thing was

那里无须买票；阅书室里又装着两个铁火炉。纵使不过是烧着不死不活的煤的火炉，但单是看见装着它，精神上也就总觉得有些温暖。书却无可看：旧的陈腐，新的是几乎没有的。

好在我到那里去也并非为看书。另外时常还有几个人，多则十余人，都是单薄衣裳，正如我，各人看各人的书，作为取暖的口实。这于我尤为合式。道路上容易遇见熟人，得到轻蔑的一瞥，但此地却决无那样的横祸，因为他们是永远围在别的铁炉旁，或者靠在自家的白炉边的。

那里虽然没有书给我看，却还有安闲容得我想。待到孤身枯坐，回忆从前，这才觉得大半年来，只为了爱，——盲目的爱，——而将别的人生的要义全盘疏忽了。第一，便是生活。人必生活着，爱才有所附丽。世界上并非没有为了奋斗者而开的活路；我也还未忘却翅子的扇动，虽然比先前已经颓唐得多……。

屋子和读者渐渐消失了，我看见怒涛中的渔夫，战壕中的兵士，摩托车①中的贵人，洋场上的投机家，深山密林中的豪杰，讲台上的教授，昏夜的运动者和深夜的偷儿……。子君，——不在近旁。她的勇气都失掉了，只为着阿随悲愤，为着做饭出神；然而奇怪的是倒也并

---

① 摩托车：当时对小汽车的称呼。

英汉对照
English-Chinese
中国文学宝库
Gems of Chinese Literature
现代文学系列
Modern Literature

that she didn't look particularly thin...

It grew colder. The few lumps of slow-burning hard coal in the stove had at last burnt out, and it was closing time. I had to go back to Jizhao Street, to expose myself to that icy look. Of late I had sometimes been met with warmth, but this only upset me more. I remember one evening, from Zijun's eyes flashed the childlike look I had not seen for so long, as she reminded me with a smile of something that had happened at the hostel. But there was a constant look of fear in her eyes too. The fact that I had treated her more coldly recently than she had me worried her. Sometimes I forced myself to talk and laugh to comfort her. But the emptiness of my laughter and speech, and the way it immediately re-echoed in my ears like a hateful sneer, was more than I could bear.

Zijun may have felt it too, for after this she lost her wooden calm and, though she tried her best to hide it, often showed anxiety. She treated me, however, much more tenderly.

I wanted to speak to her plainly, but hadn't the courage. Whenever I made up my mind to speak, the sight of those childlike eyes compelled me, for the time being, to smile. But my smile turned straightway into a sneer at myself, and made me lose my cold composure.

After that she revived the old questions and started new tests, forcing me to give all sorts of hypocritical answers to show my affection for her. Hypocrisy became branded on my heart, so filling it with falseness it was hard to breathe. I often felt, in my depression,

不怎样瘦损……。

　　冷了起来,火炉里的不死不活的的几片硬煤,也终于烧尽了,已是闭馆的时候。又须回到吉兆胡同,领略冰冷的颜色去了。近来也间或遇到温暖的神情,但这却反而增加我的苦痛。记得有一夜,子君的眼里忽而又发出久已不见的稚气的光来,笑着和我谈到还在会馆时候的情形,时时又很带些恐怖的神色。我知道我近来的超过她的冷漠,已经引起她的忧疑来,只得也勉力谈笑,想给她一点慰藉。然而我的笑貌一上脸,我的话一出口,却即刻变为空虚,这空虚又即刻发生反响,回向我的耳目里,给我一个难堪的恶毒的冷嘲。

　　子君似乎也觉得的,从此便失掉了她往常的麻木似的镇静,虽然竭力掩饰,总还是时时露出忧疑的神色来,但对我却温和得多了。

　　我要明告她,但我还没有敢,当决心要说的时候,看见她孩子一般的眼色,就使我只得暂且改作勉强的欢容。但是这又即刻来冷嘲我,并使我失却那冷漠的镇静。

　　她从此又开始了往事的温习和新的考验,逼我做出许多虚伪的温存的答案来,将温存示给她,虚伪的草稿便写在自己的心上。我的心渐被这些草稿填满了,常觉得难于呼吸。我在

英汉对照
English-Chinese
中国文学宝库
Gems of Chinese Literature
现代文学系列
Modern Literature

that really great courage was needed to tell the truth; for a man who lacked courage and reconciled himself to hypocrisy would never find a new path. What's more, he just could not exist.

Then Zijun started looking resentful. This happened for the first time one morning, one bitterly cold morning, or so I imagined. I smiled secretly to myself with cold indignation. All the ideas and intelligent, fearless phrases she had learnt were empty after all. Yet she did not realize this emptiness. She had given up reading long ago, and did not realize the first thing in life is to make a living, that to do this people must advance hand in hand, or go forward singly. All she could do was cling to someone else's clothing, making it difficult even for a fighter to struggle, and bringing ruin on both.

I felt that our only hope lay in parting. She ought to make a clean break. Suddenly I thought of her death, but immediately was ashamed and reproached myself. Happily it was morning, and there was plenty of time for me to tell her the truth. Whether or not we could make a fresh start depended on this.

I deliberately brought up the past. I spoke of literature, then of foreign authors and their works, of Ibsen's *Nora* and *The Woman of the Sea*. I praised Nora for being strong-minded... All this had been said the previous year in the shabby room in the hostel, but now it rang hollow. As the words left my mouth I could not free myself from the suspicion that there was an unseen urchin behind me maliciously parroting all I said.

She listened, nodding in agreement, then was silent. I finished what I had to say abruptly, and my voice died away in the

苦恼中常常想,说真实自然须有极大的勇气的;假如没有这勇气,而苟安于虚伪,那也便是不能开辟新的生路的人。不独不是这个,连这人也未尝有!

子君有怨色,在早晨,极冷的早晨,这是从未见过的,但也许是从我看来的怨色。我那时冷冷地气愤和暗笑了;她所磨练的思想和豁达无畏的言论,到底也还是一个空虚,而对于这空虚却并未自觉。她早已什么书也不看,已不知道人的生活的第一着是求生,向着这求生的道路,是必须携手同行,或奋身孤往的了,倘使只知道捶着一个人的衣角,那便是虽战士也难于战斗,只得一同灭亡。

我觉得新的希望就只在我们的分离;她应该决然舍去,——我也突然想到她的死,然而立刻自责,忏悔了。幸而是早晨,时间正多,我可以说我的真实。我们的新的道路的开辟,便在这一遭。

我和她闲谈,故意地引起我们的往事,提到文艺,于是涉及外国的文人,文人的作品:《诺拉》,《海的女人》①。称扬诺拉的果决……。也还是去年在会馆的破屋里讲过的那些话,但现在已经变成空虚,从我的嘴传入自己的耳中,时时疑心有一个隐形的坏孩子,在背后恶意地刻毒地学舌。

她还是点头答应着倾听,后来沉默了。我

---

① 《诺拉》:通译《娜拉》(又译作《玩偶之家》);《海的女人》,通译《海的夫人》。都是易卜生的著名剧作。

英汉对照
English-Chinese
中国文学宝库
Gems of Chinese Literature
现代文学系列
Modern Literature

309

emptiness.

"Yes," she said after another silence, "but ... Juansheng, I feel you've changed a lot lately. Is it true? Tell me!"

This was a blow, but I took a grip on myself, and explained my views and proposals: make a fresh start and turn over a new leaf, to avoid being ruined together.

To clinch the matter, I said firmly:

"...Besides, you need have no more scruples but go boldly ahead. You asked me to tell the truth. Yes, we shouldn't be hypocritical. Well, to tell the truth — it's because I don't love you any more! Actually, this makes it better for you, because it'll be easier for you to work without any regret...."

I was expecting a scene, but all that followed was silence. Her face turned ashy pale, like a corpse; but in a moment her colour came back, and that childlike look darted from her eyes. She looked all round, like a hungry child searching for its kind mother, but only looked into space. She fearfully avoided my eyes.

The sight was more than I could stand. Fortunately it was still early. I braved the cold wind to hurry to the library.

There I saw *Freedom's Friend*, with all my short articles in it. This took me by surprise, and seemed to bring me new life. "There are plenty of ways open to me," I thought. "But things can't go on like this."

I started calling on old friends with whom I had had nothing to do for a long time, but didn't go more than once or twice. Naturally, their rooms were warm, but I felt chilled to the marrow there. And in the evenings I huddled in a room colder than ice.

也就断续地说完了我的话,连余音都消失在虚空中了。

"是的。"她又沉默了一会,说,"但是,……涓生,我觉得你近来很两样了。可是的?你,——你老实告诉我。"

我觉得这似乎给了我当头一击,但也立即定了神,说出我的意见和主张来:新的路的开辟,新的生活的再造,为的是免得一同灭亡。

临末,我用了十分的决心,加上这几句话:

"……况且你已经可以无须顾虑,勇往直前了。你要我老实说;是的,人是不该虚伪的。我老实说罢:因为,因为我已经不爱你了!但这于你倒好得多,因为你更可以毫无挂念地做事……。"

我同时豫期着大的变故的到来,然而只有沉默。她脸色陡然变成灰黄,死了似的;瞬间便又苏生,眼里也发了稚气的闪闪的光泽。这眼光射向四处,正如孩子在饥渴中寻求着慈爱的母亲,但只在空中寻求,恐怖地回避着我的眼。我不能看下去了,幸而是早晨,我冒着寒风径奔通俗图书馆。

在那里看见《自由之友》,我的小品文都登出了。这使我一惊,仿佛得了一点生气。我想,生活的路还很多,——但是,现在这样也还是不行的。

我开始去访问久已不相闻问的熟人,但这也不过一两次;他们的屋子自然是暖和的,我在骨髓中却觉得寒冽。夜间,便蜷伏在比冰还冷的冷屋中。

An icy needle was piercing my heart, making me suffer continually from numb wretchedness. "There are plenty of ways open to me," I thought. "I haven't forgotten how to flap my wings." Suddenly I thought of her death, but immediately was ashamed and reproached myself.

In the library I often saw like a flash a new path ahead of me. I imagined she had faced up bravely to the facts and boldly left this icy home. Left it, what was more, without any malice towards me. Then I felt light as a cloud floating in the void, with the blue sky above and high mountains and great oceans below, big buildings and skyscrapers, battlefields, motorcars, thoroughfares, rich men's houses, bright, bustling markets and the dark night...

What's more, I really felt this new life was just round the corner.

Somehow we managed to live through the bitter Peking winter. But we were like dragonflies that had fallen into the hands of mischievous imps, to be tied with threads and played with and tormented at will. Although we had come through alive, we were prostrate, and the end was only a matter of time.

Three letters had been sent to the editor of *Freedom's Friend* before he replied. The envelope contained two book tokens, one for twenty cents, one for thirty cents. But I had spent nine cents on postage to press for payment, and gone hungry for a whole day, all for nothing.

However, I felt that at last I had got what I expected.

冰的针刺着我的灵魂,使我永远苦于麻木的疼痛。生活的路还很多,我也还没有忘却翅子的扇动,我想。——我突然想到她的死,然而立刻自责,忏悔了。

在通俗图书馆里往往瞥见一闪的光明,新的生路横在前面。她勇猛地觉悟了,毅然走出这冰冷的家,而且,——毫无怨恨的神色。我便轻如行云,漂浮空际,上有蔚蓝的天,下是深山大海,广厦高楼,战场,摩托车,洋场,公馆,晴明的闹市,黑暗的夜……。

而且,真的,我豫感得这新生面便要来到了。

我们总算度过了极难忍受的冬天,这北京的冬天;就如蜻蜓落在恶作剧的坏孩子的手里一般,被系着细线,尽情玩弄,虐待,虽然幸而没有送掉性命,结果也还是躺在地上,只争着一个迟早之间。

写给《自由之友》的总编辑已经有三封信,这才得到回信,信封里只有两张书券①:两角的和三角的。我却单是催,就用了九分的邮票,一天的饥饿,又都白挨给于己一无所得的空虚了。

然而觉得要来的事,却终于来到了。

---

① 书券:购书用的代价券,可按券面金额到指定书店选购。旧时有的报刊用它代替现金支付稿酬。

英汉对照
English-Chinese
中国文学宝库
Gems of Chinese Literature
现代文学系列
Modern Literature

Winter was giving place to spring, and the wind was not quite so icy now. I spent more time wandering outside, and did not generally get home till dusk. One dark evening, I came home listlessly as usual and, as usual, grew so depressed at the sight of our gate that I slowed down. Eventually, however, I reached my room. It was dark inside, and as I groped for the matches to strike a light, the place seemed extraordinarily quiet and empty.

I was standing there in bewilderment, when the official's wife called to me through the window.

"Zijun's father came today," she said simply, "and took her away."

This was not what I had expected. I felt as if hit on the back of the head, and stood speechless.

"She went?" I finally managed to ask.

"Yes."

"Did — did she say anything?"

"No. Just asked me to tell you when you came back that she had gone."

I couldn't believe it; yet the room was so extraordinarily quiet and empty. I looked everywhere for Zijun, but all I could see was the old, discoloured furniture which appeared very scattered, to show that it was incapable of hiding anyone or anything. It occurred to me she might have left a letter or at least jotted down a few words, but no. Only salt, dried paprika, flour and half a cabbage had been placed together, with a few dozen coppers at the side. These were all our worldly goods and now she had carefully left all this to me, bidding me without words to use this to eke out

这是冬春之交的事,风已没有这么冷,我也更久地在外面徘徊;待到回家,大概已经昏黑。就在这样一个昏黑的晚上,我照常没精打采地回来,一看见寓所的门,也照常更加丧气,使脚步放得更缓。但终于走进自己的屋子里了,没有灯火;摸火柴点起来时,是异样的寂寞和空虚!

正在错愕中,官太太便到窗外来叫我出去。

"今天子君的父亲来到这里,将她接回去了。"她很简单地说。

这似乎又不是意料中的事,我便如脑后受了一击,无言地站着。

"她去了么?"过了些时,我只问出这样一句话。

"她去了。"

"她,——她可说什么?"

"没说什么。单是托我见你回来时告诉你,说她去了。"

我不信;但是屋子里是异样的寂寞和空虚。我遍看各处,寻觅子君;只见几件破旧而黯淡的家具,都显得极其清疏,在证明着它们毫无隐匿一人一物的能力。我转念寻信或她留下的字迹,也没有;只是盐和干辣椒,面粉,半株白菜,却聚集在一处了,旁边还有几十枚铜元。这是我们两人生活材料的全副,现在她就郑重地将这留给我一个人,在不言中,教我借此去维持较

英汉对照
English-Chinese
中国文学宝库
Gems of Chinese Literature
现代文学系列
Modern Literature

315

my existence a little longer.

Feeling my surroundings pressing in on me, I hurried out to the middle of the courtyard, where all around was dark. Bright lamplight showed on the window paper of the central rooms, where they were teasing the baby to make her laugh. My heart grew calmer, and I began to glimpse a way out of this heavy oppression: high mountains and great marshlands, thoroughfares, brightly lit feasts, trenches, pitch-black night, the thrust of a sharp knife, noiseless footsteps...

I relaxed, thought about travelling expenses, and sighed.

I conjured up a picture of my future as I lay with closed eyes, but before the night was half over it had vanished. In the gloom I suddenly seemed to see a pile of groceries, then Zijun's ashen face appeared to gaze at me beseechingly with childlike eyes. But as soon as I took a grip on myself, there was nothing there.

However, my heart still felt heavy. Why couldn't I have waited a few days instead of blurting out the truth like that to her? Now she knew all that was left to her was the passionate sternness of her father — who was as heartless as a creditor with his children — and the icy cold looks of bystanders. Apart from this there was only emptiness. How terrible to bear the heavy burden of emptiness, treading out one's life amid sternness and cold looks! And at the end not even a tombstone to your grave!

I shouldn't have told Zijun the truth. Since we had loved each other, I should have gone on lying to her. If truth is a treasure, it shouldn't have proved such a heavy burden of emptiness to Zijun.

久的生活。

我似乎被周围所排挤,奔到院子中间,有昏黑在我的周围;正屋的纸窗上映出明亮的灯光,他们正在逗着孩子玩笑。我的心也沉静下来,觉得在沉重的迫压中,渐渐隐约地现出脱走的路径:深山大泽,洋场,电灯下的盛筵,壕沟,最黑最黑的深夜,利刃的一击,毫无声响的脚步……。

心地有些轻松,舒展了,想到旅费,并且嘘一口气。

躺着,在合着的眼前经过的豫想的前途,不到半夜已经现尽;暗中忽然仿佛看见一堆食物,这之后,便浮出一个子君的灰黄的脸来,睁了孩子气的眼睛,恳托似的看着我。我一定神,什么也没有了。

但我的心却又觉得沉重。我为什么偏不忍耐几天,要这样急急地告诉她真话的呢?现在她知道,她以后所有的只是她父亲——儿女的债主——的烈日一般的严威和旁人的赛过冰霜的冷眼。此外便是虚空。负着虚空的重担,在严威和冷眼中走着所谓人生的路,这是怎么可怕的事呵!而况这路的尽头,又不过是——连墓碑也没有的坟墓。

我不应该将真实说给子君,我们相爱过,我应该永久奉献她我的说谎。如果真实可以宝贵,这在子君就不该是一个沉重的空虚。谎语

英汉对照
English-Chinese
中国文学宝库
Gems of Chinese Literature
现代文学系列
Modern Literature

Of course, lies are empty too, but at least they wouldn't have proved so crushing a burden in the end.

I thought if I told Zijun the truth, she could go forward boldly without scruples, just as when we started living together. But I must have been wrong. Her fearlessness then was owing to love.

I hadn't the courage to shoulder the heavy burden of hypocrisy, so I thrust the burden of the truth onto her. Because she had loved me, she had to bear this heavy burden, amid sternness and cold glances to the end of her days.

I had thought of her death... I realized I was a weakling. I deserved to be cast out by the strong, no matter whether they were truthful or hypocritical. Yet she, from first to last, had hoped that I could live longer...

I wanted to leave Jizhao Street; it was too empty and lonely here. I thought, if once I could get away, it would be as if Zijun were still at my side. Or at least as if she were still in town, and might drop in on me any time, as she had when I lived in the hostel.

However, all my letters went unanswered, as did my applications to friends to find me a post. There was nothing for it but to go to see a family acquaintance I hadn't visited for a long time. This was an old classmate of my uncle's, a highly respected senior licentiate, who had lived in Peking for many years and had a wide circle of acquaintances.

The gatekeeper stared at me scornfully — no doubt because my clothes were shabby — and only with difficulty was I admitted. My

当然也是一个空虚,然而临末,至多也不过这样地沉重。

我以为将真实说给子君,她便可以毫无顾虑,坚决地毅然前行,一如我们将要同居时那样。但这恐怕是我错了。她当时的勇敢和无畏是因为爱。

我没有负着虚伪的重担的勇气,却将真实的重担卸给她了。她爱我之后,就要负了这重担,在严威和冷眼中走着所谓人生的路。

我想到她的死……。我看见我是一个卑怯者,应该被摈于强有力的人们,无论是真实者,虚伪者。然而她却自始至终,还希望我维持较久的生活……。

我要离开吉兆胡同,在这里是异样的空虚和寂寞。我想,只要离开这里,子君便如还在我的身边;至少,也如还在城中,有一天,将要出乎意表地访我,像住在会馆时候似的。

然而一切请托和书信,都是一无反响;我不得已,只好访问一个久不问候的世交去了。他是我伯父的幼年的同窗,以正经出名的拔贡①,寓京很久,交游也广阔的。

大概因为衣服的破旧罢,一登门便很遭门房的白眼。好容易才相见,也还相识,但是很冷

---

① 拔贡:清代科举考试制度:在规定的年限(原定六年,后改为十二年)选拔"文行兼优"的秀才,保送到京师,贡入国子监,称为"拔贡"。是贡生的一种。

英汉对照
English-Chinese
中国文学宝库
Gems of Chinese Literature
现代文学系列
Modern Literature

uncle's friend still remembered me, but treated me very coldly. He knew all about us.

"Obviously, you can't stay here," he said coldly, after I asked him to recommend me to a job somewhere else. "But where will you go? It's extremely difficult. That — er — that friend of yours, Zijun, I suppose you know, is dead."

I was dumbfounded.

"Are you sure?" I finally blurted out.

He gave an artificial laugh. "Of course I am. My servant Wang Sheng comes from the same village as her family."

"But — how did she die?"

"Who knows? At any rate, she's dead."

I have forgotten how I took my leave and went home. I knew he wouldn't tell a lie. Zijun would never be with me again, as she had last year. Although she wanted to bear the burden of emptiness amid sternness and cold glances till the end of her days, it had been too much for her. Fate had decided that she should die knowing the truth I had told her — die unloved!

Obviously, I could not stay there. But where could I go?

All around was a great void, quiet as death. I seemed to see the darkness before the eyes of every single person who died unloved, and to hear all the bitter and despairing cries of their struggle.

I was waiting for something new, something nameless and unexpected. But day after day passed in the same deadly quiet.

I went out now much less than before, sitting or lying in this great void, allowing this deathly quiet to eat away my soul. Sometimes the

落。我们的往事,他全都知道了。

"自然,你也不能在这里了,"他听了我托他在别处觅事之后,冷冷地说,"但那里去呢?很难。——你那,什么呢,你的朋友罢,子君,你可知道,她死了。"

我惊得没有话。

"真的?"我终于不自觉地问。

"哈哈。自然真的。我家的王升的家,就和她家同村。"

"但是,——不知道是怎么死的?"

"谁知道呢。总之是死了就是了。"

我已经忘却了怎样辞别他,回到自己的寓所。我知道他是不说谎话的;子君总不会再来的了,像去年那样。她虽是想在严威和冷眼中负着虚空的重担来走所谓人生的路,也已经不能。她的命运,已经决定她在我所给与的真实——无爱的人间死灭了!

自然,我不能在这里了;但是,"那里去呢?"

四围是广大的空虚,还有死的寂静。死于无爱的人们的眼前的黑暗,我仿佛一一看见,还听得一切苦闷和绝望的挣扎的声音。

我还期待着新的东西到来,无名的,意外的。但一天一天,无非是死的寂静。

我比先前已经不大出门,只坐卧在广大的空虚里,一任这死的寂静侵蚀着我的灵魂。死

英汉对照
English-Chinese
中国文学宝库
Gems of Chinese Literature
现代文学系列
Modern Literature

silence itself seemed afraid, seemed to recoil. And at such times there would flash up nameless, unexpected, new hope.

One overcast morning, when the sun was unable to struggle out from behind the clouds and the very air was tired, the patter of tiny feet and a snuffling sound made me open my eyes. A glance round the room revealed nothing, but when I looked down I saw a small creature pattering around — thin, covered with dust, more dead than alive...

When I looked harder, my heart missed a beat. I jumped up.

It was Ahsui. He had come back.

I left Jizhao Street not just because of the cold glances of my landlord and the maid, but largely on account of Ahsui. However, where could I go? I realized, naturally, there were many ways open to me, and sometimes seemed to see them stretching before me. I didn't know, though, how to take the first step.

After much deliberation, I decided the hostel was the only place where I could put up. Here is the same shabby room as before, the same wooden bed, half dead locust tree and wistaria. But what gave me love and life, hope and happiness before has vanished. There is nothing but emptiness, the empty existence I exchanged for the truth.

There are many ways open to me, and I must take one of them because I am still living. I still don't know, though, how to take the first step. Sometimes the road seems like a great, grey serpent, writhing and darting at me. I wait and wait and watch it approach, but it always disappears suddenly in the darkness.

The early spring nights are as long as ever. I sit idly for a long time and recall a funeral procession I saw on the street this morning. There

的寂静有时也自己战栗,自己退藏,于是在这绝续之交,便闪出无名的,意外的,新的期待。

一天是阴沉的上午,太阳还不能从云里面挣扎出来,连空气都疲乏着。耳中听到细碎的步声和咻咻的鼻息,使我睁开眼。大致一看,屋子里还是空虚;但偶然看到地面,却盘旋着一匹小小的动物,瘦弱的,半死的,满身灰土的……。

我一细看,我的心就一停,接着便直跳起来。

那是阿随。它回来了。

我的离开吉兆胡同,也不单是为了房主人们和他家女工的冷眼,大半就为着这阿随。但是,"那里去呢?"新的生路自然还很多,我约略知道,也间或依稀看见,觉得就在我面前,然而我还没有知道跨进那里去的第一步的方法。

经过许多回的思量和比较,也还只有会馆是还能相容的地方。依然是这样的破屋,这样的板床,这样的半枯的槐树和紫藤,但那时使我希望,欢欣,爱,生活的,却全都逝去了,只有一个虚空,我用真实去换来的虚空存在。

新的生路还很多,我必须跨进去,因为我还活着。但我还不知道怎样跨出那第一步。有时,仿佛看见那生路就像一条灰白的长蛇,自己蜿蜒地向我奔来,我等着,等着,看看临近,但忽然便消失在黑暗里了。

初春的夜,还是那么长。长久的枯坐中记起上午在街头所见的葬式,前面是纸人纸马,后

were paper figures and paper horses in front, and behind crying that sounded like a lilt. I see how clever they are — this is so simple.

Then Zijun's funeral springs to my mind. She bore the heavy burden of emptiness alone, advancing down the long grey road, only to be swallowed up amid sternness and cold glances.

I wish we really had ghosts and there really were a hell. Then, no matter how the wind of hell roared, I would go to find Zijun, to tell her of my remorse and grief, and beg her forgiveness. Otherwise, the poisonous flames of hell would surround me, and fiercely devour my remorse and grief.

In the whirlwind and flames I would put my arms round Zijun, and ask her pardon, or try to make her happy...

However, this is emptier than the new life. Now there is only the early spring night which is still as long as ever. Since I am living, I must make a fresh start. And the first step is just to describe my remorse and grief, for Zijun's sake as well as for my own.

All I have is crying that sounds like a lilt as I mourn for Zijun, burying her in oblivion.

I want to forget. For my own sake I don't want to remember the oblivion I gave Zijun for her burial.

I must make a fresh start in life. I must hide the truth deep in my wounded heart, and advance silently, taking oblivion and falsehood as my guide...

October 21, 1923
Translated by Yang Xianyi
and Gladys Yang

面是唱歌一般的哭声。我现在已经知道他们的聪明了,这是多么轻松简截的事。

然而子君的葬式却又在我的眼前,是独自负着虚空的重担,在灰白的长路上前行,而又即刻消失在周围的严威和冷眼里了。

我愿意真有所谓鬼魂,真有所谓地狱,那么,即使在孽风怒吼之中,我也将寻觅子君,当面说出我的悔恨和悲哀,祈求她的饶恕;否则,地狱的毒焰将围绕我,猛烈地烧尽我的悔恨和悲哀。

我将在孽风和毒焰中拥抱子君,乞她宽容,或者使她快意……。

但是,这却更虚空于新的生路;现在所有的只是初春的夜,竟还是那么长。我活着,我总得向着新的生路跨出去,那第一步,——却不过是写下我的悔恨和悲哀,为子君,为自己。

我仍然只有唱歌一般的哭声,给子君送葬,葬在遗忘中。

我要遗忘;我为自己,并且要不再想到这用了遗忘给子君送葬。

我要向着新的生路跨进第一步去,我要将真实深深地藏在心的创伤中,默默地前行,用遗忘和说谎做我的前导……。

一九二五年十月二十一日毕。

英汉对照
English-Chinese
中国文学宝库
Gems of Chinese Literature
现代文学系列
Modern Literature

Actually, transcending the present age is a form of escapism. And this is the path they are bound to take — consciously or otherwise — if they dare not look reality in the face yet insist on styling themselves revolutionaries. If you live in this world, how can you get away from it? This is as much of a fraud as saying you can lift yourself off the ground by your ear.

– Lu Xun
Literature and Revolution (1928)